For a Man or a Dog
A Collection of Short Stories from Carrick-on-Suir

by

Paul F. Walsh

Copyright © 2017 Paul F. Walsh

All rights reserved.

ISBN: 9781522081579

DEDICATION

For Chris & Ashlyn

Table of Contents

Introduction (Read this, it's short!) 3
Colloquial Guide (And so is this!) 5
1- The Green Door 8
2 - Going to Mass 16
3 – Storytelling 31
4 – The Bookies 38
5 – The Black Stuff 47
6 – Cooking with Gas 52
7 – First Day of School 59
8 – For a Man or a Dog 68
9 – Spuds 'n' Wudem 74
10 – Moral Dilemmas 86
11 – Coin Tossing 93
12 – It's Only Words 94
13 – Training for Vegas 102
14- Uncle Jim's Field 109
15 – Tribalism 118
16 - Kilkieran 125
17 – Segs 133
18 – The Haircut 139
19 – The Seamstress 144
20 – The Businessman 150

21 – Uncle Davy	163
22 – Gone to the Dogs	169
23 – Big Game Hunters	176
24 – Paddington Station	182
25 – Minnie	187
26 – Playing with Fire	193
27 – Tick Tock	200
28 – Chocolate Crumb	204
29 – The Big Fish	208
30 – The Bone Setter	216
31 – A Carrick Emigrant	226
32 – An Unfinished Story	234
33 – A Carrick Haiku	235
Notes	236

Introduction (Read this, it's short!)

This collection of stories started out as a few family fables that were written down for my kids. It's been years since I penned the first one and I added to the collection over time. Growing up in Ireland, I loved listening to the tales of the older generations. Who wouldn't when there was nothing else going on. Any and all family gatherings made for great storytelling occasions. The revelry surrounding such get-togethers, and the story telling that nearly always followed, were great opportunities for us kids to get a peek into the mysterious adult world of family intrigue, relationships and social interactions. Indeed, this might have been a fundamental part of our education and an essential set of lessons on our own paths towards adulthood. These days, scattered as we now are, family gatherings are more likely to happen on Skype or Facebook. As wonderful as such tools are for sharing and staying in touch, they don't make for a particularly good, old-fashioned, storytelling atmosphere. I don't want these stories to be lost to my children, nor to theirs, so I'm writing them down. Along with the stories from prior generations, I have a few tales of my own to pass along.

The title of this collection comes from my home town's unofficial slogan which goes something like this:

Carrick ... for a man or a dog!

The dots after Carrick signify a somewhat mystical, but only slightly-pregnant, pause. There's a story in here which provides my best guess as to where this saying comes from but, like all the other stories here, any semblance of historical accuracy is, at best, only coincidental. The family tales I listened to as a youngster changed with each telling so I'm just respecting that tradition of malleability in my own recounting. I am not too bothered by a little inaccuracy. I am more interested in imparting the flavor of the times, the essence of an event. And the fun and joy of growing up in and around my home town, Carrick-on-Suir.

I think I was part of a transitional generation, with a foot in both the old and the new worlds. I love all the tech advances that are such a big part of our lives today but some of the old stuff is worth remembering too. While I can clearly recall intense bouts of teenage angst, the overriding feelings I have about growing up in small-town and rural Ireland were of joy and fun. And that's a feeling worth sharing.

I hope you enjoy these tales and if so, please tell me about it. If you don't enjoy them, don't bother letting me know! That just reminds me: there might be the odd F-word and suchlike to contend with here and there. Now you have to understand that such words are an endemic part of Irish, and particularly of Carrick, speech and conversation. These words are only blasphemous and profane when the intent is for them to be that way. And that is almost never the intent in Irish usage. Despite the few words that are sprinkled around as a necessary part of the verbal seasoning, only those who know me will truly appreciate the huge amount of restraint I have shown throughout!

Slán agus Beannacht libh go léir.

Colloquial Guide (And so is this!)

Despite what you might think as you read, I have a reasonably good command of the English language. As I dwelt on the past, I found myself relapsing to a more local parsing, more akin to how I might have spoken as a child or as a teenager. Not only does this impart some youthful colloquial flavor to the stories but it's also a great excuse to overlook my real grammatical screw-ups. Though Irish, I am a big fan of the English language and I favor English English spelling. But, and because it was such a pain to battle against, I generally gave in to my spell checker's whims for correcting to American English. I sincerely apologise and apologize for this crime! You'll probably have noticed that I started that second to last sentence with a conjunction. I do that a lot too. It's how I speak, sorry. If you read some of these stories aloud (and try an Irish accent if you don't have one), you may find yourself laughing more often. I swear, it's true. Try it!

Some words in the vernacular of the day defied all the digital dictionaries so below is a quick glossary of some oft-used words and phrases for the uninitiated.

Auld or Aul' Wan is a pronunciation spelling of Old One which typically means an old woman, as in an aul' wan, with the indefinite article. However, "the" aul' wan is typically your mother because of the preceding definite article.

Mammy is the common appellation for Mum or Mom in Irish but when a boy grows "big" we wouldn't want to call her Mammy anymore in public. Then we might switch to Ma to be more grown up about it all. Don't tell anyone I told you but she's still our Mammy anyway!

Similarly, an aul' lad or an aul' fella is an old man, while "the" aul' fella is often your father. Daddy is the paternal appellation, again abbreviated to Da for a big boy. The definite article can also be used for someone other than a parent if you designate the target. The aul' fella over there, when you nod in the direction of said aul' fella, wouldn't necessarily mean your father.

Yer Wan or Yer Man is Your One or Your Man, meaning that lady or that man, right over there, the one I'm pointing at by nodding my head and raising my eyebrows towards when I'm talking about them to you. And very often behind their backs, of course! I know, it can be confusing.

Both Irish F words are used here and there but, just for reassurance, nothing much worse than that.

I have a special relationship with God, as do many Irish Catholics. I use a mispronounced and misspelled version of His Son's name occasionally. This means that I'm not taking the Lord's name in vain and it is therefore okay. I have a special dispensation for this, as you'll see in some of the stories.

There are some "focal as Gaeilge", i.e. words in Irish, used throughout. While the translation is usually provided, I have mostly ignored pronunciation guidelines. Please ask an Irish person, everyone knows one.

Some of these stories may appear to wander a bit. Okay, some of them do wander a bit! I claim that I'm trying to capture the style of my father's, occasionally excruciating, storytelling technique in some instances. He would often weave another couple of stories throughout the main story and it drove us crazy trying to get him to get to the end of the original story. I want to impose that on you too. Of course, it could just be that I'm getting more like my father as I age. In other cases, I'm rambling on to give you the lie of the land because it means something to the story later on. If you're getting a lengthy description of some little rural road in Ireland, stick with it, it'll all make sense in the end. In still others, I didn't realize I was wandering but I decided to leave the story that way anyway.

As the stories were written at different times, and over the course of several years, you may find snippets of information in one that you already heard in another. Feel free to fact check me but hold on 'til we're having a pint together to tell me about it.

That's about it, I can't think of anything else to warn you about. If you're ready, go for it!

1- The Green Door

Growing up in the country was tough. With everyone in Carrick having great adventures all the time, living in Skough wasn't much fun if you didn't have a car. And, at sixteen years of age, I didn't have a car. Surrounded by small family farms as we were, I saw the children living on those farms driving tractors from an early age. That meant they got hold of the family car at a young age too. Since we weren't farmers, the aul' wan and the aul' fella saw no point in giving me the keys to the one and only family car. Sometimes, I blamed my grandfather for us not being farmers and I cursed him for the consequences that bestowed on me. For consolation, I told myself that not being surrounded by the smell of cow slurry every day was a fair tradeoff. Any time I wanted to go to town though, that line of thinking didn't make me feel any better about the situation. Fortunately, I had plenty of energy, so jumping on a bike or thumbing a lift to Carrick wasn't that big of a thing. I did that a lot. Sometimes, I walked the whole three and a half miles to town. Then I played soccer with the lads in the park, or we might go for a walk up the hills behind Carrickbeg. As I grew older though, I found myself wanting to head out to the pub or to the dance hall more often. If there was any chance that a girl I fancied was going to some event, I would have made the journey on hand and knee in the hope of running into her. Living in the country, if you wanted anything resembling a social life, you had to endure a few hardships.

One day, I was sure that a girl I liked was going to a dance at the Ormonde Hall. To us, the Ormonde was a glittering, romantically-lit edifice of enchantment and entertainment. Only years later would I notice it was a simple concrete block structure, with its corrugated roof supporting the ubiquitous disco ball of the era. Simple though it was, the glittering lights held the promise of adventure and romance. I can't remember the pub the gang arranged to meet at that evening but then, there were a lot of pubs in our small town. Nowadays we pay a lot more attention to underage drinking but in those days, so long as you were nearly tall enough to pass muster, and brazen enough to be mortified if someone questioned your age, you had no problem being served a pint. I was both. While I don't recall much of the early evening's activities on this occasion, I'm sure I enjoyed a few pints before going to the dance. At the Ormonde, I probably spent the night strutting my stuff and looking as cool as could be ... mostly while hanging out with the guys! Of course, I would then have been disgusted with myself for not asking the target of my affections to dance all night. Regardless of what little success I might have had on the night, the one thing I know for sure is that I would have hated the late-night journey back to Skough. I would spend my time on such walks berating myself for my lack of action, my spinelessness, and God knows what other shortcomings I thought I might have. The angst would ebb and flow with each and every step on the way home. But forgive me, I digress. This isn't a love story!

Our house in Skough was just around the corner, and up the road a bit, from the Faugheen Bridge. This bridge spanned the enormous fifteen or twenty-foot width, and two-foot depth, of the Lingaun River. This bridge and the Lingaun were the hub of my rural playground from when I could toddle. This little river had the best brown trout I've ever tasted and the chill of the water in the swimming holes would nearly stop your heart on a warm summer's day when you first jumped in. I spent endless childhood hours fishing and swimming along my favorite spots up and down the banks of this river. The best fish I ever caught came from right under the bridge. A beautiful golden-brown thing, with red spots and a yellowed side fading to a bright white underbelly. The smaller kids paddled in the shallow waters across from Barry's Mill while we older ones learned how to swim in a slightly deeper spot about fifty yards upstream from the bridge. Once we could swim well, we graduated to the Turn Hole, still further upstream from the bridge. And upstream from here was the Black Hole. Logically, I told myself, it really wasn't bottomless and though I fished it, I was more than a little uncomfortable even thinking about swimming there. Walking the banks of the Lingaun was a pleasant thing to do. The sally grass growing in the fields bordering the river provided a sour and juicy treat. Along with crab apples, blackberries and wild strawberries, you wouldn't lack for snacks wandering its banks at the right time of year. It was almost idyllic, except for one thing ... Tommy Wall's bull!

Tommy and Willy, brothers, owned the land around the river and, as they were our neighbors, we had to treat their land with respect. Their cows were big, strong muscular looking animals. Herefords, I think. They were burly brown and white beasts, and they were noticeably different to the more genteel looking black and white Friesians that comprised the more popular dairy herds in the vicinity. The big bull though was a beast among beasts. I never stared it down long enough, nor from close enough range, to be sure but I'd swear there was a glint of evil red in his eye. Unless it was "working", it often had an entire field to itself. Usually the big bull was in one of the fields that bordered on the Lingaun and very often, the location of the bull dictated that we went in the opposite direction. There were occasions though when some combination of bravado, desire or stupidity induced us to go to a favored fishing spot. Regardless of the bull's presence, and despite his obvious mastery over the domain. Further down the road, the variety was less fierce. Past Barry's Mill were the gates to Ballycastlane, the entrance into my Grand Uncle Jim's farm. And still further down, the lodge and gates guarding the entrance to Castletown House. This is one of Ireland's most beautiful estate homes, a Palladian mansion, though for the most part without public access so you'll just have to take my word for it. We used to sneak in the back way, through the fields, to fish the pond there. And we could never resist taking a quick look at the grand house and its beautiful gardens. The narrow, twisting stretch of road between Castletown and Cregg Bridge has a cool shadow cast over it, even on the brightest of summer days. The tall stone walls on either side of the road meant that you were always walking in a shady coolness along this stretch. These walls enclosed the original expansive lands of the Castletown House Estate. The density of tall trees growing behind the walls provided a green backdrop to the stonework of craftsmen long since departed. In the old days, game wardens patrolled the grounds to ward off townsfolk hunting with their terriers and snare traps. A doorway in one of the high walls allowed the gamekeepers access from the lands on one side of the road to those on the other. I'm not quite sure how accurate this memory is but when I was a child, I think the sturdy wooden door and frame still had a peeling coat of green paint. Regardless, we always called it The Green Door.

The Green Door was of note because there was a ghost story that went along with it. Somewhere in the mists of time, as it often the case with such tales, a man was coming home from Carrick. He'd probably had a few pints that night because, although he had a bicycle with him, rather than ride it, he was walking alongside it. This would have been the darkest part of his journey home, with the high walls and the darkness of foliage overhead allowing nothing more than a dappled moonlight through at best. Did he have a light on his bike? Nobody knows for sure but he was probably feeling pretty good as he came up this twisted stretch towards the gates of Castletown. The effects of a hard night's drinking might be starting to wear off in the cool night air and the worst of the journey was already behind him. As he came upon the Green Door, he noticed it open and the old gamekeeper was standing by it. Leaning against its frame. In passing, he tipped his hat with an "Evening, Sir" to the gamekeeper. "Evening", replied the gamekeeper, as the two nodded in exchange. The man with the bicycle thought no more of the brief encounter. He still had some ways to go and so he continued on his way. The story falls into disarray from this point. There are variations of him fainting, and not. Some say he was already gray before the encounter, while others say nay. But the terror in the tale comes from the fact that the Green Door had been nailed up for many a year. And there hadn't been gamekeepers at Castletown for still more years than that!

Coming forward to more recent times, my night of teenage trauma at the Ormonde Hall was crowned by the lack of traffic between Carrick and Skough at this late hour. I was already tired and the folk that might have picked me up after the pubs closed were already fast asleep in their beds. I probably entertained myself on the long trudge home by reliving every missed opportunity where I might have done something more than I had, to advance my romantic intentions. The self-inflicted torture of such thoughts can only be enjoyed to the fullest extent by a young mind. The time passed unnoticed in this fashion and, as I crossed over Cregg Bridge, I knew I was entering the home stretch. Unfortunately, that meant that I was now getting closer to the Green Door. At this point in the homeward trek, even love, lust and the anguish of unrequitement couldn't direct my mind away from thoughts of ghostly gamekeepers. Of course, I didn't believe in ghosts, there were no such things. But in the dark of deadest night, it only took the surprise of an occasional owl hoot to have me imagining things writhing in the moon-mottled shadows along this stretch of road. What things of hell were hiding in the bushes and hedgerows that might force me into the vaporous arms of an apparition from days gone by? And where on earth, or in hell, might such damned spirits take to me to? I was an avid reader of horror and science fiction back then so most things unimaginable were not only possible but perhaps even probable in these witching hours. Especially when the bloody Green Door had yet to be passed on the way home.

I know my breathing shallowed as I entered the first walled stretch of roadway. I knew it was only a few more turns before I would have to face my fears up close. My heart rate was already increasing and there was a pressure in my chest, made worse by the knots in my stomach. As the fear mounted, I thought I heard a car.

Was it possible?

It was!

The engine noise grew and I turned around to face the car, yet to come around the corner and drown me in the blessed light of its beams. Back in those days, just about everyone picked up a hitch-hiker in rural Ireland. I knew I was saved. Turning to face the oncoming headlights meant my cherubic visage would encourage the most mean-spirited of drivers to stop and pick me up. As the car approached, I watched the light creep up the walls, banishing the demons along with the shadows. I turned on my most angelic look, with just a hint of an innocent smile. And I stuck my thumb out in anticipation. The car made the turn, main beams blinding me. It was travelling at a nice slow speed. That was a good sign. Probably an older gentleman with a few pints under his belt. They always stopped. Redemption was at hand.

But he didn't!

The dirty old feckin' bastard! What was wrong with him? Didn't he see I was terrified and needed a lift? This never happens! How was it possible? I turned and sprinted as hard as I could, to get as far as I could along the demonic tunnel, while the car's headlights still lit the way. If the driver looked in his rearview mirror, and could see me pounding along at full tilt, I probably looked more like a drunken lunatic than the scared-shitless teenager that I really was. Unfortunately, I didn't make it to the Green Door before my lungs gave out and the car's tail lights vanished round the next corner. I hunched over, hands on my knees to prop up my heaving torso. I was fucked! The combination of the sprint and the terror had me gasping for breaths that my lungs couldn't take. My head was pounding. Was this some kind of divine revenge for my lustful ways? Was I about to get flung through the Green Door into the abyss? I was finally getting enough oxygen to come upright again. And my head had stilled enough for me to realize that the sooner I got underway, the sooner I could get this nightmare behind me. With fresh, raw steel in my mind but water in my veins (or was it alcohol!), I stood erect. And I forced one foot in front of the other. I rounded the final turn with my head facing hard right. The Green Door was on the left and, I reasoned, if I couldn't see the spectre then it wasn't there and I might safely pass. I was pretty sure I was going right by the point of greatest menace when my foot hit a pot hole and I stumbled, turning my ankle. Aw shite! My head whipped around and there it was, right there beside me in the dark: The Green Fucking Door!

Except for one other occasion, soon to occur, the unimaginable terrors that coursed through my mind in those moments have not been equaled to this day. Somehow, I managed to get my legs moving again. The Green Door was behind me one more time and I was still alive. Thank God! By the time I reached the gates of Castletown, its tall stone walls now behind me, the moonlight again showing me the way through the shadows, I was coming back down. As I approached the gated entrance to Uncle Jim's, at Ballycastlane, I was pretty close to normal again. This really was the home stretch, a safe and sane stretch, and I moved on briskly. I was far more comfortable and confident now. Despite the pain in my turned ankle,

I was hitting a good stride to finish off the last leg of the journey when the hot breath of a beast from hell hit my face! And right behind it, a bellow so loud that I was certain, this time, that my life was at its end. Every muscle in my body reacted so viciously to the danger that I found myself in the ditch at the opposite side of the road. The terrors I had experienced at the Green Door were nothing. The beast had tricked me. I was a goner. Truly fucked. For sure!

Fortunately, the beast was not the one of my imagination, nor was it something that had escaped through the gates of hell. It was Tommy Wall's bloody bull with his head hanging over a five-bar gate. Right by the roadside and right beside my ear.

That feckin' bull!

2 - Going to Mass

Growing up in Ireland almost guaranteed that you were going to attend a lot of masses. And I did. Organized religion was so integrated with the fabric of our lives that we hardly noticed how big a part it played in our early development. Church and state were as one. It was all part of the adult authority system that dictated how we should live. Respect was due to the clergy, priests and nuns, along with doctors, teachers and bankers. Respect was due to our parents, our grandparents, indeed all our elders and betters. And, of course, the Garda Síochána. And all just because. Catechism or religious instruction was part of every child's curriculum. The school day started with a morning prayer, though I can't remember now if it was in Irish, another big part of life for Irish school children, or English. Some of the highlights of our young lives were based on religious milestones. I didn't know anyone of my age who wasn't baptized as a baby so that, in primary school, we were all marching in lockstep towards our First Holy Communion. A truly momentous event in our young lives. This major milestone was anticipated with great longing and trepidation. The trepidation came from the fears created by of years of indoctrination. Sorry, I mean religious instruction! We had to learn all about what was and wasn't a sin. In advance of receiving the Blessed Sacrament for the first time, we were going to have to go to our First Confession. Confession is that wonderful catholic sacrament where we tell the priest about all the bad things we had done and then, we are forgiven and our souls are miraculously scrubbed clean again. This meant that, for our First Confession, we had to confess every single sin, from every day of our entire lives. Now I was the bane of my mother's life. I had done so many bad things that I was about to have to account for that I was in mortal fear of being struck down by a heavenly bolt of lightning. On the spot, right there in the confession box. At the very least, the priest would be horrified by my evil history and he would probably flay me alive, in the middle of the church, in front of everyone. Ma would be mortified. However, if I managed to survive my first visit to the confessional, there was an upside. For our First Holy Communion, which quickly followed our First Confession so as to avoid sinning again before taking the Blessed Sacrament, we got to dress up. Better yet, we got to go to this big party afterwards. And then, best of all, we went around to collect money from relatives, friends and neighbors. Surely all this good stuff was worth the risk of being struck down.

Girls got to wear pretty white dresses and veils, while the boys were treated to their first suit and tie. Albeit a disgustingly childish suit with short pants for most of us. I don't remember too many of the details of my deliberations ahead of my first confession, selective amnesia perhaps. Besides, there is a lawyer-client privilege thing about confessions so I don't have to share everything. But I do remember it being weeks of terror, as I mentally adjusted my list of sins up and down, in practicing for the big event. We were coached, cajoled and threatened about God knowing everything so there was no point in hiding anything from the priest. I think it was at this age that it first occurred to me that God might have a sense of humor. In any case, the buildup was a roller coaster of emotions and I finally decided I'd better come clean. We were having our first confession at Faugheen church. Up to this point in my life, this little hamlet was a place of joy for me. From a very young age, the shops, the church and the water pump, where you could slake a huge thirst with the coldest of water, were all a mere walk from home. We often wandered over to Kattie O'Shea's thatched cottage for gallon sweets, cough drops, acid drops and lollipops. Kattie's was also a pub. It had a big open-hearth fireplace and the smell of the wood and peat turf fire, mixed with the heady essence of a pint, is a fond olfactory memory to this day. The darkness of the pub, around the back from the little sweet shop, was comforting. Usually, you'd find a few auld fellas back there, sipping a pint and having quiet conversations with only occasional nods and grunts. It felt very calm back there and whenever we went around the corner for a look, we kids respected the silence and warm solemnity by being quiet ourselves. I used to love a bottle of County Cola at Kattie's. We thought it was way better than the American stuff and we used to pretend we were drinking Guinness, and that we were drunk. That stuff would strip the lining off your throat if you guzzled it at too fast a pace but you couldn't help yourself sometimes. Da told me that Kattie used to slice the top off a marrow and dump sugar into the middle. Then she'd put the top back on, tie it all back together with baler twine, and hang it from the rafters in the thatched roof for I don't know how long. If you were lucky, you might be there on the night when she took it down and gave everyone a shot of whatever it turned into while hanging there. I never had a shot of that stuff. Kattie's was a place to be though.

The feelings of joy at being in Faugheen were at serious risk now though, as the entire class sat in the church pews, awaiting the religious ministrations of our priest in that dark wooden box. I had by then spent several more days refining my list of sins. Both to ensure complete disclosure, and to order them in such a way that I could quickly build up to the worst ones early. I thought that if I could maybe finish off with a few harmless ones, that would trick the priest into thinking I wasn't so bad after all. Of course, God would know that I was trying to trick the priest so I wasn't sure if I should add "priest tricking" to my list of sins now too. On the big day, my nerves were completely shot and, thank God, I wasn't the first to have to go into the box. The first few of my classmates that had to go in to the dark before me, to confess their sins, were girls. They were back out in about two minutes. I couldn't believe it. Were they that bloody good that they could do all the "Bless me, Father, for I have sinned" stuff AND an Act of Contrition, ALONG WITH their list of sins. And they could do all that in only two bloody minutes? I was surely fucked. Oh no, there's another sin to the list, I'm fucking swearing in my head in the Church. Aw Jaysus, I just did it again!

Never mind, I thought, girls are good and boys are bad so the lads will take much longer. When the first of the boys went in, I started counting in my head and the bloody bastard was back out before I made it to two hundred. When the first lad came back to the pew, I couldn't even concentrate on trying to find out what penance he had to do. Was it three Hail Mary's and an Our Father or what? I was wrecked. I was thinking I'd be in there for half an hour recounting my list and I'd probably have to become a priest, or maybe even a bishop, in order to atone for a load of guilt that big. Whilst in the worst throes of this latest bout of anguish, Mrs. O'Shea tapped me on the shoulder. The signal that it was my turn to go to the next empty box. A confession box is a three-compartment wooden structure, usually ornately carved and very holy looking. The confessionals were often parked in the darkest corner of the church so the good people could sneak in and out to have their souls cleansed. Though there are glassless windows in the door of each compartment, the darkness of the interior is maintained by the use of heavy velvet curtains, somber in color, religious royal purple was often the choice. The priest sits in the center compartment and he swivels back and forth between the two outer boxes, dispensing forgiveness and penance like someone feeding grain to chickens. The center compartment has a grille on either side of where the priest sits. Each grille has a little wooden panel that slides shut, so the priest can hear sins at one side, while blocking out the other side. As I opened the door and went in, I realized there was a friend of mine starting off his confession at the other side. And I could hear him! Names will not be mentioned, Pat, but suffice it to say that I knew this fella was guilty of at least as many transgressions as I was. But that was not what his story sounded like from my side of the box. After trotting out a few harmless things about making his mother mad and not saying his bedtime prayers once or twice, he was done. Jaysus, I couldn't believe it! The lyin' little shite! For penance, he only picked up three Hail Mary's, an Our Father and a Glory Be and he was out the door in mere minutes.

My turn …

"Bless me, Father, for I have sinned and this is my first confession, Father."

"Welcome, my son.", was all he said to start.

It was Father Kelleher and he used to frighten the bejaysus out of me with his deep voice. Ma loved Father Kelleher. I think he married them, baptized me and now, I thought, he was about to murder me.

"But if you want forgiveness, you'll have speak up there now, my son.", he continued.

"So I can hear those sins, you know …", rumbled the priest into my confusion.

Of course, I was only whispering so the fella in the box at the other side wouldn't hear me. But that was the end of that notion. I upped the volume, closed my eyes, and carried on by starting the whole process again. The priest mumbled his response to my scripted opener and I was on again …

"I misbehaved on my mother three times, Father, and twice on my father, Father. I used a few bad words one day, Father. Oh … and I had bad thoughts, Father.", went the promptly revised, and greatly abbreviated, version of my first confession.

"And what bad thoughts did you have, my son?" said the priest.

Aw Jaysus, that last one was a bad one to pick for my hastily reduced list. I never knew you could be interrogated in the bloody box.

"I had unkind thoughts about some of my friends, Father, and I called my sister names behind her back, Father. In my head, Father.", I miraculously recovered.

I wasn't about to let him trip me up at this stage in the game. After all the really dirty thoughts I had had, on far too regular a basis, I'd be there all day long confessing!

As it turned out, I only picked up three Hailos, an Our Father, and a set of Glory Bes for penance. I promised Father Kelleher that I would do better for the next time, and I was out that bloody door in under two minutes. No sign of a lightning bolt anywhere. Woohoo! And phew!

After that bout of mental trauma in the confession box, I figured that First Holy Communion was going to be a breeze and indeed, it was. I did suffer some major guilt pangs heading up to the alter to receive the host. After all, God knew that I had severely curtailed my sin telling in the confessional. Did that mean I wasn't worthy to receive? I figured that God was smart enough to know where I was coming from though. Once He fixed that privacy problem, I would come clean but meantime, I thought He'd forgive me the transgression of omission in the confessional. I was heading to the altar!

The Communion rigmarole was a good one. All the parishioners came up the center of the church and knelt at the marble railing across the front of the altar. With all the kids making their First Communion, the church was packed with family and friends. The priest passed along the marble rail, chalice of hosts in hand, dispensing one onto the tongue of each child. He was accompanied, in lockstep, by an altar boy who kept a silver platen under the chin of each communicant, just in case a host was dropped on the way to the parishioner's mouth. The altar boy was a friend of mine and the little shite rapped me in the Adam's apple with the platen, just as the priest was dropping the host onto my tongue. What with my neck craned to receive the host, the rap of the platen on my Adam's apple, and the dryness of the host, I nearly gagged and the host wound up stuck to the roof of my mouth with the panic of it all. I thought I was going to choke and I had to put my finger into my mouth to dislodge it. Now, unless you were a priest, touching the host was not allowed in those days so I knew I was on a very short plank here. Even God's sense of humor was potentially being stretched at this point in the proceedings. However, nothing happened and my guilt at touching such a holy article had subsided in time for me to enjoy the big tea party afterwards. We had the biggest, creamiest doughnuts I ever had in my life. I was so relieved at surviving the whole bloody affair that I can hardly remember anything past the good stuff: collecting all the money, getting that damn suit off, and heading out to buy sweets!

Despite my shaky start to this whole religion thing, I actually liked going to church in those days. It was around that time, and with the encouragement of Mrs. O'Shea, my favorite teacher, that I became an altar boy. That job had a bit of glory attached to it and you could make a ton of money doing weddings and funerals. People always felt generous around a wedding or a funeral so the altar boys could pick up a nice little envelope from the parties involved. If you had to go to mass anyway, there was no harm picking up a few quid every so often either. Sometimes, you'd even get to sneak a sip of wine in the sacristy. This wasn't a problem for us, as it had to be blessed by the priest during mass, before it became the blood of Christ. We also got to wear this really cool uniform, consisting of the surplice and soutane. Though for years I thought the latter was called a sultana and I thought that was just more of God's joking with us. The other thing I loved about church was hymns but especially those hymns sung in Latin. Back then, I thought I had this amazing soprano voice. While I enjoyed singing in the local choir in Faugheen, it wasn't until I went to boarding school that this became a much bigger thing for me.

Mrs. O'Shea advised my parents to have me sit the scholarship exams at some of the regional boarding schools and I did. My folks hadn't a clue about some things but they seemed to pick the right people to take advice from. I think I sat the exams at two or three of these schools but, for whatever reason, it was decided that I would take the scholarship from Mount Melleray College, in County Waterford. Ma and Da couldn't afford to send me there at full price but winning a scholarship saved them a ton of money and I got to escape from home. Frankly, I knew nothing about the place but I was very impressed when I saw the student quarters with all the football fields, the handball alleys and the basketball court. There was a small church attached to the student buildings but I was even more blown away when we went up to see Mount Melleray Abbey. It was all simply magnificent, with its towering, high-ceilinged church and the massive hewn-stone buildings. The place even had a gift shop, selling all sorts of relics, crosses, rosary beads and religious paraphernalia. God was big time here. A superstar even. Who knew!

Mount Melleray is home to the Cistercian order, or Trappists, as some know them. The teaching staff was a mix of priests from the monastery, and some lay teachers that came in from the real world on a daily basis for class. I had a very correct English English teacher that was great, an ebullient Latin teacher, and an Irish teacher that was a gas. When they wouldn't serve us, he even bought me and the lads a pint in Minnie's, a pub in Dungarvan, one summer. Needless to say, there was a strong church presence surrounding everything here and, outside of class, student life was organized under the auspices of priests from the monastery. It didn't take too long to get over the trauma of leaving home at the ripe old age of ten or eleven, as enough other traumas were quickly brought to bear on our young lives to distract us. If I thought I was getting enough religion in my life up to this point, Mount Melleray was about to take it to a whole new level. We were awakened in the dark of night and had to rush down to the bathrooms to wash our faces. In ice-cold mountain spring water. The older boys had to shave and I'm not sure if they were just no good at it, or if it was the coldness of the water, but they often finished up with nicks and cuts all over their faces. There was a task I wasn't looking forward to growing into. Once we were washed and dressed, beds made drum-tight, it was off to the little student church, where we attended mass every morning. Yes, every single bloody morning. If it wasn't for the coldness of the chapel and a bit of hymn singing, I probably would have fallen back asleep there every time. After mass we piled out, en masse, and swarmed the refectory for breakfast. Everything here had a funny name. It was like we were in a different world. We ate in the refectory and the open area that was central to all the major rooms where we ate, lived and studied in was called an ambulatory. All a bit over the top, I thought at the time, but the religious message was being delivered consistently too. No matter where you went, short of the boot locker room (which could have used some divine intervention), there were holy pictures on the wall. And holy statues in alcoves, and around corners here and there. They were on stairs, in the dormitories, and what have you. The refectory was one of my favorite rooms though, and breaking real bread was my favorite religious thing to do. So long as it was buttered. A lot of our food came to our table by virtue of the work of the monks in the monastery. Our bread was baked fresh every day in the kitchen, the milk came from the dairy herd that the monks tended, and so on. We ate well but we ate the same boring menu, week in and week out, all the time. We pined for those little extras from the outside world. And that brought a whole other dimension to the educational curriculum. You could trade your breakfast bowl of cornflakes for another fella's fish fingers at supper time, for example. Or, if you managed to bring in some outside contraband, you could trade a scoop of peanut butter for a dip of another's lime marmalade. At breakfast, bread with peanut butter and lime marmalade was a thing. There was some serious learning and education going on here. Aside from the odd beating we took in a fight, and given the mandatory bit of the bullying that all boarding school kids will tell you about, there were only two incidents that stood out as grossly unfair during my time in boarding school.

There was a prefect at the head of each long dining table in Melleray. A prefect was a senior student that had gone over to the dark side. Though still students themselves, they helped the priests run our lives. You couldn't trust a prefect. Mostly these were older clerical students, intent on becoming priests. The rest of us were missing even the sight of girls so we could never understand what was going on with these prefects. Did they really want to do more of that deprivation stuff? Anyway, the first student to the right and left of the prefect at our long, long dining tables were assigned food dispensing responsibilities and I was one of them. The food was delivered in bulk to the head of the table and we got to dish out the individual servings to the rest of the table. Reserving a nice portion of those offerings we liked most for ourselves, of course. To our friends, we could be selectively heavy handed with the good stuff as we walked along the length of the table, doling out portions to our fellow students. We weren't beyond accepting a little token appreciation for such positive dispensations so those willing to offer a little payback might find an extra-large helping of chips, or a bonus pat of butter, on their plate. One evening for supper, I think we were having sausages, beans and chips, I was standing up pouring the tea for the rest of the tribe. I'd pour and the student seated next to me would pass the full cup and saucer down along the line. Next thing, with no warning, I had the most searing pain in my arse that I ever felt. The bloody priest had skelped me, with a quick and powerful stroke of his blackthorn walking stick. It was a cut stroke, fast and with venom. It caught the outer layer of the cheeks of my arse so finely that the pain it drew defined a whole new level of excruciation for me. The prefect stepped forward to defend me right away but it was too late. I was in agony and I shot into my chair so fast that I forgot my arse was in so much pain and the hard landing on the seat caused even more. That bloody priest was losing it because a few of the other tables were rabble rousing and he went a bit mental because they weren't listening to him. When he finally lost it, he went around flailing his walking stick at anyone that was standing, for a legitimate purpose or not. He was the second in command at the boarding school and he was usually a nice, calm fella. But you have to watch out for any fellas that are made feel a bit too small from time to time. No apology either. My education continued!

The only other time I was unjustly persecuted at Melleray was by the chief himself. To us younger kids, he was a really big, really tall man. A bull amongst sheep he was, and we saw him as the ultimate authority. A dictator even. And one that we all feared. There was a showing of Franco Zeffirelli's Romeo and Juliet (I was madly in love with Olivia Hussey at the time) in the student study hall but myself and another lad were called out. Jim, he was from Cork city with the accent and everything, and I were called out of the proceedings and asked to stand in the ambulatory. While we waited for what was to come next, we snuck whispered comments out of the sides of our mouths to each other. Neither of us had a clue what was going on and we were trying to figure out why we were called out. Myself and Jim were classmates and decent enough friends but we hadn't recently indulged in any joint activities that might warrant us being called out together. Anyway, the chief came along shortly afterwards and accused us of stealing scalpels from the science lab and cutting things with them. I hadn't done this and indeed I didn't even know what a scalpel was at the start of this encounter. When I asked the chief what I'd even do with one of those black plastic things, he only glared at me. I mistook it to mean spatula, and Jim was sniggering off to the side at my ignorance. Anyway, the big fella just took it to mean that I was being a smart arse and so we were both marched off to his office. Aside from missing Romeo and Juliet, we had to stand and wait while he went out to the hedgerow to select a nice whippy wattle to dispense further punishment with. He slowly peeled off the leaves and twigs from the primary tool of punishment while we watched. Bloody mental torture too, it was. Jim was called into the office first and he came out with tears in his eyes. Never mind the red eyes, his hands were reddened and swollen from the skelping they took.

"How many?", I whispered to him as we passed, him on the way out and me on the way in.

"Six on each fuckin' hand.", he whined in his Cork City accent, as he kneaded his tender palms together.

In I went and, and just for the record, I restated my innocence all over again.

"I didn't even know what a scalpel was, Father!", I proclaimed one last time.

"Well consider this the punishment for something you didn't get caught doing on another occasion.", he adjudicated, and I got my six on each hand too.

I was grinning through the tears at that one. He was pretty quick, the chief, but I was feeling the heavy injustice of it all too. I simply wasn't guilty this time. Was this more of my education? And if so, just what was it they were trying to teach me?

There were many good times at Melleray too though and being called up to sing with the monks at the abbey was among the best. I'm not sure what religious celebration it was but I can remember one such excursion being positively transcendent. Myself and a fella from Wexford, John was his name, were two of the best sopranos in the student choir. We got to attend such events to counter all the baritones amongst the ranks of the auld monks and priests. The mass was in Latin, as were all the hymns, and I kid you not, we sang like bloody angels. It's a pity there weren't cell phone around back then, I'd love to hear a recording of the day to see if I was as good as I like to think I was. Or maybe I wasn't and it's better not. The atmosphere in the high-ceilinged church, the heavy volume of the monks singing, the power of the ancient Latin, all served to highlight and accentuate the penetrating, angelic quality of our soprano voices. That's how I remember it anyway but we did get a round of applause from the crowd. People were clapping and I had never seen that happen in a church before. It was just one of those special experiences for me, the memory of which still raises the hair on the back of my neck. However, despite the joy of events such as this, and all the good friends I made, I was almost glad that they closed the school down. The abbey and all the buildings are still there but the boarding school is no longer a school. There was something not quite right about kids being locked up in such a highly structured environment for years on end. I'm not saying it didn't have its positives and I'll admit that the secular part of the educational process was pretty good. The rest of the program though probably didn't meet the objectives, theirs nor ours, since most of us just weren't buying into the religious side of things. By the time I was done there, I'd had my fill of the mass, the rosary, benediction and an authoritarian rule of law that didn't always show respect for truth and justice. Finishing up in Melleray was a mixed emotional bag for me but mostly, I saw it as being set free. After completing my Inter Cert there, I figured I had done my lifetime's quota of mass, praying and penance.

After my three years in boarding school, I went on to finish my secondary schooling at the Christian Brothers School, the Mon, back in Carrick. This wasn't a total escape from the religiosity of the Irish educational system but at least it was day school. We didn't take the Christian Brothers as purveyors of the word of God as seriously as we did the priests and monks in Mount Melleray. It's funny how accepting we all were of the religious orders dishing out corporal punishment like it was good for us. Most of us who went to the Mon will remember the leather strap that was used for such purposes. Funny thing, religion. Regardless, I had decided that I still loved God, that He still had a sense of humor and, given what I had endured, that He wouldn't mind me skipping mass on Sundays to play soccer down the lanes with the boys. The other great thing about the Mon was that we had to go up the road, to Greenhill, for French class. This was the all-girls school, run by the Sisters of Mercy. You couldn't escape religion, girl or boy, in Ireland back then. The girls had to wear these maroon or burgundy uniforms and I'm sure some of those skirts weren't that short off the rack. This was more my kind of religion. Aaaah, the memories!

While I had been a bit of Leeds United fan when Johnny Giles was with them, I was obliged to follow QPR, it being a family tradition based on where my grandparents lived in London. Once I started going to London for the summers, all my friends there were QPR supporters. The stadium, at Loftus Road, wasn't that far away and, once I attended my first game, I was an R for life. This was just another religion and we had our Gods in the form of Stan "the Man" Bowles. Stan was a bit of a maverick. He'd get into trouble every now and again but he could dazzle on the field and he could score. I wanted to be all that. Unfortunately, my soccer skills were seriously lacking. There were a few decent footballers among the local tribe in Carrick though. One of the lads had had a trial with Man United and the best of us went on to have a great career with Irish and European clubs. They were good and, with great regret, I knew I wasn't that good. Still, soccer was our new religion and the times we spent on Sunday mornings, down the lanes at the back of the Main Street, were great. The two best, or the two biggest or loudest, players would divide and pick the teams, one man at a time, alternating. Of course, the best players were picked first and, since this was your peer group, you knew exactly where you were in the pecking order. Every now and again, you might have felt you were picked out of order by one or two places but, for the most part, you knew exactly where you were perceived to be in the overall skills hierarchy. There were no medals for just showing up in those days and that helped you understand, and eliminate, any delusional tendencies you might have. You couldn't fool your friends and there was no fooling yourself because of that. You recognized your limitations early and you made quick decisions about staying for fun or moving on to something you might be better at.

This combination of all this education boiled down to it being a question of soccer versus mass on a Sunday morning. Pondering such questions gave me some valuable insights on the direction my life might, or might not, take going forward. At this point, I already knew I wasn't going to be a priest. Nor was I going to be a professional footballer. What might be next? Such are the joys of the formative years. You wind up growing into an adult with a mixed religion of God, football, women and drink. What with the sense of community, and the opportunity of breaking bread with our fellow man, now I look at going to the pub with friends to watch a match as being akin to going to mass. Sure, isn't it all nearly the same thing!

3 – Storytelling

Stories in our house were always told with nods and winks, furrowed brows and thoughtful, maybe even wistful, expressions. Allusion, illusion and delusion were a part and parcel of every family tale that was ever told. What was **not** said, under the guise of a wink or a raised eyebrow, was often as important as what was said. The more drink that was imbibed before the telling of such a family fable, the more translucent the fabric of truth became. Every story from the past was an adventure, a mystery and, it seemed, an epiphany. Almost as though the teller himself just realized the import of the bombshell being dropped. Moreover, stories told after a funeral were considered even more significant, since this information bore the burden of being "passed on" to the younger generation, as yet another member of the older generation was laid to rest. For the most part, sexist or not, men seemed to do most of the telling. My grandfathers bequeathed the art of storytelling to my father and he, in turn, tried to do the same for me. While my father seemed to do the telling, my mother was always on hand, attentive and alert for any errors, of either embellishment or omission. Regardless of the degree of clarity my father chose to apply for any given rendition, and even with my mother's storytelling safety net deployed, I was often dizzy with a lack of understanding of the tale being spun. I knew I couldn't ask too many questions; as any hint of under-appreciation, or any lack of understanding on my part, would interrupt the process of recollection and draw the wrath of the teller upon me. Such wrath was typically displayed as thinly disguised disgust, as if my lack of comprehension could only be put down to an unexpected bout of stupidity on my part. Stories were made all the more confusing if the gathering was larger, and especially so if the onlooking participants spanned the generations. Toss in a few aunts, uncles, and one or two of the grandparent's generation, and you had a confusion of scattered thoughts, opinions, corrections and exclamations that made it impossible for a young and logical mind to absorb barely the essence of the story. Fortunately, the same story was often retold at each family gathering. And if you combined fragments from all these renditions, you usually had a fairly good outline of some haphazardly half-remembered reality.

Storytelling was de rigueur after a death, particularly in memory of the dearly departed one. Kilkieran cemetery, sitting on the slope of the hills above Skough, is home to some ancient Celtic High Crosses and, because of that, it's on the tourist map of all those interested in such things. While the crosses in Ahenny are equally well known, the two sites are in such close proximity that if you're going to the bother of visiting one of these fine examples of Celtic antiquity, it's only a few minutes up or down the road to visit the other. Being local, they were all just "auld crosses" to us growing up. No more than ancient background color to the grand vista we had across the Suir valley and the surrounding mountains. Though we did use the base of the big cross as a seat from time to time, we considered them important enough that we would never think to desecrate them in any way. The cemetery and its crosses served as a backdrop to an occasional picnic, or as a place to take a drink break during a hillside ramble. Towards the back of the cemetery, and on the lower slope of the hill, is St. Kieran's Well. Even before the place was cleaned up and designated as historically significant, you could get enough of the grass and the weeds out of the way to imbibe the coldest, freshest water that a hillside spring could provide. After the restoration, the well became a stone-surrounded highlight of the cemetery. The water from this blessed well is attributed with miraculous powers of healing for such ailments as headaches. Our young minds expanded this faculty with the power to cure anything related to the head and I wondered why my grandfather didn't come to bathe his shiny dome with its healing waters. If people were "sick in the head" why wouldn't their mothers bring them here and douse their heads with the well water? While an occasional tourist, typically weighted down with large cameras, could be found wandering the cemetery, they were not too big an affront to the locals. If they threw a few coins in the donations box, they might even be welcome. The donations help with the upkeep of the cemetery and I sometimes wondered how often it got robbed, being out in the country as it was. Aside from us kids playing there every now and again, and for the most part, the place was peaceful and quiet. It was more important to me though, as my ancestors are buried in the Walsh tomb, right beside one of the ancient crosses. From an early age, I recall standing at the wrought iron railings surrounding our stone crypt, peering through the bars, reading the epitaphs and trying to imagine how important a life my great grandfather must have lived to be worthy of spending eternity in such a beautiful place. And where did all that wealth go when, now, I was the one in great financial need! Even from a very young age, having this testament to local Walsh history in Kilkieran gave the place a great sense of belonging for me. It is where my grandfather and grandmother are laid to rest. My mother and father, along with uncles and aunts, are all together there now too. It's where I'll be going one day though I'll be breaking tradition a little, since I asked my wife to cremate me before bringing me back to Ireland. That way, getting me there won't cost so much. My mother would be proud!

While we're on the topic of death and burial, I should point out that this is not as gloomy a subject for me as you might imagine. Despite our tormented national history, or perhaps even because of that, the Irish are generally a witty and jovial lot. Our family was no different. Funerals certainly bring an abundance of tear shedding and wailing but they were also times of friends and family coming together to remember and celebrate the life of the departed one. Kilkieran is a particularly good spot for a funeral as Maloney's pub is just a few minutes' walk down the road, at the cross of Skough. And our own house wasn't much further down, on the road towards Carrick, from there. Bereavement should not be suffered alone and there was never any fear of that happening in our family. You couldn't walk the streets of Carrick without running into some substantial number of relatives. I had aunts, uncles and cousins galore but the biggest of family gatherings were guaranteed to be at family funerals. Because of that, the biggest and grandest of storytelling sessions were in the pub, or at home, after a funeral.

As I matured through the years, hearing the same stories told again and again, my knowledge and understanding of each tale grew. Though I'm still suspicious about the accuracy of most of them. Along with my own lapses of memory, I'm pretty certain that each tale was tweaked with each retelling. The bigger the audience, the more tweaking was done, as everyone present contributed their own slant. In not wanting to speak ill of the dead, funeral stories were respectfully adjusted to elevate the reputation of the central character, the person in the box. I would not be remiss in thinking that some of these tales grew to the point of being potentially excellent material for a Hollywood script. Not this one I'm about to tell you about though, this one is totally true and accurate!

My grandfather, Patrick, or Paddy as some knew him, grew up in the big house in Ballycastlane. Our house in Skough was built on a half-acre of the farmland that surrounded the big house, and that at one time supported the big house. If there's any truth to this story, I was almost a farmer's son. Traditionally, Irish farms were passed on to the oldest son and my grandfather was the oldest sibling in his brood, as was my father in his. The big house was torn down many years ago, and I remember, as a child, playing with my cousins in the rubble of its foundations. Its walls were so thick that you could shelter from the rain in one of its window openings. Was it three or four stories tall? I'm not sure, I have never even seen a picture of the original structure but regardless, in my grandfather's early years, it was the majestic center of a working farm. And home to our family. In the lee of the house were the stone stables and outbuildings that supported the workings of the farm. In my Grandfather's time, ploughs were horse drawn and chickens, wandering the paddocks, ate far more spiders and flies than the grains and processed feed that fattens their descendants today. The color of an egg yolk was more vibrant then, and chicken giblet soup was more a meal than a drink. I think the field at the back of the stables was used to grow kale and mangels, as a winter feed supplement for the animals. No wonder there wasn't any problem eating red meat back in those times. Milking the cows by hand was practiced right up to the time of my childhood. Not being exposed to farming activity every day, it was always a bit of an adventure to visit my cousins at milking time. Playing on a farm usually involved helping out in some way but it wasn't without some trepidation that I took my place at the side of one of these sizeable beasts. Sitting atop a three-legged stool, with a bucket placed between your knees, was how cows were milked then. Despite the cute, girly names bestowed on each cow, they were all fearsomely big animals and the prospect of a stomping hoof coming down on your foot was no laughing matter. My cousins laughed at my fears but things usually settled down within a few minutes of my getting the right stroke and pressure going. The alternating rhythm of the hands on the teats served to deliver streams of warm milk into the bottom of the bucket. Sooner or later someone would direct a jet of milk to somewhere other than the bucket. More often than not, it came in my direction. And of course, we couldn't resist sending a shot into our own mouths occasionally. With food like this I don't really know how tough it was but you would often hear remarks to that effect in any story from those days.

When my Grandfather was a young man, it sounded like him courting my Grandmother wasn't totally accepted by his father. Storytelling hints, suggestions, and innuendo all seemed to point in the same direction. I could never clearly decipher what the storyteller's thought might have been in my great grandfather's mind but there is no question that he seemed to harbor some level of dissatisfaction in his eldest son's choice of a bride. During the course of telling the story, there would be more knowing looks and raised eyebrows, indicating that this might have been a long running battle between father and son. As each subplot was revealed, it became more and more apparent that things were always going to come to a head. One day, my grandfather was out ploughing the fields, perhaps even the one that the house I grew up in would later stand on. There is a rhythm to farming that may change from one generation to the next as new technologies are applied but the pace of change was slow. Then, there would have been an expected number of hours that Paddy should be out in the fields for. On this day though, Paddy was seen leading the horse back to the stables, no plough in sight, and much earlier than expected. His father was watching proceedings from one of the upper floor windows and he may have watched just long enough to build up a good head of steam. Finally, he could stand it no more. He opened the window and yelled at Paddy, wanting to know what the bloody hell he was doing back so soon. Paddy, on the other hand, had been doing some thinking of his own and whatever time he had spent alone in the fields allowed him to come to some conclusions about the state of his life. How long this exchange went on for we have no way of knowing but Paddy freed the horse of the tackle and he released him into the paddock during the course of his father's tirade. While we don't know exactly what words were exchanged, the parting blow delivered by the old man, as my grandfather headed towards the main gates, ran something like this ...

"If you go out that fucking gate, Paddy Walsh, don't ever come back."

He went out the gate. And he never came back. And I never became a farmer.

To this day, I don't know if this was a planned departure for my Grandad but in any case, my grandfather moved to London and was with my grandmother 'til the day he died. They now rest together in Kilkieran Cemetery and we are around to bear witness to their lives. With my own parents now gone, it seems like we will never know the full story about my grandparents eloping to London but maybe that's for the best ... there's nothing wrong with having a bit of mystery in a family tale.

4 – The Bookies

The Grand National is the greatest horse race ever. It is a grueling steeplechase over fences and obstacles that neither man nor beast should have to take on. The death defying speeds, particularly amidst the stampede of competitors that make up the field in this spectacular event, is beyond any sane challenge for horse and jockey. Indeed, the Grand National might perfectly define the phrase "jockeying for position" by any measure you'd care to apply. Though the race is run in England, in Ireland it's of such great note that it's a bit like Christmas for the bookmakers. It is an event for the masses. For the many who didn't care to gamble from one end of the year to the next, they would come in to place a bet on their favorite horse in the Grand National. I didn't know what "off track betting" was when I left Ireland, as it was the norm for us growing up in Carrick. There were as almost as many betting shops as fish 'n' chip shops around town. The betting shops were small family businesses back then and each had its own peculiar damp and newspapery smell. The racing pages from the daily newspapers were thumbtacked to the walls and above the bar-high shelves that surrounded the room, all by way of giving the punters access to the latest information on horses and riders. Along with local races from Punchestown and Leopardstown, the exotic names of faraway race courses in England were on everyone's lips and most kids were quite familiar with Cheltenham and Chepstow. And of course, Aintree, the home of the Grand National. I'm sure there were laws about such things, even back then, but it was very common to see children placing bets on behalf of those legally entitled to do so. It might be for parents, grandparents, or even for elderly neighbors who had neither the time nor the inclination to make the journey to the bookie's. With the year-round practice of placing bets, everyone was used to seeing us kids come and go, so it wasn't very difficult to place a bet on

Grand National day for yourself. Comparing it to the modern world of more tightly imposed rules and regulations, I think the old-world way had a lot of common sense attached to it. Everyone could tell when something was a bit off then and if you chose to be misbehave, the word always made it back to the delinquent child's Mammy. And Mammy usually took care of family business as necessary. Now, I really look back at the whole experience as a part of my early education. We got to study the geography of race courses around the country and beyond. Our math skills had to be capable of handling betting odds and we were well able to figure out our winnings on place bets and accumulators. Most importantly, we had to develop the social skills necessary to ensure that the bigger kids didn't steal our winnings. The educational benefits were only enormous. All in all, you'd struggle to find the equivalent knowledge and experiences at any third level institute of learning that I've ever been exposed to since.

I'm not sure the weather statistics will support this but my enduring impressions about Irish summers are of endlessly long, hot, lazy days, each one filled with adventures. It was a gloriously long season peppered with swimming, fishing, bicycling, soccer, picnics, beaches and all the wondrous things that you might imagine. One other significant thing happened most summers and that was the return of our Granny and Grandad, my father's parents, from London. Because our house in the country was a little bigger than the townhouses we all came from in Carrick, and because our house was home to fewer kids, they typically stayed with us. This was a big win for us over the cousins, one I'm sure we couldn't hide all the gloat from. What it meant was that we got the grandparents all to ourselves for lengthy periods of time and, most importantly, we were there when they first opened the suitcases full of exotic sweets, biscuits and confectionary from England. I fully understand and appreciate how this childhood training made for some of the shallower elements of my adult character but, quite frankly, I don't care! My Grandfather, Paddy, was a big man, tall and stocky. He had the bombast to go with that imposing frame and he sucked on filterless cigarettes during my earlier years. Because my mother and father smoked filtered cigarettes, I thought my grandfather must have rolled his own. I would collect the butts from my parents' ashtrays and break out the remaining flakes of tobacco to save them up for my grandfather's visits. To his credit, he humored me every time I handed him a big plastic bag, filled with partially burned tobacco flakes. I really thought he was rerolling and smoking my "burnt offerings" for years. My grandmother, on the other hand, was a diminutive creature and while my grandfather was the big stick of this pair, she was the quiet and deadly one. The puppeteer pulling all the strings, the mistress of guile. Ostensibly she was a delightful creature, full of mirth and smiles that were only enhanced by the port wine stain on her cheek. This birthmark was easily hidden by makeup but you could tell it had no bearing on her view of herself when it was exposed. I wasn't my grandmother's favorite grandchild but that only made me work tirelessly in an attempt to secure that vaunted position. Though it really didn't matter, she was my Granny and I loved her anyway.

This summer was starting out like any other and, like so many previous holidays, Gran and Grandad were staying with us. There was a wedding of some relative up the country that my grandparents were attending and, since they had only recently arrived, we kids were anxiously awaiting their return from the event. We wanted to hear more stories of our cousins in England, and of the great big world outside Carrick. They returned, as expected, later that evening. In fact, we were given special dispensation on our usual bedtime so we could await their return. When they got back, we could tell something was a little off with Gran. She had that look on her face when she came in the front door that told you everything hadn't gone quite according to her plans for the day. We had seen her display worse though, so it was more likely just one or two little things were causing her some mild irritation. The possible cause of this irritation came through the front door moments later, in the form of my grandfather. He may have had one pint too many! He was smiling, affable and full of good cheer. He wanted to hug everyone and he was telling us all how great we were. My grandmother was not amused. As the banter waned and the conversation leaned towards more serious notes, my grandfather began dispensing advice to us all. I can't remember what wisdom he imparted to anyone else present, as he singled me out for special advice on marriage. He suggested that the path to salvation was to stay away from women and to put my pants on backwards to ward off their evils. Indeed, he went further and suggested that I should consider the priesthood as a means of staying clear of the ravages a woman can inflict on a man. I was of such a hormone raging age that this was the very last advice I wanted to hear. So frightened was I that my grandfather's words were a portent of things to come that I prayed to God for months afterwards that he wouldn't let me become a priest. I had some very religious moments during this phase of my life and God was usually very obliging in delivering on my requests. This one was a big ask and I was hoping for the best.

The timing of this wedding episode was co-incidental with my grandfather's heart attack, which struck him down only a few days later. This big, strong man was laid so low that, for the first time in my young life, I was endlessly worried. He just didn't look right. His face was pale, his breathing so labored that I feared going to sleep in case he died while I slept. An absolutely unbearable thought. We moved an armchair from the living room to the kitchen, the heart of the home, so that he could sit by the fire and partake in the daily babble of conversation. Though he continued to be weak, he could position himself on the armchair such that breathing was easier for him and, with time, he recovered from his pallor and his voice returned to its usual room-filling bass. As his condition improved, I took some comfort from this terrible event. Going back to England was now out of the question, at least temporarily, and we got to have his company for a longer period of time. He and I spent many hours in conversation during that summer and I was glad to have had that time with him. He alternated his time between the bed and the armchair, with occasional forays outside the front door, where he patrolled my mother's flower beds. We all adjusted to this new situation very quickly. It seemed like this was going to be the new norm and my grandfather seemed to also accept that this was not all bad. He began to enjoy his life again, albeit one with limited mobility.

Now Paddy was big into the horses and he had developed a betting system that he thought was both foolproof and profitable. He had this large format accounting ledger. It was a slender volume of wan paper, divided by red and blue lines. He spent weeks studying the form of several horses in order to select those that would be inserted into his system. These were typically horses with longer odds but once they made the grade, according to Grandad's qualification system, they were entered into the ledger and he would start betting on them. He continued to bet on them until they won. Once that happened, he would then toss them out, replacing them with fresh contenders. I'm really not sure what metrics of form were analyzed before he felt a horse worthy of being added to the ledger but the theory was that a good horse would win a race shortly after being entered into his book. If that were so, and the longer odds paid off well, then any horse winning within three or four races, sometimes more, was profitable. The analysis of form was his daytime hobby and it wasn't long before he asked me to take his first bets to the bookies. Other than an annual fun flutter on the Grand National, I had sufficient math skills, and an understanding of odds, to realize that I wasn't going to make a career of gambling. Because of that, I really wasn't very interested in learning his system. While the heart flutters along with a bet on the National, there were too many other activities that got my heart fluttering to warrant being drawn into gambling. The opportunity to enjoy the flutter at someone else's expense was a whole other matter though. If Grandad was footing the bill, I was certainly going to enjoy placing the bets. Besides, it was an excuse to "have" to go to Carrick every day, rather than do whatever other activity my mother thought more appropriate than playing around the streets in town. The bonus was that Grandad let me keep the change and if he won, I got a little cut off the top. I had become my Grandad's runner!

After a few weeks of placing my grandfather's bets, I became very adept at calculating winnings but I was also beginning to think that my grandfather's system wasn't as profitable as he thought it was. In cahoots with my cousin, I voiced the evil thoughts that had been percolating in my brain for weeks now. I was thinking that we should become the bookie and pocket the proceeds from this doomed system. Next day, the heart really fluttering now, we didn't place the bets but hung out in the bookie's 'til the last race was run. Not a winner among the lot! We took off to buy all the sweets and goodies we could until the last penny was spent. Well not quite, I calculated the exact change that would have been left over after placing the bets and brought it back to my grandfather, as proof of my absolute honesty. Along with my condolences on another losing day. I think I was awake half the night in anticipation of the next day's betting activity. Grandad had added two new horses to the ledger since yesterday and none were knocked out so it was going to be a big haul. I could hardly contain my excitement as he worked through the numbers and yes, when he produced the list, I knew it was going to be a big pay day. Off I went to Carrick again, Grandad's money in my pocket. It would soon to be all mine. I did not place the bets once again and I was so confident of a positive outcome that I didn't even bother to hang around the bookies while the races were underway. Upon going back to the shop in the afternoon, I was (and you knew this was coming didn't you!) absolutely flabbergasted to find that all but one of the bloody horses had won or placed. I was fucked!

We picked through the money in our pockets, and in our money boxes, but it was coming nowhere near to what the winnings should have been. We were bankrupt. It was one of the most harrowing days of my life, trying to figure out how to explain this one when I got home. Grandad had been waiting for the big win and today was the day. He'd have been listening to the radio and getting the results over the course of the day so I could just imagine his beaming and expectant countenance as I walked in the door later. I can't remember who gave me a lift home from Carrick that day but it was one of the very few times I was almost hoping not to be picked up. I even thought about running away from home, maybe to Waterford. They'd never find me there. By the time I pushed in the big steel gate on the driveway, I had concocted a story about not getting a lift to town, and having to walk all the way, missing the first two races and deciding not to place the bet at all. Whatever gibberish came out of my mouth, my grandfather called me on it right away and asked to see the money. When I produced fistfuls of change, he knew exactly what I'd done and, weak or not from his heart ailment, I got a tongue lashing. He made me swear that I'd pay him back. Within a few days, we'd made up and I was back to running bets for him but outside of that, and to this day, I have no interest in gambling. That summer proved to be both the beginning, and end, of my dual and duplicitous careers as a runner and a bookie.

Later that summer, during August, my folks went out for a drink with family and friends at The Old Mill, leaving me to babysit my sisters, and to keep an eye on my grandfather. By then he had taken to going to bed early with the newspaper, so he could study form for the next day's betting activities. Sometime between eight and nine o'clock, I made him his usual mug of strong sweet tea and I delivered it to his bedroom. He was dozing, head back, mouth open a little to allow his wheezy breath to escape more easily. I put the tea down on the dresser and shook him awake by the arm. Groggy for a bit, he awakened to what was happening. He grinned and picked up the yellow mug for the first sip. Acknowledging it to be to his taste with a nod and a smile, he grunted his thanks and I went back down to whatever TV program I was watching. As I left, I let him know that I'd come back to get his empty mug later. When I went back, perhaps half an hour later, the mug was half full but cool. Grandad was lying in his usual sleeping position; head back, mouth slightly agape. I couldn't hear him breathing. I can't remember if I took the mug away, I think I did, but I know I left the room and closed the door. I think I got the girls off to bed, telling them to leave Grandad alone, as he was already asleep. And then I went to bed myself. I was worried sick that Grandad was dead. I'm not sure if I fell asleep or if my mind simply shut down but the next memory was of my crying mother shaking me awake to tell me Grandad had died. I just knew it.

Ireland is a great country to die in. I'm sure there are many others too but my experiences of death in Ireland are overwhelmingly positive because of the support of family, friends and neighbors. Despite the late hour, people just, somehow, show up. I really have no idea how this all happened back then. There were no cell phones, no internet, no means of instant communication but out of the woodwork, all the right people seemed to appear. All saying and doing all the right things to help out. Jack, from up the road was there to take care of my grandfather. His daughter was calming my mother. Several others came along to help, some with food and drink. How are people so prepared for these kinds of happenings? There was also a nun from Owning, young and quite pretty. Despite the sad circumstances, I couldn't help but be infatuated. And don't tell me that wasn't God and Grandad having one more prank at my expense. It all just had to be retribution for my ill-fated career as a bookie. And perhaps for my prayers about not becoming priest throughout that summer.

5 – The Black Stuff

For the most part, I felt very fortunate growing up with both a town life and a country life. I was born in Marian Avenue, the end house on a row of terraced homes in Carrick, with a view of The Green. It was my grandparents' house and it was where my mother grew up. I think I was waved out the front window to show the world I had arrived but, of course, I don't remember that. By the time my earliest recollections cut in, I was already a brat. A gurrier even. You had to be, those were not always the gentlest of times. Now I'm not talking Dickensian hardship here but of my two distinct upbringings, my town life was probably the tougher of the two. But it's a life I remember with great fondness. While I was learning to swim, fish and commune with nature in Skough, I was learning how to take abuse, give it, and to pick myself up off the ground again in Marian Avenue. While casting a fishing line was the morning activity in the country, sculling along behind the back of a dirty, dusty, black and moving coal truck was part of the afternoon's adventures. Our Mas used to give us the height of shite for ruining the soles of our shoes from being dragged along the street. Nanny's house was small but it seemed to absorb as many people as could pass through the front door. Climbing the concrete steps would take you to a front door that was often wide open and almost never locked when not. And even if it was, you might find the key on a piece of string inside the letterbox flap. To the left of the door was a narrow staircase leading to the upstairs bedrooms and the only bathroom. On the right was the parlor that had been converted to bedroom duty for as long as I could remember. It's the room I was born in. The kitchen was so small that we called it the scullery and it had the back door leading out to a small, walled back garden that was dominated by the coal shed, with my Uncle Davy's pigeon coop built on top of it. The shed alternated with homemade kennels as home for whatever dog was the family pet, guard dog, or hunting companion at the time. There was a succession of dogs at No. 35 over the years but Bonzo, a mongrel terrier, is the earliest one I can remember.

The other side of the scullery was the living and dining space. The old coal-fired range was always alight, and this is where most meals were cooked so maybe it was part kitchen too. Whatever it was called, it was the hub of the house and it was where all-comers gathered for a cup of tea or a bottle of stout, as circumstances might dictate. Cooking was done in large pots atop the range and the smell of bacon and cabbage still does things to the neural networks of my brain. My grandfather, Tommy, was often parked by the fire, head tilted towards the radio on the shelf just behind him. Here he would suck an endless series of filterless Woodbine cigarettes down to the point of burning his fingertips. The top door on the range was often open, so that the glowing coals provided both real and visual warmth to the room. Tommy would often poke the coals with the poker to help the fire settle before tossing in another shovel of coal from the scuttle. There were always little eruptions about who had responsibility for filling the coal scuttle and emptying the ashpan, which was located underneath the burner cavity. The metallic clunk-whack as the rack was rapidly beaten first one way, then the other, caused the burning embers to settle and the ash to plume lightly into the room as it was dislodged from beneath the burning coals and into the ash pan. Some of the discarded ash was used on gardens and flower beds, though I have no idea if this was a good thing for the plants.

Along with being the family hub of my mother's side of the family, Nanny's house was also a great place to dump us kids off to on a Saturday night. When my mother and her sisters decided on a night out, we kids were often dropped off in Marian Avenue. It wasn't called babysitting back then but that's what it was and my grandmother found herself with a houseful of kids on many a Saturday night. While we loved Nanny, it was our least favorite place to spend a parent-free night. In the earliest years, there was no TV at my grandmother's house so it wasn't as entertaining as we would have liked. However, kids being kids, we soon managed to find ways to entertain ourselves. Very often, that meant things were going to get crazier and louder as the evening wore on. As tiredness cut it, you could be assured of a few squabbles between siblings and cousins. The odd bit of pushing and shoving, and maybe a little bit of a fight every now and again. The result was that someone always ended up crying and Nanny had to intervene to straighten things out. Peace would only reign for a short while before something else erupted. By the time the parents came back to collect their respective broods, Nanny would have had enough. Then the adult children, our parents, would have a bit of a squabble with her for a while before everyone took themselves off to their own homes.

Families, being what they are, would not allow such petty things to stand in the way of a good Saturday night out and so things continued in this manner for a while. There is no question that Nanny was getting the short end of the stick in this deal so she then had the daughters bring her a few bottles of stout when they dropped off the grandchildren. And before they took off for their own night at the pub. This was unusual, in that porter was considered a man's drink. When she was out, Nanny usually drank tiny bottles of a locally popular light and bubbly pear drink, Babycham. A champagne perry they called it, and I think it's still available today. For these child-minding evenings, however, stout was the tipple of choice. The stout was delivered in the smaller half pint bottles, these being considered more appropriate for a woman to drink. Perhaps she wanted the porter so as to keep Grandad stupefied as well, as there was no way he was going to drink perry, champagne or not. Nanny, ever the lady, had a delicate little half pint glass for her porter and she would only pour it to half full, adding to the look of gentility about the whole affair. On one particularly memorable night, or at least the early part of it was memorable, Nanny did something very unusual. She had this thick walled, small glass that she took down from the cupboard, and she brought it over to her chair by the range. Putting the glass aside, she stuck the poker into the hot coals of the range, and then went out to the scullery to fetch the sugar bowl. Adding a spoonful of sugar to the glass, Nanny then pulled the poker from the fire. It had a reddened glow about the tip of it, from the heat of the coals. She poured some porter over the sugar in the small glass, as we kids watched on with amazement. Next, she stuck the hot poker into it! The porter sizzled and spat with the heat from the poker and Nanny just proceeded to stir. The sizzling abated, she returned the poker to the coals and handed me the glass. Holy shit!

Poker stout. You have no idea of the deliciousness of this concoction. As the oldest, I got the first glass but in turn, we all watched, fascinated, as she repeated the process for the rest of the kids who were considered old enough to partake in the ritual. Though I'm not sure there was a low cut-off age, I think the volume was simply adjusted downward for the younger ones. I'm sure I remember a toddler getting to drain the few remaining drops in the bottom of a glass even. Needless to say, this provided great entertainment for the grandchildren, as the warm brew was administered to each of us in turn. We were made to promise to lay down for a while after we got our dose of the dark nectar. I can remember lying down on a comfy armchair, with a blanket and a cushion. The next memory was of being woken up by my parents when it was time to go home. This became a highly anticipated diversion for us kids and, for a very brief spell, Marian Avenue was the place to be until someone gave Nanny up. Someone opened their big mouth. Now you might be able to make some kind of medicinal argument for a whiskey-dipped finger soothing a sore gum but porter and sugar? Ma and her sisters went mental and the warm sweet porter went away. That said, and purely from a health perspective, you understand, I probably paid a bigger price for consuming sugar, rather than porter, over the years!

6 – Cooking with Gas

You can't beat cooking with gas. Any chef will tell you that the responsiveness, that fine degree of control, on a good gas burner can't be matched by infrared, induction, radiation, convection or any other method of heat transfer. We were very sophisticated in rural Ireland when I was growing up and we had a gas cooker (stove) in Skough. By coincidence, a gas cooker was also the cheapest cooker you could buy but I'll stick with the justification being the more sophisticated demands of country cuisine. We had a back kitchen, or scullery, and the cream-colored cooker took pride of place against the back wall. The yellow gas cylinder that fed its flames was stored in the cupboard off to one side of the sink. Not to disparage all other forms of cooking, I also loved the big coal burning range in the adjacent main kitchen but when I felt the need for speed, the gas cooker was the only way to go. I almost always felt the need for speed. I'm not sure if you can find the like of it today, what with the need for fancy range hoods to exhaust all the lovely cooking smells these days, but our cooker had an upright rear panel that supported the "grill" that jutted out over the top of the stove. This grill shouldn't be confused with the North American term, indeed there they would have called this a broiler. The grill on a gas cooker housed a rectangular pan, with a mesh tray insert, so that you could load up a couple of pounds of sausages, or rashers of bacon, to be seared from the top down by naked flames of burning gas. We weren't interested in eliminating the fat from our food back then, and maybe we shouldn't be doing that now either, but that's what happened with the grill. As the bangers and bacon were teased and seared towards perfection, the exuded fat all dripped into the bottom of the grill pan. Ever frugal though, we saved all the grease for later use in the frying pan. The grill was there or thereabouts at eye level for an adult so, as a child, I had to drag out a kitchen chair to watch my creations bubble, sizzle and brown under the grill. It was a thrill to watch them as they progressed to a level of culinary perfection that cannot be matched by any other technique.

"Clean your plate, there are children starving in Africa!" was a common refrain, as my mother encouraged her brood to eat. I don't ever recall having too much trouble cleaning my plate and the older and heavier I got, the more I wished I hadn't. My earliest memories of real food were of big thick rusks, floating in a bowl of hot milk, with a melting glob of golden butter atop the rusk. On a cold Irish winter's morning, the warmth of this breakfast is only exceeded by the warmth of the memories it brings back. As we grew older, we graduated to such feasts as just-past-soft boiled eggs with slim slivered slices of toast, or soldiers, for dipping in the buttered yolk. Big thick slices of loaf bread went under the gas grill to be toasted, on one side only, then on to be heavily buttered so that nuggets of yellow butter remained interspersed with the molten liquid gold that stretched, deliciously, across the entire surface of the slice. Despite how good all this was, my favorite was, and maybe still is, a big plate of chips. Before fast food restaurants made the French fry ubiquitous, we cooked them at home, using potatoes harvested from our own back yard. My love of chips saw me cooking them myself from a very early age. And you couldn't cook better chips than with a big pan of lard. On a gas cooker.

A child playing with a gas stove? It's too late to call child services, Ma is cooking with gas upstairs now. But that wasn't too unusual in those days and frankly, I didn't ever feel that I wasn't totally in control of the gas cooker, even as a nipper. From both parents, I had many hours of patient training on the dangers of fire. We were coached, while quiet young, on filling the big range with an assortment of coal, turf briquettes or wood. And, of course, a few burns along the way taught me lessons that were far more rapidly remembered and far better ingrained. Graduating to the nicely controlled little gas burners were nothing after that. My training started early on the gas cooker too though. Ma was well capable of deciding which of her brood could do what, and when. The gas stove had a small, permanently lit pilot light in the center of the four burners. A wand off to the side was brought close to the pilot light and pushing upward on the ring at the top of the handle released the gas and allowed the wand to come alive with a little plume of fire. This little flame, at the tip of the wand, was then used to ignite the burners. Ma started out by training me in the use of the wand and we then graduated to lighting the gas burners with slender, folded strips of newspaper. Running from the permanently smoldering range to the gas cooker with the burning paper taper, you had to make sure that no blackened ash or embers fell to the floor. Finally, we learned to light the burners with matches and cigarette lighters. All these backup techniques were required in case the pilot light ever went out. Or in case we changed the gas cylinder and had to reignite it. Let's be real here, there's no better training for the real world than the real world and Ma was not shy about getting us involved as soon as she thought us capable. Of course, she was a bit selective about which freedoms to grant us along the way but, by and large, she was quite open minded for the time. For me, however, I just wanted the freedom to cook whatever I wanted, whenever I wanted to, so getting "Ma certified" on the gas cooker was a big deal. I knew I was certified when one of the first requests she made of me to independently work with the gas stove was to light her cigarette off the wand! She liked a lie-in on a Saturday morning and, this particular morning, I had already delivered a cup of tea to her bedside table. The kettle was boiled on the gas cooker, of course. She had her cigarettes but no matches and I couldn't find a box of matches anywhere so she gave me one of her cigarettes and asked me to light it off the wand. Can you picture it happening these days? A kid strolling down the hall towards his mother's bedroom puffing on a cigarette! I wasn't doomed to smoke 'til many years later but it still cracks me up to think that this might have been the start of my bad habit. Now you can call child services, maybe they can still help.

But we digress, let's get back to cooking. Once she knew that I knew what I was doing, it was open season on the gas cooker. You get a great feel for food, and for the whole experience of cooking, when you work with a gas cooker. It's such an intimate, second by second interaction with the process that you become one with the whole event. And it is an event. Under the grill, you have a clear visual of what's happening. On an open pan, you employ all the senses. You can see, prod, poke and roll the food throughout. You can touch, tweak and tickle those burners, virtually instantly, to take the food in the direction you want it to go. The smells and sounds surround you. Cooking this way so involves and engages the senses that it becomes an intimate experience. You become one with the food, leading up to it becoming one with you. Okay, I'm getting a little carried away now but, to this day, I like to see, smell and feel while I cook. I know I'm only talking bacon and eggs here but who can resist a good breakfast platter? And an omelet, still sizzling on the pan, going straight to the grill (broiler) to be fluffed up and to have the cheese browned? Come on, you can almost taste it, can't you!

It is a tenet of old school engineering that you always ask the laziest person in the room to figure out the most efficient way of doing anything. That's me! My early exposure to cooking with gas has made me a master of one pot or one pan cooking. If I'm preparing a meal that requires more than one pot or pan, I need a sous-chef. And I don't do clean-up very well so minimizing any work on that front is good too. The ultimate culinary successes of my early years came from the chip pan. A perfect plate of chips, served on a warmed plate, all being hot enough to release vinegar vapors that will cause you to gag and tear up, is the foundation of my culinary skill set. It won't be a surprise to anyone that an Irishman loves his potatoes and I do. There is almost no bad way to prepare a spud; hot or cold, peeled or not, whole, cut, mashed, julienned, you name it and I'm pretty sure I'll love it. My mother's roast potatoes stand out, as do my Auntie Josie's mashed potatoes, but I can do chips better than anyone. They say it takes ten thousand hours to become a master of anything, I started young and I think I've done the time.

The traditional chip pan was an open pot with a mesh basket. And it was filled with lard, not the polyunsaturated chemical fats du jour that we are encouraged to use today. Seems like I was a whole lot healthier back then too. Regardless of your take on which fats might be healthier, we all eat fries every now and again so, when you do, you may as well eat the best fries you can. There weren't any animal factory farms back then either so we were looking at lard from pigs that ate what they were supposed to eat for the most part. Even when penned, they happily foraged about in the mud and the grass, and they enjoyed a life out in the rain and shine, so believe me when I tell you: this was the best of lards. The beauty of lard is that is goes solid again after each use, making for easy storage of the chip pan in the oven. In our house, woe betide the person that didn't align the handle of the basket with the handle of the pot before the lard solidified. The beauty of gas is that it quickly takes it back to cooking temperature when you need a fix of French fries. The whole process is quicker than going to the drive through and the results on the palate can not be matched. Modern home fryers have lids and filters that deny the necessary sensory feedback for making the best chips so I still keep an old-fashioned pan on hand for when I really want the best. Kerr's Pinks, British Queens, King Edward's, Records and Golden Wonders were all grown in our garden. Each one had its own unique taste, texture and mouthfeel. I can't find these in my local produce section now but the same process applies, regardless of the type of spud being used. Less experienced practitioners will often test the temperature of the pan by tossing in a single fry, though some don't even know what to look for when that single sliver of starch hits the hot lard. The more experienced know instinctively when the temperature is just right. They know that the raw chips must be dry before being piled in. The visual in doing chips is very important. The light golden color of the perfect chip is a delight to the eye but, despite the lightness in color, each piece must be cooked to fluffy perfection, all the way through, on the inside. The smell that wafts from the pan changes as the chips approach being done. The periodic lift, rattle and shake towards the end of the frying cycle sneaks up on a sound that is just right when the little golden pieces are done to this required level of perfection. These are chips! It goes without saying but the plate must be warmed to maintain a perfect serving temperature. Just ahead of dumping these delicious things on the plate, the final vigorous shaking removes the excess lard. The ticklishly light tink and clink sounds, as they hit the plate, are the final guarantee that you've done it right. Vinegar, malt of course, must be applied promptly and must be applied BEFORE the salt so that the salt can adhere, in volume, to each and every vinegar-wetted chip. The only thing you can do to improve on this gourmand's delight is to quickly place a fistful of hot chips inside a slice of heavily buttered round side of a crusty, fresh Carrick loaf. You now have a chip buttie that will delight your senses beyond all compare. The taste and flavor explosion in the mouth is accompanied by the drizzle of melting golden butter that will wind its way down your chin, and between your fingers. Only to be licked off towards the end of each heavenly mouthful of sandwich. Now that's how you do chips.

The chip pan, however, isn't a one trick pony. You can pretty much do anything you like with it. Sausages are great, sausages in batter are even better. Deep fried mushrooms are awesome. Fish and meats, of course. I've done bacon in the chip pan and one of my favorites, scotch eggs are unbelievable. One of the most challenging experiments in deep fat frying proved to be eggs. Eggs in a chip pan! Sure you can, it's like poaching but in hot lard instead of water. You need to keep the temperature down a bit or you'll wind up with an explosion of bubbles that make a real mess of the basket. The possibilities are only endless.

I don't have a gas stove today but I still miss it. You just can't beat cooking with gas.

7 – First Day of School

I remember our house as a place of excitement. There were yelling and screaming matches, we sang, we played, and we fought. We laughed and cried. We talked about the neighbors. We worried about what the neighbors were saying about us. We always got dressed up for mass on Sunday and Ma always made sure we had clean underwear before we went out. In case we were in an accident, you know! Da was the calm one, Ma was the excitable one and I took after Ma. While Da was the acknowledged brain of the family, it didn't take me long to figure out that Ma might be the smarter one and she was definitely the one pulling all the strings. Family circumstances dictated an early exit from school for my mother. There were a lot of smart women in the country back then but it seems like only other women and children could see it. The Irish inheritance was that men took the lead, women followed, and children were to be seen and not heard. At home, Ma was having none of that shite! Neither for herself, and certainly not for her kids. I don't deny that she missed seeing a few of the trees in the forest but, for the most part, she was a feminist in her daily existence, well before that became a thing to be. I'm not selling Da short here but Ma was special. She knew she had missed the boat with education and she wasn't going to let that happen to her offspring. She was willing stuff into my head with an intensity that probably spoke to the sense of deprivation she herself must have felt. I had to learn the alphabet before any other kid my age. I was at a chalkboard doing arithmetic before I could even say the numbers. I was reading comics, food labels, fairy tales, recipes, newspapers and magazines on her lap before I had the physical ability to run away. It all sounds a bit intense but I loved it.

Was I a Mammy's Boy? Absolutely!

It all worked too because I wasn't much older when I could handle any set of numbers that any hapless visitor could scribble on my little chalk board. Ma invited everyone who came through the front door to test out her little math prodigy, her show pony. Addition and subtraction, a piece of cake. Multiplication and long division, not a problem. You want to make those numbers bigger, go right ahead. Of course, I liked impressing adults with my amazing skills so I was quite happy to play the role for her. Reading was equally important in her eyes, and her efforts on my behalf gave me a lifelong addiction, for which I am grateful. It got very interesting when she set about teaching me Irish though, since she barely had two words of the language herself! I'm sure my early pronunciation was abysmal, given her lack of knowledge of the language, but she tried nonetheless. Some years later, an Irish language teaching program, Buntús Cainte, appeared on TV. TV was a big heavy box of antiquated electronics, with a small screen, and a grainy black and white image in those days. I can clearly remember Ma trying to beat Máire and Aileen, the show's presenters, to the translation with each new lesson. This woman, my Ma, was teaching herself Irish in her efforts to give me a head start.

This all went down before I started school. And I mean even before I began our rural version of kindergarten. Junior and senior kindergarten were dubbed "Low Babies" and "High Babies" in Ireland, if you can believe it. Now there were some disadvantages to this early head start in academia, chief among them being an ego that gave birth to a bit of mental laziness. That still gives me a bit of grief every now and again. Despite Ma giving me such a great start, she was a bit overprotective and she was most reluctant to let me out into the real world. As much as she was trapped, we were a single car family after all, she wanted me trapped too. In the absence of other distractions, I was hers. For that, and who knows for what other reasons, I didn't start school at the appointed age. Nor did I start at the commencement of the school year. I may have to take some of the blame for this too. Since I was such a Mammy's boy, I just didn't want to leave home and go to school. However, the day finally came when I was going to be dragged there, kicking and screaming, whether I liked it or not. Part of the problem was that I wasn't the typical country kid but rather some funny hybrid of a townie and a culchie. While surrounded by family, both in and out of town, I gravitated towards town. It was where most of my cousins were and it was where I liked to spend my time playing. As it happened, I wasn't going to town for my schooling. I had to go to Newtown National School which was just a walk away from my house. This school was, and still is, a small two-room schoolhouse near Ahenny, home of the ancient Celtic high crosses. While I recall the emotion of heightened panic on the big day, augmented I'm sure by my mother's panic at having to push me out into the real world, I really can't recall too much of the detail of the preparations for the event. I know things would have been a bit frantic and I know that my mother's stresses would have been echoed and multiplied in my young mind. We walked the couple of miles to the little hilltop school together, probably hand in hand most of the way. And I do remember that it was grey but it wasn't raining. For whatever reasons, I wasn't starting at the end of the summer, like most normal kids did. I think my start was after the Easter holiday, so I was going into a class that had been together for a couple of terms already. This may have been a planned process to "get me used to" school before "really" starting the following school year. I never did ask how that all came about when I had the chance. In any case, here I was, not wanting to go to school in the first place, and having to go in with the school year already well underway. I was a little stranger joining a class that had been making friends for most of the school year already. Talk about stress!

As we rounded the last turn before the school, by Kennedy's house, the Newtown woods were just hiding the school building from view. The panic escalated. I wasn't saying anything but I really didn't want to be here. Why couldn't I just go back home and write on my own chalkboard? I had plenty of books and things to do at home, why couldn't Mammy just carry on teaching me herself? I don't think I said anything but I think my feet might have been dragging still more as Ma pulled me up the steps to the gravel yard in front of the school building. From the perspective of a little five year old, the building was imposing. In reality, it was a tall but small rectangular edifice, with an even smaller two door porch protruding from its middle. Built in 1868, the walls are thick and made of stone. The roof is a dark grey-blue color, shingled with slate from the local quarry in Ahenny. Inside, it was a high ceilinged, two-room school house, catering to no more than about 50 or 60 students from the surrounding countryside. The little porch was also divided, with a door on each side that allowed the pupils from the respective junior and senior classes to enter the appropriate room. The two rooms housed multiple classes and a coal burning fireplace took center stage at the head of each room, serving as the primary heat source during wintery Irish weather. Irish weather, being what it is, meant that the fires were burning pretty much the whole time while school was in session. The toilets were in a separate little brick building, further up the yard. These were also divided into two rows, one on each side, and I think one side had miniature toilets for the little kids, while the other had standard toilets for the bigger kids. The doors of each stall faced the elements and, with the gap at the bottom and top of each stall door, this was a great inducement for practicing regularity at home, rather than letting your rear end face the elements at school. The school building itself looked like it was set in a carved hollow in the hillside. The hill above the school was swathed in blackberry brambles, thorny furze and fern, all interspersed with natural rock outcrops. The boundary of the school yard was a barbed wire fence that separated us from the evergreen backdrop of the

Newtown woods.

It's hard to imagine that this little school, with such a small population, helped form the minds of some very bright, some very nice, and some very accomplished people. I think Mr. Thompson was the headmaster when I started out but I was going to the other room and my teacher was going to be Mrs. O'Shea. Imposing though she looked on that day, as I grew up, I realized that both she and my mother were petite. I am sure all the other teachers were great too but I had the great fortune to see Mrs. O'Shea become the headmistress when I changed rooms from the little kids' side to the big kids' side. When she became headmistress, she too moved to the other side so I had Mrs. O'Shea throughout most of my primary school years. I can't recall too many times over the years when she lost it with us, though God knows we gave her cause on a daily basis. For the most part, my memories are of her smiling and encouraging, cajoling and guiding. It was she who guided my parents towards having me sit scholarship exams at some of the regional colleges and boarding schools when it came time for secondary school. She still makes little cameo appearances in my mind that make me smile. One lunch time she, and I think it was Mrs. Phelan, were having lunch at her desk in front of the fireplace. I came back in from play to get something or other from the schoolbag at my desk. Whatever conversation was underway between the two teachers, she paused me on the way back out to ask if I knew what the steering wheel of an airplane was called. I guess flying wasn't the norm back then but I recall it being a serious question. "A joystick!", I fired back, very matter of factly, and very sure of my knowledge from years of reading those little 64 page war comics. I was continuing on my way back to the playground when she called out to me again. When I turned, I could see the disbelief on both teachers' faces. They thought there was something funny, in the humorous sense, about my answer but I could also see they were taken aback, and totally disbelieving. Retroactively analyzing this with an adult mind, and to someone with little knowledge of airplanes, the connotations and potential innuendo of anything being called a joystick must have been hilarious coming from such a young mouth! However, at that age all I could see, with great embarrassment, was that they didn't believe me. I took serious umbrage at their disbelief. At home that evening, I reconfirmed the term with my father and, first thing next morning, I marched right up to Mrs. O'Shea to proclaim the accuracy of my terminology. All backed by some serious paternal authority, my Da.

"He was in the army one time, you know!", I proclaimed as proof of his military wisdom.

She let me vent for a few minutes, with I think a hint of a smile on her face, and then she informed that she had looked it up later, confirmed that I was correct. And then she apologized to me! Right there and then, I knew I loved Mrs. O'Shea and that she was the greatest teacher of all time.

On that first day of school, however, all I could feel was that she was taking me away from my Mammy. Standing outside the porch, Ma and Mrs. O'Shea discussed my first day at school. I could hear the clamor of the teacher-less kids inside and it struck terror deep to the core of my little being. I needed an escape route. Taking off down the steps and running down the road just didn't seem like the right approach but there was this big laurel tree, right there in the front yard. I sneakily made my way closer to the base of its trunk and when I saw them, heads together, deep in conversation, I made my move. Hidden from view behind the trunk, I made my way up to the lower branches. In mere seconds, I was twenty feet up. Okay, maybe it was only ten feet but it looked like a really big tree from my diminutive perspective back then. Regardless, I was now up and out of reach of the two most dominant women in my life at that moment. They both raced over and my mother, mortified as she would have been, tried yelling and screaming. That wasn't working so Mrs. O'Shea calmed my mother down first, before turning her cajoling attentions to me. I was having none of it; I was staying in the tree. The pupils inside were now darting into the porch to see what was happening. The antics in the school yard were far more interesting than the times tables, or whatever might have been occupying their attention before I showed up to provide the day's entertainment. Now I was truly done for. Not only had I made a holy show of myself with the teacher, and all this in front of my mother, but now all the pupils were a mass witness to my antics too. This day was going to go down as one of the most humiliating episodes of my entire life, no question. Mrs. O'Shea's continued coaxing finally had me, with huge reluctance, climbing down from my safety perch. She got rid of my mother quickly and held my hand as we walked towards the porch. The burning embarrassment of it all, could it possibly get any worse? It could, all eyes were upon me when we entered the classroom. The gross indignity of it all burned, as did my face, well past being introduced to my fellow students. My face burned still redder when I was seated at my wooden desk with the other "low babies" and beside a girl. Low babies? And a girl! I was beyond mortified.

Our little desks were a thing to behold though. Grainy wood, with the softer parts eroded by the palms of past pupils kneading their márla (plasticine) so that the harder, winter age lines of the wood stood proud of the surface. Sliding brass cover plates hid the little ceramic inkwells, each white vessel containing a small pool of the black-blue ink that we dipped our pens into. You can't beat a nib and ink pen for refining hand writing skills. That was all to come later, however, and outright embarrassment and humiliation was the overriding emotion of my first moments at school. My adventures for my first day in school weren't over yet, however, I still had one more card to play.

My first school work consisted of playing with márla for twenty minutes and then we had to draw a star. I filled the entire page with a large, jagged-edged, round and yellow outline and promptly downed my crayon. Mrs. O'Shea asked me what I thought I was doing, because everyone else was still working away on coloring in the neat little five-pointed things on their pages. I told her I had drawn the sun, that the sun was a star, and that this was how it looked, big and round with flaming edges. Right away, I think Mrs. O'Shea knew I was going to be trouble! After all this exhausting work, I can remember how delighted I was when the break was announced. Because of my earlier time-consuming antics, this was likely not too long after I had taken my seat for the first time. But I still wanted out of this hell hole. At play time, I remember standing alone in the playground, under the watchful eye of Mrs. O'Shea. While almost everyone else had someone to run around shrieking with during the break, I probably chewed on a fingernail and stared at the ground. Alone. Whatever I did, I managed to impart enough peace of mind to Mrs. O'Shea that she went back to the classroom after about five minutes of keeping an eye on me. I gave her another few minutes, just to be sure she was staying inside, and then I was off down the steps. I think I ran the whole way home.

Of course, I was hardly in the back door when Mrs. O'Shea turned up at the front door. I had been in the middle of trying to convince my mother that this really was the right time to be home from school.

"We got to go home at lunchtime today, Mammy. And I ran all the way home, Mammy, so as to save you the bother of coming all the way up to Newtown to collect me!", I reasoned.

I knew she wasn't buying my story though and when I heard Mrs. O'Shea's voice at the door, I knew I was toast. I ran and hid under the bed. I could hear the mumbled conversation at the front door but I couldn't make out what they were saying. I had visions of being dragged out from under the bed by the heels and being hauled back to school by the ear lobe. Oh God, could things possibly get any worse. Fortunately, that didn't happen. And a good job it didn't. I just don't think I could have taken any more abuse on that day. When the conversation stopped, I heard the front door close. I scampered quickly from under the bed and across to the bedroom window. I peeped out under the corner of the curtain to see Mrs. O'Shea closing the front gate on her way out. She was going back to school without me. Was it possible? Was I safe? No, now I was probably done for, Ma would kill me. After Ma closed the front door, I could hear her footsteps coming up the hall. She waked into the bedroom, where I was cowering on the floor, by the front window. She was even calmer than usual. Especially given the gross nature and the sheer enormity of my misbehavior. I was after making a holy show of her. But I knew from the resigned look on her face, hands resting on her hips, head slowly shaking from side to side, that I wasn't going back to school today. And she didn't even kill me. Phew!

I don't recall much of what happened the rest of that day but I didn't go back to school until the following morning. This time, although still very reluctantly, I managed to stay for the full day. Come to think of it, I don't remember too much of what happened for the rest of that first school year. I was still mortified at having to sit beside girls. I was in regular battles about why my drawings were a bit different from everyone else's. And I was bored out of my mind by low babies arithmetic and reading. But things took a great turn for the better at the start of the following school year. I was bumped right over the high babies class and into first class. How cool was that, I wasn't a baby any more. This was a whole new beginning for me and maybe this school thing wasn't so bad after all!

8 – For a Man or a Dog

It's not official but it's bloody great. There is no amount of money that you could put down for anyone to come up with a town slogan as good as this:

Carrick ... For a Man or a Dog!

But what does it mean?

Half the kids today probably couldn't tell you but I know! Or at least I know what my grandmother's interpretations of it were. And let me tell you that Nanny had half a dozen different ways to slay you, or praise you, with that one little saying. Yes, there are for this phrase, like all things Irish, multiple meanings. What's the use of a word or a phrase if you can't torture the minds of your audience and leave them with feelings of total uncertainty. Many a comment from Nanny would leave you musing, or writhing, with a lack of understanding as to what she might be on about.

Carrick is a small Irish town, straddling the River Suir. Carrick-on-Suir, or Carraig na Siúire in Irish, is made up of two parts. Carraig Mór (The Big Rock) makes up the bulk of the town and it sits on the Tipperary side of the river. Carrickbeg, or in Irish: Carraig Beag (The Small Rock) is the smaller "half", across the river, and this side is in the County Waterford. While the population made it past eleven thousand back in the mid-1800s, it has declined since those times. For as long as I've been around, it has meandered up and down between five and six thousand townsfolk. Anyone connected to Ireland's history will tell you that hard times are not unknown in the country, and Carrick has had maybe more than its fair share over the years. Located as it is, about halfway between the larger town of Clonmel and the City of Waterford, Carrick may have been passed over more often than it deserves. That treatment has only served to polish the granite though, and its people are the real Rock of the Suir. I know we all think our own are great but in the case of us Carrick people, we're right! The town is also no more than a stone's throw from the County Kilkenny border. You can hardly imagine the atmosphere in the pubs on an intercounty match day. Of course, when we can't find someone else to fight with, we fight amongst ourselves. The town supports two GAA (Gaelic Athletic Association) clubs on the Tipperary side of the river, the Swans and the Davins. While across the bridge is St. Mollerans, in Carrickbeg. There is not a lot of choice in these matters, you're just born into supporting one team or another. And I was lucky enough to be born across the road from the Swan club.

Despite the glorious history of the Carrick Swan Club, as a child, I seem to remember feeling a little intimidated by some of the Davins' history too. The club was named after Maurice Davin, one of the founders of the GAA. This fella was the sports superstar of his era. An amazing athlete, whether it was running, jumping or flinging weights down a field, Maurice Davin was considered the best athlete in the world in his day. To cement his place in history, he co-founded the GAA. We won't even touch the politics of those times but suffice it to say, Maurice Davin is one of Carrick's most famous figures and you'll be walking in some real historical footsteps if you take a wander up to the Davin Park. I have to stop going on about the Davins now though ... my Auntie Jean, may the Lord have mercy on her, would only kill me!

The fame doesn't stop there either. Still on the sports front, another famous son of Carrick is the cyclist, Sean Kelly. He now has a square in town named after him, and a sports center. In his day, he was the best professional cyclist in the world rankings for years, and was known throughout Ireland and beyond. In Carrick though, he was the

King, and half the kids in Carrick grow up thinking they will one day follow in his footsteps. Or maybe bicycle pedals is more apt. The Captain, Bobby Power, was another force in the world of cycling when I was growing up in Carrick. The local Carrick Wheelers Cycling Club has shepherded a lot of local talent to the national and international stage over the years. One that is already taking a run at it these days is Sam Bennett. Sam was born in Belgium, where his father played soccer professionally at the time, but they moved back to Carrick and he's a Carrick man. One of our own. On Sunday mornings, when we were supposed to be at mass, I used to play soccer with his father and his uncles down the lanes behind the Main Street. Unfortunately, their skills, neither soccer nor cycling, rubbed off on me. They are, however, still rubbing off on the more talented kids coming up through the ranks today and it won't surprise me to see other sports heroes emerging from our little town over many years to come. Young Michael O'Loughlin is looking pretty good these days too.

We can't talk about famous Carrick people without mentioning the Clancy Brothers. Now as a youngster growing up in Carrick at the time, you couldn't admit out loud to liking either the Clancy Brothers or stout. That was the music and the drink for the "old" people. But I loved both anyway. And I still do. If you haven't heard the music of the Clancy brothers, you should be ashamed. They went on to great fame and fortune in America and around the world and you just have to listen to their music. I'm telling you … go listen! These guys, for God's sake, were a big influence on Bob Dylan. I think Bob even stayed in Carrick with them one time. Aside from their great music, I met Paddy Clancy for the first time at my father's workshop in town. Da could fix anything and there were a lot of farmers in and out to him over the years. Machines and equipment, tractors, bailers, trailers and God knows what were in and out of the yard to have things welded, fixed and modified. I can't remember what Paddy brought in that time but it was great to meet a famous person. Paddy had a farm about half way between town and my house, in Skough. He went into farming back in Carrick, after years of being famous and singing in America. He had some of the coolest looking cows anywhere. I have no idea what breed they were but they weren't the usual Friesians and Herefords that everyone else had. In the years that followed, Paddy often picked me up on the road when I was walking home from Carrick. I don't know if he ever knew my name because he always referred to me as "Petey's boy". I was okay with that. And glad of getting the lift. It wasn't too long a walk from Paddy's farm to home for me. One night I was coming home from the pub, three sheets to the wind, and Paddy stopped to pick me up, just past the railway gates. After being acknowledged as Petey's boy again, I knew I was in safe hands. This time though, instead of dropping me off on the road by his farm, he just kept going, chatting nonchalantly as he did. Jaysus, I couldn't believe it. Where was he going? Next thing you know, he's wishing me a good night outside my own front gate. Then he turned around and went home. Nice man, Paddy Clancy.

There is now an annual Clancy Brothers Music and Arts Festival in Carrick, on the June bank holiday weekend. Worth adding Carrick to your schedule if you're touring around Ireland at the right time. In fact, regardless of the time of year it is, you should plan on spending a day or two in Carrick. It's a great place, with great people, and there's a lot more color there than you'll see if you only pass through. Believe it or not, there is now a world-famous tractor parade along the Main Street at Christmas. Known as The Christmas Tractors of Carrick-on-Suir, it's a parade of farmers tractors, all lit up with Christmas lights. An amazing sight to see. This was started by a local farmer, Stuart Downie, and he talked a bunch of his mad friends into joining him for the event. I swear to God, it's a real thing and it's gone viral. We even had it shown on a local morning news show here in Toronto. We have singers, artists, actors, writers and all sorts of talent in our town and the environment continues to deliver today. Some may only be known locally but, over time, it has proven to be quite the talent pool and any visitor to Carrick will have fun discovering our home-grown stars. Sometimes, it's hard to believe what the people of this little town can do but it's great. Carrick ... for a man or a dog. Though we should probably figure out how to add women into the phrase too, somehow, since they have, more often than not, led the charge in Carrick. That one might be a good topic of conversation in the pub on a Saturday night! When you come to Carrick, be sure to check out the Ormonde Castle, and the Heritage Center. Take a stroll by the Suir and wander its streets. Save a night for one of the local theatre and musical society performances. And be sure to keep your eyes open for the work of our local artists and crafts folk. Come see us.

Okay, enough of beating the tourist drum, what is that little saying all about? And how did it come to be?

There is a little historical confusion as to what it really means. Did we proudly coin it ourselves? Defining it pridefully to mean that you could easily find a good, strong, hardworking dog, or an equally stout man, in the town of Carrick. Our town was known for both. Though that definition must come with apologies to animal lovers everywhere, as our fighting dogs may have been the start of the legend, way back in the day. Or was it a phrase applied less kindly applied to our town by outsiders that were hinting that our men were more like dogs? There might have been the odd one of them too, I suppose. Regardless of what its true origin and meaning might be, if the expression is used by a local, in a praiseworthy manner, there is no greater compliment to be paid to a Carrick man. Used caustically, there is no greater insult. It is an expression that I heard many times growing up, used both admiringly and sarcastically, and sometimes ruefully or wistfully. This is even more true when the phrase is used by Carrick women. If Nanny did the "for a man or a dog" thing to Uncle Davy, sometimes it was nothing but pure caustic. Poor Uncle Davy was withered by the passing of the remark and you knew he was about to get lambasted by her. Said by any Carrick woman to a Carrick man she was proud of, you knew the lad would be looking forward to washing the dishes for her that night! Now do you know what it means?

Regardless of its many nuances, it really is a great expression. And a fantastic encapsulation of all that our little town is about. It brings intense emotion to bear, one way or the other, depending on the tone. It sums up the past and the present. And it holds out hope for enduring well into the future. It may not be official but that slogan really captures the essence of our town. And it gives me a little dart of proud pain in my chest any time I hear it. Or even when I say it to myself.

Carrick ….. For a Man or a Dog!

9 – Spuds 'n' Wudem

Despite growing up eating weeds that were growing out of cow pats, every time I go back to Ireland I have an eating plan for the holiday. I need a doner kebab, with extra garlic sauce, and I need that within 24 hours of landing. Smoked cod and chips is another must-have within the first few days. Irish Chinese food is quite different to Chinese food anywhere else on the planet. And it's good, so that's on the menu too. My sister usually does bacon and cabbage for me, along with floury boiled spuds in their skins. No way I'll make it through the first week without an Irish fried breakfast, you can't beat that black and white pudding. I try not to think about the cream cakes but when you're in a country where the cream is real, what can you do. I know I'll succumb to devouring a few of those along the way too. It's not that I don't appreciate haute cuisine but really, I'm just a fast food gourmand. And the Irish fast food is the best. Ireland maybe isn't the first place that comes to mind when you think of a gastronomical vacation but it might be a mistake not to have it on your list of the best places to visit, just to eat. Mountain raised sheep that are nearly wild, grass fed beef, and dairy products made with the milk of grass fed cows. And I haven't even mentioned the seafood. My mouth is watering as I write. Of course, you can have a drink there too!

You can't get too far away from the ocean in Ireland and I miss that now. When I'm not in a hurry, I still prefer twisty, tree-lined roads to monotonous straight-line highways. One of the biggest differences between the Ireland of my childhood and my home in North America today is with the sweetness of things. Everything, and I mean just about everything, is far too sweet here. My sour palate came from growing up in a place where almost everything was sour. Or, at the very least, not sickeningly sweet. Our back yard in Skough was a productive garden most years, with neat beds of carrots, parsnips and onions. There was, as you might expect, a large area devoted to furrowed rows of potatoes. While green bean stalks climbed the stick and string supports that Da had constructed, with way more precision than was necessary. He was like that. In the random spaces and corners that remained, Ma poked in other plants and shrubs. Growing things in Ireland is easy and Ma was a green fingered goddess when it came to making things grow. She would throw things into the compost heap and have a fruit bearing tree growing out of it next season. She always had a plethora of pots out the back. These might have starter twigs poking out of them, or they might contain plants that she grew from seeds, or from an overripened fruit. Indoor plants, outdoor plants, trees, flowers, you name it, she was growing it out the back. All these containers were arrayed along the path, where she could keep an eye on them from the kitchen window. Anytime she spotted a plant she liked, she'd break off a stick, jam it in a pot of soil and, like magic, a new tree, shrub or plant appeared the following season. I think she gave most of them away because much of the selection in her nursery pots never made it to the garden. Some of those that did get planted, however, included currant bushes, with red, white and black fruits, gooseberry bushes, and rhubarb stock. All sharp and delicious. Past the original planting, nothing was ever fertilized with anything other than cow manure from Uncle Jim's field. And we never heard of pesticides in those days so we're talking some pretty clean and healthy foods coming from this garden. A basin of soapy water might sometimes be used to discourage whatever insects might be attacking her plants, along with a bit of ash from the fire pan for the hydrangeas and roses. Salt was used on the slugs and boiling water for the ants. Though I don't think the ants did anything to her plants, she just didn't like them. My sisters and I happily feasted our way around the garden each summer, eating the little "thinnings" from the rows of carrot and parsnip seeds. We dined on spring onions and baby Spanish onions. Finishing up our work in the vegetable garden, we moved on to a dessert of goozegogs (our vernacular for gooseberries and you pronounce the gooze like ooze!) and those sharp currants. And Ma's truly tart rhubarb tarts were beyond compare. The cornucopia didn't stop at the end of the garden, it just got better beyond.

I rarely brought snacks when I went wandering the hills and woods around our house. There was always something wild growing that could be eaten. I wouldn't have allowed my kids to do the same thing at that age, at least not without supervisory company and a cell phone, but those were different times. In those days, wandering the rivers and hills was a very normal and routine way for country kids to amuse themselves. With adult hindsight, especially given Ma's overly protective nature, it is even more amazing that we were allowed to wander around stuffing potentially poisonous things into our faces. My mother was a townie though so she really didn't have a clue but, that said, I really have no clear recollection of how we learned what to eat either. And, more importantly, what to avoid. I know it wasn't my parents, since I taught them more about what was good to eat in the wild, than they me. I can only assume it was the younger kids watching what the older kids did. Some were learned by trial and error but to say that we carefully tested out new treats with very small samples sizes makes the process sound way more sophisticated than it was. More often than not it was done on a dare. I remember Tommy, my cousin from town, going out foraging with us one day. And we didn't know we were foraging, by the way. He had no idea what he was doing, he was from town after all. But he was really enjoying piling nature's bounty into his face. He came across this gorgeous looking plant with a thick central stalk, covered with an oval shaped cluster of red berries at the top. He crammed the whole thing into his mouth before we could stop him and he was already throwing up before we could even yell out a warning.

Fortunately, he didn't swallow too much but boy, was he ever sick! My Auntie Eileen nearly killed me for trying to poison her son. I have no idea what that plant is called but even now, I'd still recognize it at a thousand paces on a grey and foggy day!

Not every trip was fraught with danger though and for those of us who grew up in the environment, foraging while indulging in a sunny (really, that's how I remember it being!) summer's stroll in Ireland was a thing. One of my favorites was Sally Grass, often to be found naturally occurring in the damp shaded glades by the edges of woodlands. And also in meadows filled with cow pats! I think it's of the sorrel family and I have no clue where the Sally Grass name comes from but that's what we called it. Finding a big, leafy green cluster of this deliciousness was a joy. You needed to have enough juicy leaves to cram your mouth full all at once. And then, once you started chewing, the flood of sour liquid it produced would have you puckering your lips like a duck's arse in a cold lake, on a wet day in January. It was feckin' delicious, I tell you! My walk to school was a wonderland of fresh, wild food. The little wild strawberries that grew in the dyke across from our house were just the appetizer for those that grew on wall of the Brunnock's house, across the road from Mrs. Fitzgerald's, where the bounty was beyond compare. The delicate little plants had travelled all over the sun-drenched face of the stone wall surrounding the house and they didn't mind us picking a few on the way back and forth to school. I was later to be very grateful to Mrs. Fitzgerald for a much more serious thing. One time during a particularly bad winter storm, I think she may have saved my very young life. It had been pouring rain for days and the Lingaun River had broken its banks somewhere upstream so that it was now hurtling through the fields and across the Faugheen road just a little ways down from her house. It wasn't like that on the way to school but on my walk home, here I was, stuck on the wrong side of this torrent. It was quite the sight, like the rushing waters of Niagara Falls but now, here it was in Faugheen. The ditch (hedgerow) on one side was completely washed away but there was an old timber post fence on the other side, being held together by horizontal strands of barbed wire. This seemed to be holding up well against the flow. I had to get home and I knew it was pointless to try walking straight through this flood, I'd get washed away in it. However, I was eyeing up the strands of barbed wire and thought that if it was just my legs on the strand of wire below the water, that I'd be able to hang on to the top strand and shuffle my way across, without the deluge sweeping me off down through the fields. I was practicing on the dry section of barbed wire fence, just off to one side of the flow, when Mrs. Fitzgerald came out waving a tea towel in my direction. Jack, her husband, was right behind her looking at least as anxious but maybe not quite so flustered. However, by the time Mrs. Fitzgerald made it to the side of the river opposite me, she had an air of calmness about her that was just serene.

"What are you up, Paul?", she calmly inquired.

"I was going to climb across the fence, Mrs. Fitzgerald. To get home to me Mammy, you know.", said I with equal equanimity.

"Ah, hang on there now a minute, son.", says she, "And Jack will get the tractor to take you across that. It might be a little bit dangerous." Understatement is endemic in Irish colloquial conversation.

Despite my protestations about there being no need, as we didn't like to impose, she quietly persisted. Finally, she brought me around to thinking that it might even be fun to see how the tractor would make out going through the raging river. Jaysus, bloody good job too! The tractor started off at one side of the road and by the time we made it across, it was close to being dragged into the field at the other side. When I told Ma the story, she was bawling her eyes out and we had to rush back over to Mrs. Fitzgerald to thank her. There was great talk and crying, big hugs all around and I was wondering, just a little, what all the fuss was about. It wasn't until some years later that I realized what Jack and Mrs. Fitzgerald had done for me that day. God be with them both.

Up around the next corner, on the road to Newtown, was another one of Tommy's and Willy's fields. Just inside the five-bar gate was the biggest goozegog bush you ever saw. We loved them when they were small and sour but they were even better when they ripened up and were tinged red, almost sweet. The technique for getting over a five-bar gate was well developed by all of us. You ran up to it, grabbing the third and top bars with each hand, then you pushed hard while leaping off the ground at the same time. The end result was that you flew through the air and landed upright at the other side. Sometimes the bull was in the field so you hastily executed the same motion in the opposite direction. If it was all clear though, you could fill your pocket with enough goozegogs to get you through the school day. Much better than the moldy old cheese sandwich that you might have in your lunch bag if it was only Friday and Ma wasn't going shopping until the Saturday. We passed the Kirby's house on the way up and Mrs. Kirby was renowned for her currant bread. Her lads, and Bee, went to school with me and I was always begging them for a bite of her buttered currant bread. There was an orchard by the side of their house too and there was one apple tree that produced the biggest, juiciest apples I ever tasted. I was very jealous of the Kirbys sometimes. Up at the school, the feasting continued. The most truly sour thing I ever ate in my life were the sloes that grew on the thorny blackthorn bush at the far end of the school building. You'd get reefed by the thorns trying to pick them but my slashed and bloodied hands were only a testament to how much I loved them. I preferred blackberries while they were still red. They were sourer that way and you could fill your mouth up and suck on them for ages. Up at the top of the hill behind the school, there were these little pale green plants that grew along the fringe of the woods. The leaves looked like clover leaves but bigger, and lighter in color, and each cluster stood taller, each triumvirate on its own stem. You could eat the leaves and the stems. Nobody knew what to call them but that didn't stop us devouring these sour and juicy creations by the fistful. My mother's flower bed had something that looked quite similar to these, except they had pink flowers in spring and summer. I tried eating those one day. They were delicious too and I ate a whole bunch off one plant before she came out and boxed my ears. I don't know if my ears were boxed because she thought I might poison myself or because I destroyed the look of her flower bed but I was more careful in selecting a few stalks, leaves and flowers from each of her many plants on future excursions. That way she wouldn't know I was still grazing her flower bed. There were hazelnut trees in some of Uncle Jim's fields and a cherry tree but the best was the Spanish Chestnut tree that was by the driveway up to his house in Ballycastlane. You had to roast these on the fire and they were good.

This might have been the healthiest I ever was in my life. Not only was I living on the diet of a hunter-gatherer but all our meat and dairy products came from the grass-fed herds in the fields surrounding our house. It wasn't until years later that I came to understand that this wasn't the case everywhere. In Canada, for example, I have to pay a heavy premium for butter made from the milk of grass-fed cows. And it's a "Limited Edition", since the outdoor growing and feeding season is much shorter here. In Ireland, if the cows weren't eating the grass all the time, we'd be choking on it! Nor was this bounty limited to country life, there was more great stuff that I got to eat in my grandmother's house. Stuff that Ma never made at home. There was a fella from the County Cork that came around the streets of Carrick in a van selling drisín, or drisheens in the anglicized form, which gives you a better idea of the pronunciation too. We have this way of saying "d" in Ireland that is more like a "dh", similar to the English "th" sound but with a "d" instead of a "t" at the front. Nobody else can do this right. Somehow, we can't manage the English "th" sound in the same way though, and we make the "th" sound more like a "d". Go figure. Anyway, drisheens were a blood sausage and I loved a big feed of drisheens off the frying pan when Nanny was cooking them. While I wasn't a fan of it myself, I think this fella used to sell tripe too. Grandad loved a good bowl of tripe and onions, in white parsley sauce, with lots of salt and pepper. Everybody had bacon and cabbage, with boiled spuds, in those days. The lump of bacon in Ireland is brined and I haven't found a good substitute for it anywhere I've travelled. Indeed, you can't even get floury spuds the like of what we had at home. The brining and the subsequent boiling process somehow imparted a translucent perfection to the thick ring of fat surrounding the tender, melt-in-your-mouth, pink meat of the bacon. The cabbage had to be boiled in the bacon water, of course, so that every mouthful had the flavor of the bacon fat. When eating this fine meal, you had to have a piece of meat with the fat attached, along with a heft of cabbage, and then you'd top that off by adding a chunk of flowery spud at the end of the fork. The whole forkful, with a bit of everything on the plate, had to go into your mouth at the same time for the true experience. And, of course, you had to douse the spuds liberally with butter. A joyous medley of flavors to be sure and it's one of the meals that I enjoy every time I go back home. The corned beef and cabbage that is the traditional Irish meal in America is a regional thing. I guess the corned beef was cheaper when the Irish emigrants set up shop on this side of the pond. And they wouldn't have been able to get the right bacon anyway. There were other funny things that happened at Nanny's house too. Out in the country we had our milk delivered in bottles but in Marian Avenue, Jimmy Sexton came around with milk in a churn. Jimmy had a little sweet shop up by the West Gate but I think he had a small farm on the hills above Carrickbeg too. After milking the cows, he came around with the milk churns in the back of his mustard colored Mini. It was a little panel van, no windows in the back and just two seats in the front. Jimmy would have a couple of churns in the back. The stainless-steel scoop had a long handle and that hung over the lip of the churn. He would dip the scoop deep down into the churn, give it a swirl or two, and then scoop up the milk. Each full scoop was a pint. The women would come out with their big glass jugs and ask Jimmy for a pint, or two or three, depending on what they wanted and how big their jugs were. I don't even know where to get raw milk nowadays, it might even be illegal in many places, but this milk was creamy and delicious like you can't imagine. I loved going to Jimmy's shop for an ice-cream cone too.

While bacon and cabbage is at the top of my list of favored Irish cuisine, coming close behind were my mother's Irish stew, made with beef or mutton, it didn't matter. I think there might have been what they called spring lamb at the time too but we always had mutton. It was cheaper, I think. The mutton had more fat and, good as it was in a stew, a slab of mutton was even better roasted in the oven. The outer layer of fat would turn into one big crispy sheet of crackling that you could chew on for hours. We also enjoyed liver and onions, roast sheeps hearts, steak and kidney pie, and another one of my all-time favorites: cold pressed ham and tongue. This was a staple in our house around Christmas time and other holidays. The tongue was delicious hot too, the only melt in your mouth meat I know of. Along with her meat, Ma used to get bones, from Kehoe's the butcher, to make soup. The range was always alight in our house and the further away from the burner box you'd place your pots, the longer and slower the cooking process. The soup was always far away from the hot coals so that it felt like days went by before it was ready. And smell would only drive us crazy waiting for the first helping. While the soup was great from the first helping to the last, as we worked our way down through the big pot, it got thicker. By the time we got to the bottom quarter of the pot, I was making soup sandwiches. I'm not joking, you'd slather this really thick, bottom of the pot, soup onto big buttered slices of Carrick loaf and then slap another slice of bread on top of it. We used to get the loaves from Galvin's bakery in New Street, or from Kiely's over by Pearse Square. Ma would sometimes give me soup in a flask (thermos) for my school lunch and I always took some buttered bread along to dip in it or to make soup sandwiches with. That was some soup. And then the dogs got the bones.

Ireland is great for fish too. We were only a few miles away from the sea but the River Suir provided an abundance of trout, salmon and eels. I fished its tributary, the Lingaun, for trout but Ma thought they weren't good because the tannery truck used to take waste up to the slate quarries and she was convinced it was going into the river. I remember seeing the Glen River in Carrick one time, it was blue. The Glen was close to the tannery, and the whole bottom of the riverbed was pale blue. Like a Caribbean ocean it was. This pale blue background made the fish stand out and very easy to catch but you couldn't eat a fish out of that kind of blue water. Who knew what pollution was in it that made it blue. Out by our house though, the Lingaun was crystal clear, and cold, so I had to argue with Ma to have her cook the bloody fish. After all, weren't we drinking gallons of the water every time we went swimming in the Lingaun, how bad could the fish be after that? Turned out they were delicious. Da knew a fella up in Treacy Park who was a fisherman and every now and again he came home with a salmon. The River Suir in Carrick was a very entertaining place. We had the New Bridge and the Old Bridge, along with the quays that ran the length of the river in town. At one time, there was a small building on the Old Bridge. It was called the Nail House because it housed a man who made nails. I have a fistful of nails from Da's workshop that he said were made there. I have a souvenir of the New Bridge too. We were sliding down the ramp on the Carrickbeg side one time and I ripped my hand on some thorny bush on the way down. It had reefed out a nice V-shaped lump of flesh and, when we inspected it, we thought we could see the bone inside. It nearly made us sick so I pushed the flap of flesh back in, made a fist, and we carried on playing. Besides all the kids and casual fishermen on the banks, we had a great number of real fishermen who went out on the river in their little black cots to net salmon. The cots were all made locally. They were small wooden craft, tarred black, I think. They were pulled up on the banks for the most part but it was great to watch the fishermen going out with their nets. A boat on either side of the river, with the nets drawn between them. Anyway, Da used to come home with a fish every now and again, sometimes amidst hushed whispers to Ma, like he was running booze during prohibition or something. I'm not sure what the subterfuge added to the flavor but, no question, a salmon baked in the oven of the coal fired range was something special.

Not to be outdone, the fast food industry in Ireland had me hooked from an early age too. Everyone cooked with tallow, lard or butter in those days and you just couldn't beat the flavor imparted by real fat. Fish 'n' Chip shops were the staple for many years in Ireland but eventually, we started to see the emergence of such exotic things as doner kebabs and taco fries. God, they are awesome too! I still haven't found Chinese food that is better anywhere than that we had in Ireland. You can't beat a chicken curry and fried rice, except maybe with an order of curry chips if you're in a hurry. The smoked cod and chips is the best and don't even mention the sausage or hamburger in batter. It doesn't stop at the dinner either, the desserts are really good too. If you've never had a "99", or an apple tart that is actually tart, get ready to ruin your diet. And you'd only kill for the pastries, all made with real whipped cream. My mother used to make a fruit cake that would lodge in your stomach and feed you for a week. Never mind that you might be merry from the booze in it. Sherry trifle too. I'd better stop now, I'm supposed to be starting a diet this week.

Ireland doesn't seem to have much of a culinary reputation on the worldwide stage but, and I admit I may be just a little biased here, I've eaten in a few places around the globe and I think it stacks up very well. Go there and see for yourself.

Oh yes, wudem, what is that?

Whenever we asked Ma what was for dinner, she'd crack a big smirk and say …

"Spuds 'n' wudem!"

She then waited for us to react, and we usually obliged.

"Ah Ma, c'mon, what's really for dinner?", we'd wail. Much to her amusement.

Wudem is a corrupted abbreviation of "with them" so spuds and wudem was potatoes and whatever was on the plate with them!

10 – Moral Dilemmas

Daoine gorm is an Irish phrase and it means 'Blue People'. This is how we referred to the dark-skinned people of Africa in the Irish language. That may have come about because, in Irish, the devil is "an fear dubh", or the black man. I know we wouldn't have wanted to call anyone else by that name so blue people would have been a much nicer way to go about it. In the Gaeltacht these days, I wonder what they call the blue people in the Avatar movie? The Gaeltacht is a collective term for the small Irish speaking areas of the country. The first time I can consciously recall realizing that there were people who weren't pale, pink and blotchy, like me, was when I went to primary school. We had a little statue of St. Martin de Porres off on a side table. The little porcelain figure of St. Martin had him standing on a little money box that was built in to form the base of the statue. I had never heard of St. Martin before either but it turned out he was big into collecting donations for the starving children in Africa. Once I heard there were starving children in Africa, I was horrified. I mean really, really distressed. How was it possible? What with all the spuds in the fields and the cows being milked every day? How could there be kids starving in Africa when people in Ireland were taking good food off the table after dinner and feeding these leftovers to the dogs and the pigs? I immediately emptied my money box and brought its entire contents to school so that St. Martin could buy food for these poor children. One day, I had no money left, so I brought in a banana for St. Martin to send to Africa. Mrs. O'Shea told me that I couldn't put it in the money box and she made me eat it. I was scrounging pennies everywhere I could for the next several weeks when I found out that St. Martin had died and gone to heaven hundreds of years before. Now I thought that someone was trying to put one over on me. Even if he was a saint, how could he be buying food for starving children in Africa if he was already dead himself?

My donations stopped but I was still worried about those poor children. Now, when my mother told me to clean my plate, because there were starving children in Africa, I did. Though it was only years later that I wondered how me cleaning my plate could help a poor starving child in Africa. Some childhood habits stick and I know this one probably didn't do much good for my waistline over the years.

Now if black people were daoine gorm, or blue people, what was I? Was I part of the daoine bándearg? The Pink people? And what were all those English people? They were as pale, pink and blotchy as we were. What did we call the people in Japan and China? They were all a slightly different color too. It was the first time in my life that I had ever thought about defining people by the color of their skin. The daoine gorm thing still puzzled me though. I managed to reason my way through the black-blue skin color conundrum by another Irish anomaly. We called a Kerry Blue a Kerry Blue, instead of a Kerry Black or just a Kerry. This most Irish of dogs was obviously black but their fur was so black it almost appeared to be a lovely blue in the sunshine. On the other hand, some black people weren't dark enough to be blue, they were a lighter brown color so what did we call them? And what about all those people in India? And why did we still call the original people of North America Indians when it was a mistake on the part of that gombeen, Christopher Columbus, who had no idea where he was at the time. Then they called some people white but they weren't exactly white. They were all shades of pale and pink and sure, if you got a tan, what were you called then? What did it mean if you got a sunburn? The whole thing was one big mess in my mind and I was far better off not thinking of people in terms of color at all, like before. Besides, in history lessons, I was learning all about how the English were screwing us Irish over for centuries so I had to deal with burgeoning nationalist feelings that were driving me a little bit crazy too. And that proved to be a far bigger dilemma for me at the time. One that would occupy my thoughts throughout my primary and secondary education, thanks to how the history books were written.

The first and biggest mistake the English made when conquering Ireland was in not having English fellas write the history books for the schools. All you had to do was slant it a bit in the favor of the English, to make them look less heartless, a bit kinder towards the conquered Irish, and then make sure all the poor Irish kids went to school. We'd have been conquered in mind as well as body, in only a generation or two. That didn't happen though and, by trying to deny the Irish a bit of food, freedom and learning, they just got our backs up. All in all, it wasn't the smartest move for the colonization process. I had another big challenge in rationalizing the fact that my father, despite thinking he was an Irishman, was born in England. During history lessons, I was a rabid green Irish nationalist but as soon as I got home, I had to love the English again. Otherwise I'd have to hate my father and I knew that was a sin. The big philosophical question of the day for me was this: was he Irish or English? To make matters worse, his parents still lived in London and I loved going there every summer. They were born in Ireland but they had been living in England for years. Were they Irish or English? Many of my aunts and uncles, from both my mother's and father's side of the family, were living in England now so I had a cartload of English cousins. Was I supposed to hate them too? Of course, I couldn't, I loved them. Later on, I got a cousin that wasn't as pale as a mushroom like the rest of us. Her Dad was in England but she lived with us in Carrick. She learned Irish like all the rest of us, and she grew up sounding like we all did in Carrick. We all played together, naturally, since she was one of our own. Anyway, except for my cousins with English connections, maybe I could hate all the other English? That didn't work out either. I also had lots of English friends from going to my grandparents in London every summer. We used to go down to the QPR games at Loftus Road together and we were all "hoops" so I couldn't hate them either. In fact, we spent all our time hating supporters of all the other football clubs and we didn't care what color or race they were, it was the color of their scarves that was the thing. The more I thought about it, the more I realized that all this hating-by-color stuff was bloody stupid, very hard work, and maybe it wasn't worth the effort.

One time there was a Protestant that visited Carrick from England. He wasn't hanging out with our gang so we forgot all about him when he went back home and we never saw him again. I remember meeting my first real Protestant when I went to boarding school, at Mount Melleray. I had heard there was a Protestant among us and I was shocked when I first met him. All of us Catholic boys talked in whispers about this Protestant that was in our school. We couldn't figure out why a Protestant would be in a Catholic school. Was he going to convert to the real religion or what? Even though he was Irish, he sounded a bit English, or at least he had some kind of ponsey accent, and that confused us even more. He showed up at mass but he didn't go to communion so we were sure there was something funny afoot. As it happened, he was a nice guy, and he was good at soccer and basketball, so we soon forgot that he was a Protestant. There was another fella from the Seychelles. He had darker skin than your typical pasty faced Irish lad and he had wavy black hair. At first, we didn't know what to make of him either. But holy Jaysus, wasn't he a nice fella too! So he also became part of the gang. The only other funny foreigner there was an American. He had an American accent and everything. We couldn't believe it, he sounded just like someone on a TV program. Turns out he was cool too so we all got along. The only bastards in the school were our own so we had learned all about not being racist and bigoted in the very first term. Amazing the education you could get in a boarding school. While learning that being different was okay, cool sometimes even, we probably didn't realize this had all happened 'til much later.

Despite all the bad stuff that happened in some religious institutions, our school was pretty good. We got the odd bit of corporal punishment that wasn't deserved, and I think those priests and monks might have enjoyed dishing it out a bit too much at times, but otherwise, a religious boarding school wasn't the worst place you could spend a few years. We did however suffer from an overdose of mass and prayers. First thing in the early hours of the morning, last thing at night before bed, and more than twice on Sundays, for God's sake. It was all too much. You just couldn't handle the number of hours of praying, all the masses and religious instruction. We got a decade's worth of religion in every year. No wonder I didn't want to see the inside of a church for years afterwards. It's even a battle to get out the door for mass on Christmas now, even though I love the old Christmas hymns. My mother-in-law tells me that I'll turn back to it all the closer I get to the grave. She may be right, we'll just have to wait and see.

In our house, Ma was the boss. It didn't matter how smart we all thought Da was, nor did it matter that he was the one making all the money. Ma ran things and we all knew it. If Da was giving her any guff, the next bit of Sunday steak he had for dinner was cooked like shoe leather. I'm not joking, I used to bring strips of it to the Castle cinema on a Saturday afternoon sometimes. It was tougher than beef jerky, and I didn't even know what beef jerky was in those days. It was so tough that you could chew on only a couple of strips for the duration of the entire film. It wasn't only that Ma won the argument, she was also going to make you pay for having the temerity of starting the argument in the first place. Ma thought she never started an argument. After all, if you didn't argue back at her in the first place, there wouldn't have been an argument, would there? Ma did the silent treatment better than anyone too. She would get this constantly-smoldering look of pique and anger on her face if you had decided to go up against her. It could stay there for days if things weren't sorted out to her total satisfaction. Indeed, she often kept it up for another day or two after things were resolved, so that you knew not to cross that particular line again. While I was often the subject of such annihilations, I was also special. When Ma and I weren't engaged in open warfare between each other, I was a pawn in other arguments, and sometimes those were between Ma and Da. I know, I know, the child psychologists would have a field day but I think I picked up a few useful insights along the way too. Not the least of which was: be very wary of women! However, I wasn't stupid either and it didn't take me long to figure out how to leverage the situation to my own advantage. When Ma used me as her weapon of choice, I'd often play along. You scratch my back and I'll scratch yours, mar dhea!

I knew where Ma had learned her lessons from. Both my grandmothers were in charge too. And it didn't matter what the men were like. One of my grandfathers was strong and loud, while the other was a much quieter soul. Regardless of their demeanor, they were both under the thumb of my grandmothers. With all these lessons, and despite the patriarchal nature of Irish society, I knew there was a hardened steel in the core of women. Since Ma was the one coaching me for life, I picked up a few hints and tips on what to do along the way. I wanted to be the boss, just like Ma. As I got older and learned more about the rest of the world, I realized it wasn't that way for all women. And I didn't agree with that. But now I was in awe of what Ma, and both my grandmothers, had achieved. In those days, things were even more biased against women achieving all they might want. I still find myself taking Ma's position in the modern world but it doesn't always seem to be perceived the same way coming from the mouth of a man. Maybe it's a similar challenge to the whole color thing and we shouldn't be making opposing sides out of such things at all. Regardless of color, gender and whatever other alignments we choose to make, perhaps we should just all be nice to one another.

I do enjoy the conundrum my upbringing creates though, and it is this: if I take charge of things like Ma did, am I behaving like a male chauvinist pig? Or am I being a true feminist!

Epilogue
My early memories of tolerance, acceptance, equality and inclusion may not match reality to the extent that we might wish for. This story was written some years before my cousin, Lol, started her #IamIrish project. I think my childish memories were far kinder than the reality. I am an avid follower of Lol's project and I encourage you to check it out.

11 – Coin Tossing

Coin Tossing

My wit is not as quick
My skin is not as white
But living where my tongue is tied
You sometimes feel like shite

The summers here are hot
The winters bright and long
And when it rains I think of home
With words of Clancys' song

I'd kill for fish 'n' chips
An' I'd murder for a drink
If I could have them both at home
I'd be there in a blink

I love it here it's true
But still I'm from the Bog
If you come from where I came from
You may be Man or Dog!

12 – It's Only Words

You probably knew, and would have expected, that there would be the odd f-word in a collection of short stories by an Irish fella, didn't you? You may have stumbled across a few examples already but this story is all about the f-word, and other terrible things, so if you're offended by the word, you might want to skip this one. On the other hand, what do you know about the little f-word? If you're not aware of this great little word, stick with the program. You might even find yourself adopting the little f-word; instead of those childish sounding "frickin" and "effin" choices that you've been lumbered with up 'til now. Aside from the odd f-word, we're a fairly religious lot in Ireland. But we've learned how to skirt around blasphemy too. We are a race known for our linguistic gymnastics and we know how to untie our tongues. I'm a big believer in that whole freedom of speech thing. So is Ireland, it's in our constitution too. However, the legal lads in Ireland are the same as everywhere else, and they do do a bit of backtracking when it comes to protecting against anyone undermining "public order or morality or the authority of the State". That sounds a bit religiously authoritarian to me but morality is a big thing in Ireland too so you'd have to wonder how it all comes together in real life. Suffice it to say that we don't often see the Garda Síochána out with a checkpoint to ticket citizens for the odd bit of swearing. I'm almost regretting putting that down now; those robbers in government will be thinking they're onto something with that notion!

My take on the whole thing is that you'd have to want to be blasphemous or profane, in order to be so. You'd have to have that intent, up front, to make use of such otherwise-useful words for that purpose. In daily speech, it would be very rare to have such intentions. Who among us that grew up in Ireland doesn't remember some adult saying about us:

"Ah Jaysus, leave the poor little fecker alone, he's only playing!"

Nothing sacrilegious there. No bad intentions at all, in fact. Wouldn't you only love your Nanny to be protecting you from an over-protective mother in that fashion!

Anyway, to be profane, you'd have to be taking a swing at some sacred or religious thing. Blasphemy is the same, you'd have to be doing something sacrilegious or knocking God, or something like that. It's fair to say, even today, that the majority in Ireland still wouldn't want to do that. And certainly not without good reason, like where he might deserve a bit of stick for not looking out for us. And I'm sure The Big Man himself would understand that and He might not even mark us down for another sin because of it. The courts in Ireland, and anywhere else for that matter, can't even figure this stuff out. Except in places where they say this word or that word is banned and just flat out illegal, regardless of intent and meaning. That's a bit over the top to my way of thinking. It's a bit dictatorial almost, isn't it? The worst thing you can say about the big f-word, in my opinion, is that it might be considered by some to be vulgar. Maybe there are a few sophisticated people who can claim the higher ground here but I haven't met too many of them along the way. And a bit of well-placed vulgarity might be just the thing to take the wind out of the sails of some gasbag with notions of grandeur anyway.

Now that we're talking about God and everything, we should probably cover the one about taking the Lord's Name in vain. Despite us having to learn, recite and repeat the Ten Commandments in school all the time, I didn't notice how it was spelled for ages. I spent years wondering why I would have to inject the Lord's name into my veins. And was I supposed to do that, or was I not supposed to do that? And how would you do such a thing? Wasn't it enough that we had to eat his body and drink his blood at mass every Sunday but now he wanted us to get an injection too? I finally worked it out, of course, but it had me going for a while. I loved watching western films at the Castle Cinema when I was young. Mainly because that's all that was on. Though sometimes we'd get a Hercules film, where he'd be throwing a spear through half a dozen Roman soldiers with a single throw. That was great too. We'd go to the matinee on Saturday and, this one time, in one of the western films, there was a fella called Jesus. But they called him something like Hayzeus. It sounded totally different to the spelling. I thought that was their sneaky way of saying Jesus, without actually taking the Lord's name in vain. Sure, weren't we doing the very same thing ourselves? We'd often say Jaysus, rather than Jesus, so as not to be sinning. The Carrick Musical Society put on Jesus Christ Superstar one time and I was worried that the town would be hit by a lightning bolt or something. It never happened and the show was only great. Anyway, I always thought God was a bit of a joker myself, what with making children go through the whole First Confession thing and everything. I'd be praying with great ferocity and He wouldn't always come through for me when I'd place a bet on the Grand National, for example. In fact, it felt like He'd always let me down when I was the most desperate for a bit of cash. I think He's a bit of a Character, to be honest. I even wondered if He might have a bit of Irish in Him.

All that said, and in particular as a child, I was worried about taking the Lord's name in vain way more than I was about any f-word you might fling around. But then I realized something. If I hit my thumb with a hammer and I cried out "Jaysus", I genuinely wasn't expecting God to bring his wrath down on the hammer. It was only a stupid hammer after all, and the operator was more the problem. And since I was already suffering, I didn't need any more His wrath coming down on me either. And there you have it. There was no blasphemous intent in the use of His great name, and therefore no sin. Now to be fair, I'd always throw in a few extra sins at confession, like admitting to taking the Lord's name in vain a few times. So as to keep things in balance, you understand. Maybe there were a few times that I didn't mispronounce His name enough or something. Or maybe I really kinda half-wanted Him to strike someone down if they did me wrong in a really bad way. And I knew that was wrong, maybe even a sin, so I'd have to admit it during confession. I figured the deck was generally stacked in my favor though. After all, I'd done so much praying, hymn singing, masses, benedictions and decades of the rosary that I must have had a bit of extra in the state-of-grace bank. However, there were those times when I needed to tone things down. And that's where the little f-word comes in.

The little f-word is "feck". That's it, just one little vowel away from the other one but it's a totally different beast. It has all the versatility of its big brother and can function as a noun, a verb, an adjective, an interjection, or an adverb. Feck is a miraculous little Irish word that is so versatile. While the big f-word might have a primary association with sex, feck's primary association is with stealing or throwing things. I have no idea how this came to be but that's what it is. So, for example, we might have thought about fecking (stealing) my Uncle Davy's bicycle while he was in the pub. Or, in the alternative sense of the word, we might be guilty of fecking (throwing) a rock at a window in the derelict building round the corner. Now it has a similar linguistic versatility to its big brother in that we could also ... feck some feckin' bricks from the building site to feck at the old windows in the aforementioned feckin' derelict building, so long as the old fecker, the watchman, wasn't there keeping an eye on it! You get the idea, it's a noun, verb, adjective or whatever you need to fit the situation. However, the really big thing about "feck" is that fact that it falls well below its big brother in the pecking order of swearing intensity. It is a far more socially acceptable, and less severe, word to use in a more delicate setting. While very young children weren't allowed to use either word, as we grew older we got to slide the occasional feck into our conversations. Until the auld wan got used to it, you know, then we could build up to the big one. The psychology and interplay that brings about introducing the word in adult company for the first time is so wonderfully delicate that it's the stuff of a good thesis. Can you just imagine the workings of a child's mind as he says his first, not in anger, "feck" in the presence of his mother? My own personal technique is to slide it out the side of my mouth in a more hushed tone than the words that surround it. Now we usually didn't start with our mothers, of course, you would be far wiser to test drive it with another adult first. I think my practice sessions were with my Aunties, who giggled riotously at their sister's child graduating to big boy words. The giggling was all I needed to prop up my courage to give it a go in the company of my mother. Though I don't remember the details, I know I chose the perfect moment of impact, and then I quietly slid my first feck out the side of my mouth. It didn't work; I got boxed around the ears. But not too hard, and that was a good sign. I had broken the ice and was paving the way for a lifetime of swearing, Carrick style!

Feck is uniquely Irish and you may even find yourself adopting it. I'm promoting this excellent word for use everywhere, as it's a great substitute for the other one if you are in the company of those of a more sensitive nature. I can't hardly wait 'til I hear it in the wild in North America!

The nuances don't stop with the child-adult divide; there is also some gender differentiation. Women, by and large, don't swear as much as men. They are, however, far more vehement and effective when they do. If Ma was swearing at us, we knew we'd done something that really pissed her off. My wife swears so rarely that I sometimes wonder if she ever heard the words growing up. But when she does pull out the f-guns, I know I'm about to be buried under a mountain of shite. That said, and regardless of their own use of such words, I think an Irishwoman appreciates a good verbal technician. One well versed in the art and timeliness of swearing. You can even do swearing with tone! In my youth, I was exposed to elocution lessons and was making great efforts to complete my "ing" pronunciations in my daily conversation so that my truncated fuckin' became a far more eloquent fucking, with the "g". Around that time, I was availing of every opportunity to hang out with the gang in Carrick. We were at that great age where it was okay for the boys and girls to all hang out together. In such gatherings, we practiced our slowly evolving social skills. Conscious of my elocution lessons, one day I was merrily "effinG" my way through a conversation when this particular target of my affections remarked that my swearing was like poetry. Come on now, is it any wonder that the f-word became a lifelong companion for me!

The religious divide is perhaps more interesting than that of gender. I mean how could you possibly swear in front of a priest or a nun? Through the course of my education in Ireland, I was heavily exposed to both secular and clerical educators so, along with the f-words, taking the Lord's name in vain would be seen as a big thing in such company. Here again, my more tolerant take on the whole thing is that you have to look for the intent. For the most part, I think God has more important things to be getting on with than listening out for a few Irish gobshites calling on him to help their team score a goal or something of that nature. Whatever words you might choose to start out with, suffice it to say that the same rules apply with the clergy as they do with any stranger. Start out slow and slide in the lesser words to gauge the reaction first. And certainly before running headlong into your usual repertoire. One time, I recall being very worried about what might slip out with the excitement of going to an

Ireland soccer game in the company of a priest. It turned out that I couldn't even compete! Though, in fairness, he wasn't wearing his collar at the game. While I've heard a few of the clergy, and even one very cool nun, light up the conversation over the years, it's fair to say that they mostly practice what they preach and they leave most of the verbal gymnastics to us lay folk.

Way more challenging than the clergy is meeting a new girlfriend's mother for the first time. That's a job you don't want to screw up but you couldn't go through life not being able to swear in the company of the future Ma-in-Law, could you? The technique remains the same but you needed to be a bit more cautious and patient here, especially if you were hoping to keep seeing the girl for any length of time. Beyond that is consideration for how you might want to raise your own kids. Had I been raising my kids in Ireland, I don't think it would have warranted a second thought but I was conscious of the negative perceptions that might arise in Canada so I promised my wife I'd do better when our son was born. It didn't last for long but I did try. For maybe a day or two anyway! In some wonderfully weird and elegant way, my kids did the same to me as I had done to my parents. Stern on the outside, on the inside I was giggling my arse off, when my son quietly slid out his first f-word. Meantime, the wife was going apoplectic. Though I think she too was doing just a little giggle on the inside. Growing up on this side of the Atlantic, they didn't have the benefit of broad exposure to feck so they had no option but to make the leap from angelic baby talk to the big f-word. As it was for us with our parents, my kids are more linguistically prolific with their own friends than they are with us. But isn't that the way it's meant to be?

Despite my advocation for the f-words, big and small, it's ironic that I have found myself exposed to conversations where I thought another was at it too much. Amazing as that may sound, I guess we all have self-imposed or cultural limits. And I have to remind myself of that when gauging my own use in the company of those who may not know me so well. I have just a touch of a bias against women swearing as a matter of rote, for example, and I think children should advance slowly in the space. I think it's less a sexist thing and more an expectation born of my mother's philosophy. And what Irish son doesn't expect every woman to be a copy of his mother! I recognize that my perspective is all part of the skewed biases from my upbringing, along with the more recent conditioning from decades of living on the other side of the pond. While some do it to the point where I might feel a bit uncomfortable at times, I generally do not speak out. After all, I might be making others uncomfortable at times too, though that would never be my intent. At the end of day, it's often more about tolerance for each other, and not applying our own lens to judge the life and actions of others. This is only kindness and there's nothing wrong with being kind to each other.

If you even get to visit our wonderful little isle, I hope you will enjoy not only its greenness but that you will be open to its full spectrum of colors, visual and aural. After all, they're only words.

13 – Training for Vegas

Little did I realize that growing up in Carrick was just training for Vegas. Sunday was newspaper and comic day in our house and we brought a big bundle of both back from Tobin's Newsagents on Sunday mornings. We'd pick them all up after mass in St. Nicholas. My father always said that anything you could read in those scandalous Sunday newspapers from England was going on in Carrick. That look on his face, when he said that, told me that it was all about sex, drugs and rock 'n' roll. I wondered where in Carrick it was all happening because I wanted in!

Smoking is right up there as one of the few regrets of my life but I still have to laugh about how it all started for me. I'd love to say I was about four years old, though more likely I was older, when I first puffed on a real cigarette. I did have one practice run earlier though. I rolled up a sheet of newspaper to about the width of a cigarette and lit one end of it in the open fire. The tip was still alight when I sucked vehemently on the other end. I was all about vehemence so everything I did was done vehemently in those days. Unfortunately, vehemently inhaling rolled-up burning paper wasn't a great idea and I was nearly asphyxiated on the spot. It was hot, it burned the throat out of me and I didn't know if I was going to die from the heat and pain of it. I was so racked with coughing and spluttering, and trying to get some air into my lungs to replace the acrid plume, that I couldn't even scream for help. I thought I was a gonner. This is right up there as one of the top three most traumatic memories that I experienced as a child. The earliest incident was when, as a baby, my uncle Tom accidently (I think!) threw me into the open fire at Granny's house. We were in London at the time, and the doctor had to be called to treat the burns on my arms. I remember getting a stick of English chewing gum, it had a yellow and green wrapper with white stripes, as a consoling treat. While they applied some kind of smelly liniment to my arm, I chewed away furiously on the gum but it didn't work. I was burned, for Jaysus sake! Another was when I was in my friend's house in Marian Avenue. Teddy and I were kicking a little blue plastic ball around the floor. Nora, his mother, was getting the dinner ready at the same time. I saw a spot of water on the floor. A nice little gob of water that had dripped from the boiled bacon his mother had just taken from the pot on the range. She had put the boiling pot down on the floor in front of the range. I deliberately jumped on the water spot and wound up going arse over head when my foot slipped from under me. When I landed, my right arm went straight into the pot, up past the elbow. Jaysus, it was hot. Boiling hot. Back to Nanny's house across the street I went, screamin' like a herd of banshees. With poor Nora, distraught, coming in my wake. Teddy was bringing up the rear, wanting to know if we were playing ball any more. More doctors, more wailing and gnashing of teeth, more cajoling treats to stop me crying, etc. Now that I think about it, there were a couple more incidents that would vie for the top terror spots. Ma and Da were going out one afternoon and she told me she was going to buy me a bottle of Cidona, a local sparkling apple drink, but only if I was a good boy. I was asleep when she got home but, even then an early riser, I went down first thing the next morning to find my Cidona. There was a different looking green bottle in the cupboard and I thought that must be it. I screwed off the cap and took a big swig. Oh, mother of God! I was instantly puking my guts up; my tongue was burning and I thought I was dead. It was feckin' bleach! Where were my child-prodigy reading skills that day? Anyway, back to the first cigarettes.

I always tell this story after a few pints so you might have heard it before but it took a bit of time after inhaling the burning paper before smoking looked even remotely appealing again. One Saturday morning, my mother asked me to light her cigarette off the wand on the gas cooker. I was supposed to just rotate the tip of the cigarette in the flame and then blow on it to get it going. Feck that for a game of cowboys, I was ready to keep it going the real way so I sucked on the filter, more than a few times, as I slowly made my way down the hall. The half inch of ash probably gave me away and Ma gave me a clip around the ear after taking the cigarette out of my hands. I could hear her and my Da laughing as I ran down the hall. You just couldn't do my mother a favor sometimes! Funny enough, despite living with two smoking parents, it was many years later before I took my first real puff. There was a small gang of us round the back of the fire station, in Pearse Square. I remember the decision to take a fag (that was the vernacular for cigarette round our way) being of great import. A serious occasion, without a doubt, since Ma would seriously box my ears again if she found out. And besides, I didn't have the money to support a regular habit. Nonetheless, I can recall the weighty gravity, absolutely massive it was, of the decision I was about to make. Though I knew next to nothing of addiction at that age, it still felt like a life changing decision. But I wanted to be part of the cool, and very grown up, smoking fraternity so I took the fag. I don't think I inhaled much of that first cigarette but that was the start of my addiction. I've quit many times over the years since but I have been repeatedly lured back and it doesn't seem to matter that the habit now makes me a social pariah. And they are ridiculously expensive now to boot. Feck!

What followed that first cigarette can only be described as a life of crime. I'd be stealing the longer butts from the ash trays at home and sneaking out the back for a quick puff. I would purloin the occasional smoke from my father's pack when I worked at his workshop down by the Ormonde Hall. Surely, he knew, it got to the point where he must have been buying twice as much when I was around. Loose change lying around the house, sometimes in the bottom of my mother's purse, was really just my found money, wasn't it? The loose change thing was a winner because we could buy single cigarettes at Paulie's, down by the chapel. Sometimes, we'd pool our pennies to buy a smoke and then we'd sit on the log outside Paulie's shop and share the one smoke between us. Very social it was. While some of the old people smoked filterless, we preferred the filtered type. But we needed the bravado of smoking a popular Extra Size brand which, though the same length, were fatter and stronger than many other cigarettes of the day. Most days however, we took one or two fags from whatever pack Paulie had open. A smoke was a smoke. In fairness, it took more than a few years of occasional smoking to get me hooked full time. I came to the Mon, the Monastery was the local Christian Brothers School, for the last couple of years of secondary school. Being new to the school, the perfect place to make new friends was the bicycle shed because that's where the smokers went. I didn't have any smokes that day, and no money to buy any, but one of the lads gave me one. My first new pal at the Mon is gone now, may he rest in peace, but I still remember him fondly. It was at the Mon, about age fifteen, that I really became a properly addicted and regular smoker. Even though we didn't have social media and the internet to educate us back then, I think I knew I had an addictive personality. If I search for the silver lining here, knowing that I had this all or nothing penchant, I never went near drugs, thank God. Except for alcohol, of course!

While I'd had a few sips of this and that along the way, the first public pint I remember having was at the railway station in Waterford. It was me and my cousin, Pa, and I have no recollection of why we picked such a location. We were probably hitch hiking our way back to Carrick. We were both underage but he was taller than me so I got questioned by the barman. I must have been indignant enough on the day because I wound up with a pint of a local Irish ale in front of me. God, it was great! A few years before, while I was at boarding school in the County Waterford, I went back to school one time with a big lemonade bottle full of poitín. Me and a fella from Dublin hid the bottle in the row of evergreens on the walk to the schoolhouse. Every morning, on the way up the hill to school, me and Frank would have a quick nip. We wanted the bottle to last a long time though, so we'd only take a little nip and we showed up for class only invigorated, rather than tipsy. The first time I got drunk, however, was way more interesting and it was in Ballyneale, a few miles away from home. I might have been sixteen but maybe not, I'm not sure. It was some kind of field day, though my recollections of anything outside of puking my guts up in the beer tent are severely limited. After that, I managed to talk the barman into giving me one more pint, to rinse my mouth out as it were. The next thing I remember is walking along some country road, hopefully in the direction of home, and I found myself on my hands and knees in the ditch, trying to dispose of my innards in the weeds. I felt bloody awful and I wanted to die. I have no idea how I made it home that day and I have no idea what my mother did but it probably wasn't pretty. She must have known how embarrassing it all was though because I don't ever remember her bringing it up again. And she was a great woman for throwing all your dirty laundry in your face in the heat of a good row. Needless to say, I swore blind that I'd never drink again. But I did. And that meant that I had to swear that same oath a few times since.

The great thing about drinking is that it can turn anyone in to a fool so we're all wise to the fact that it might be our turn next and that tends to soften the reproach. I remember going into The Old Mill to meet up with my father one time and on our way home, we had just crossed the road at the bottom of New Street, right across from the guards' barracks. Guard is the local term for an Irish policeman, or policewoman. Officially they are the Garda Síochána, which translates to Guardians of the Peace. Next thing, the Sergeant stepped out onto the road and raised his hand. My father muttered something, probably a curse, and slowly pulled over. He had the window down by the time the Sergeant slowly came around to the driver's side window.

"How's she cuttin', Pete?", asked the sergeant, as he tilted his cap back on his head to rest his elbow on the window ledge.

"Grand, Sergeant, and yourself?", my Dad, coyer than usual, replied.

"I'm fine, thank God.", said the Sergeant, "Were you enjoying a pint this fine evening?", he went on.

"Just one or two, Sergeant.", came back from the auld fella.

After a few minutes of this convivial exchange, the Sergeant decided my father was okay and wished us a good evening. My father wished him the same and the Sergeant passed on one last instruction as my father put out his hand to wind the window back up.

"Keep her well under 30 now, Pete.", was his last instruction. And Pete did.

I'm not sure many would agree with that approach these days but the Sergeant was generally considered a great man in our town. Well respected, and kind when he could be. He knew stuff about maintaining the peace that you wouldn't find in the typical police training manual these days. I think I might even have had an afterhours pint beside him myself some years later. The excitement in afterhours drinking wasn't in the wild party atmosphere or anything of that nature, since the door was locked and most of the lights were turned off. Rather it was the whole illicit nature of the affair since all we were doing was having one or two extra pints in the company of old men. And most of them said nothing anyway. I should add that the Sergeant's cap was off though, so he wasn't on duty. There's a right way to do the wrong things, you know. These and other memories of drinking in Ireland have a warmth that have made them worthy of several retellings over the years. And no, just to be clear, I don't agree with drinking and driving, not at any speed.

Despite a few close calls along the way, nothing really bad happen to me because of drinking. Thank God. Occasional embarrassments, yes. Family squabbles, absolutely. But nothing of major consequence blights those early drinking memories. If you can get through life without touching a drop, you're probably better off but I have to admit that I still like an occasional drink. Though I don't do it often, I now prefer to only drink in the company of good friends who will take care of me should I make the mistake of overindulging.

The rock 'n' roll part of Carrick life was vibrant too. It may be a small town but we liked to dance and party and we can do that with the best. We had musicians that were in nationally known bands and singers in our local dramatic societies that were as good as any you'd see on TV. As nippers, we'd be sneaking into the Forrester's Hall for the hops, as such afternoon dances were called. The young gurriers, like me, would be trying to look up the big girls' skirts. When they caught us, they'd kill us and then the bouncers would throw us out. By the time I reached the age of going to dances to actually dance, it was all about the Ormonde Hall. What a place! Glittering silver reflections, colored flashing lights and a big disco ball. It was the epitome of style and class in our young minds. In reality, it was a rectangular concrete shell with a half-round corrugated roof. This was where we went in search of love and the talent was nothing short of amazing. We're talking local beauty queens, nearly everyone had sexy cousins visiting from England, and sometimes even au pairs from the continent, with the accents and everything. It just was an absolute cornucopia of local and international beauties. Unfortunately, I was a bit too shy to take advantage of the situation. We had lots of pubs with music too. All kinds of bands played the local pubs and any pub that didn't have a band had patrons willing to whip out a fiddle or a song without a by your leave. I remember being shocked the first time I heard my mother singing Sliabh na mBan in Lawlor's, on Lough Street, one night. This is a song about our local mountain that overlooks all goings-on in the Suir valley and it's a bit of an anthem for our town. Along with the more raucous Two Carrick Smashers ditty! I never knew she could sing, let alone sing in public with all those people watching and cheering her on. My own early singing career was limited to singing hymns with the choir but for some reason, I could never pluck up the courage to sing in public outside the church. Though there was that time when my cousins, Tommy and Hubert, thought I sounded exactly like David Essex, as I accompanied him singing Rock On one time when we were heading out to swim in the Lingaun. I still need a pint or two to empower me enough to sing karaoke with a group these days but I'd love to have been braver on that front. Of course, there was that version of Bohemian Rhapsody that three of did in Ballyneale that time! And that not only brings us back to drinking, a topic I've already said enough on, but it also brings us forward to sex, which was the last element of the scandals that my father hinted were abounding in Carrick.

Of course, we didn't talk about sex in Ireland in those days, so you'll just have to imagine what that all might have been like!

14- Uncle Jim's Field

Our house in Skough, the green roofed bungalow, was built on a half-acre of Uncle Jim's field. At one time, it was the first house you saw when you came round the corner from Faugheen. The house has since burned down, the green roof is gone. But the solid block walls still stand strong. Nowadays it's all a bit of an Irish jungle, overgrown and multi-greened, protected by a monster green cedar barrier on each side. Stuff just grows in Ireland. I planted the Crimson King

Maple at the front for my parents wedding anniversary. I think it was their 30th anniversary at the time and we were about to emigrate so I thought Ma would like that. This house was a bit special for the time. Indeed, some of the work would be admired to this day, were it not for the fire. I was a babe in arms while the house was being built and I have this little blue scar on my index finger as a permanent reminder of the construction. I was bouncing around on my mother's knee, right by the new front door, while my father was cutting wood with one of his prized tools, a fine carpenter's saw. I managed a great big bounce while Da was on the cutting stoke and I managed to get my finger right in line with the thrusting blade. I still imagine that I saw the little bone through the flood of red blood that surged out of the sliced digit. Since I was barely over a year old, I'm not sure that this memory is real. It's more likely that I rebuilt the memory from years of my mother telling the tale. In any case, real or constructed, my memory is that my mother went frantic. No, she went batshit, nuts, freaked out, and more. She plunged right into the kind of panic attack that only a mother can when her firstborn is mortally wounded. Not that she didn't contribute to a few more accidents herself over the years but it was always easier to rant and rave when the guilty party was someone else. And especially if it was my father. When Da told of the blood, sweat and tears that went into the building of our house, he often omitted my bloody contribution to the whole affair.

I'm not sure if any architect ever had a hand in the design but our three-bedroom bungalow was pretty cool. Two bay windows protruded from the front and the big steps up to the front door made it look grander than it really was. By today's standards, it was small enough but it was well and stoutly built. The front wall of the house continued across a gap to the detached garage, making the whole structure appear bigger than it really was. There was never a crack in any of those walls over the years. My father had that mindset. He put a good foundation under everything he touched so if the requirement was oversized for an eight-inch beam, he made it twelve. Just to be sure. The walls were cork lined for insulation and the plasterer, one of the few involved in the project who wasn't a relative, did a magnificent job of creating a smooth, pink, and very flat surface. I remember the pink plaster being visible in the early years. I'm not sure if my folks had trouble making up their mind what to put on it or maybe we couldn't afford to put anything on it back then. It went on to take many colors and flavors of wallpaper over the years. As times changed, so did Ma, and the paper gave way to her color creativity when painted walls became the thing. I'm not sure where the inspiration for the lilac color in my sisters' bedroom came from but we were stuck with that for a few years afterwards. The exterior was pebble dashed and those bloody walls gave me more cuts and scrapes over the years than just about any other thing on earth. The perimeter of the half-acre the house sat on was surrounded by concrete posts, tied together by taut strands of barbed wire. That fence segregated us from Uncle Jim's field.

Uncle Jim was really my Grandfather's brother and therefore my father's uncle but we always called him Uncle Jim anyway. Being a part of that field was great though. I could make my way down to visit my cousins by going down the back way, through the fields, to their house. It was also a source of the most wonderful mushrooms you ever saw. Down in the boggy part of the field, near the Barry's Mill corner, the ground was a bit lower and it tended to hold water for a little while whenever it rained a lot. The dampness must have been good for the mushrooms though because I could fill my big white enameled bucket with them on any dewy morning during the growing season. Some of them were as big as dinner plates, while the fresh spurts of growth were made up of the cutest, whitest little button mushrooms you could imagine. Of course, I munched on the little buttons while I filled my bucket, little ones on the bottom, big ones on top. Back up the field home, I carefully leveraged the bucket back through the strands of barbed wire before throwing myself on the ground to wiggle back under the fence. Dew be damned. With two lard filled frying pans on the gas cooker, one each for the big and small mushrooms, the smell was only bordering on heavenly. A big dose of salt and you had a breakfast fit for a king. Since Uncle Jim had a small dairy herd, we often had cows for company. They'd come up to the fence by the kitchen window, barely six feet away, and look in with their big eyes, eyelashes batting at us. My cousins had named most, if not all of the cows, so we knew a few of them by name and often spoke to them as they stood looking in, chewing the cud in that relaxed way they had. Aside from having pet cows beside our house, we had plenty of cow dung for the garden. While it was, more often than not, one of my jobs, my mother was also very adept at squeezing between the two middle rows of barbed wire to get some manure for her roses come springtime. I didn't mind going for it though because the other boon of the cow pat was sally grass! Only as an adult did I discover that the "sally grass" of our youth was a sorrel, but we didn't care, it was delicious. The cow pats seem to promote the growth of the most dense, bushy clumps of the sourest sally grass leaves. I'm sure that this might be frowned upon nowadays but the new leaves grew from the middle of the plant so there was no actual cow dung on the leaves we were stuffing in our mouths. Was there!?!

Down in the far corner, where the gate to the next of Uncle Jim's fields was, there was a cherry tree. I didn't know of another wild cherry tree anywhere so this was special. Its fruits were a crimson red, full and luscious, sour as bejaysus and just the best thing you could eat when they were ripe. Further down was a cluster of hazelnut bushes, almost big enough to be called trees. I felt like a wild man, feasting on nature's bounty in Uncle Jim's fields but the best of nature's bounty was the milk and the cream from Uncle Jim's cows. And we had both aplenty when it was time to bring in the hay.

In addition to farming, Uncle Jim was the local creamery manager. We had this 1.5 liter plastic bottle in our house at the time. I remember that well because it was so unusual. The metric system wasn't in vogue yet so having this wide mouth metric bottle was definitely out of the ordinary. I have no idea where it came from but, once a week, this was the vessel I took over to the creamery to have filled with fresh cream by Uncle Jim. All the farmers from the neighborhood passed by the road in front of our house, with their big churns of milk, on their way to the creamery. It was a wonderful medley, mostly of cars and tractors with trailers. Along with those were horse drawn trailers and, best of all, there still remained a few carts that were drawn by donkeys. In search of a lift to the creamery, I was careful to spread my attentions across all the passers-by. So as not to offend anyone. But my favorites were Jack and Jimmy, since both took their milk to the creamery with an ass and cart. I liked John's horse too though; it was a big animal and the cart he pulled was bigger than all the others. If I got up on the ditch (things were a bit upside down round our way: a ditch was a brambled, overgrown stone wall or fence) by the side of our garden I could see far enough up the road to see who was coming next. If I wanted to go to the creamery with Jack and his ass and cart, for example, I could hide if it wasn't him coming down the road. That way I wouldn't have to snub someone else that I might want to go with next week. When Jack's little ass came bobbing around the corner, I would rush over to sit on one of the huge logs that made for a fence in front of our house in the early years and I'd try to look all casual, like I had no idea he was coming. They all knew what I wanted but I always asked, every time, for a ride to the creamery with them. Jack would rein in the pace of the little donkey briefly, while I twist-jumped my rear end up on to the back of the cart, always trying to minimize the bounce so as not to have the shafts bouncing on the poor little donkey too much. The gentle gait of the ass was very calming, though I doubt I was overly conscious of such mind-soothing benefits at the time. Jack, though a quiet man, always engaged me in conversation, asking after my mother and father. I can't recall what stories I might have told him along the way but riding on the ass and cart with Jack and Jimmy evokes very fond memories. Once at the creamery, I hopped up onto the loading dock with my bottle and Uncle Jim would take me around to the separator where we would fill the bottle to the brim. I always overfilled it so I could take a little slug from the top before screwing on the cap. I already had a well-developed taste for cream and the weekly visit to the creamery only fed my addiction.

Milk was delivered in glass bottles back then and there was no homogenizing process so the cream separated out on the top. The foil caps that protected the milk were easily overcome and I was chased with the wooden spoon on more than one occasion for piercing the top and sipping off all the cream. I usually claimed it was the birds pecking the caps and drinking the cream but it seems like I had my ears boxed anyway. The beauty of going to the creamery was that we had a whole liter and a half of cream to work with for the rest of the week so the milk bottles were safe then. Anyway, I was doing all the work of getting the cream so a quick slug off the top was more like payment, it could hardly be called a crime. Ma always gave me money to pay Uncle Jim for the cream. Uncle Jim told me, the very first time I went to the creamery, to put the money back in my pocket.

"Will I give it back to Ma, Uncle Jim?", I asked.

"No, that's yours now, put it back in your pocket and we'll say no more.", he replied. Holy Jaysus, is it any wonder I loved my Uncle Jim, he was a great fella.

Not yet with a well-honed criminal mind, I foolishly told Ma that of the day. Even when we found them in our flesh early, we would always let them fill up on blood first. Then we would burst them out by pinching them between our fingernails. Despite all the fun we had being up high in the hay loft, bursting sceartain blisters, and what have you, the best part of the day was when we went into Auntie Josie's for lunch. Though we had this meal in the middle of the day, it was all served on dinner sized plates, heaped high with fried eggs, bacon and Auntie Josie's mashed spuds. Josie's mashed potatoes were legendary, even better than my mother's. Though I'm not sure I should have told Ma that! Auntie Josie made her spuds with so much cream and butter, and this black pepper that was way hotter than what we had at home. The mere thought of it has my mouth watering again. The big jug of cold milk, straight from the cows we passed by in the fields, was on the middle of the table to wash it all down with. Here we were, feeding up on the milk, the butter, and the cream from the very cows we were bringing in the hay for, so they had something to feed on during winter. Wasn't is all just amazing!

Of course, it wasn't all fun and games in Uncle Jim's field. There was one incident with this field that nearly gave me a heart attack. Along with one of the biggest hidings of my life. I'm not sure if I can blame it on my mother having me light her cigarettes off the pilot light on the gas cooker or if it was the fault of the Mrs. Gorman's nephew, from England. This Englishman came to stay with our neighbor, Mrs. Gorman, one summer. He had this great accent, like some of my cousins in London, and he knew all about fire, explosions and other exciting things like that. He put on a pyrotechnic display in Mrs. Gorman's yard one day, using only fertilizer and sugar. Things were booming, banging, exploding, fizzing, smoking and blindingly flashing all over the place. It was just magnificent. In any case, I was immediately taken by fire and I embarked on all kinds of thing to do with fire. I was melting lead with Gerry, my friend up the road, to

Uncle Jim gave me the money back. I can't remember how much it was but she wanted it back from me and I had to recount Uncle Jim's words in great detail to prevent her getting her money back. Uncle Jim said the money was mine so it was mine. Ma had no choice then but to let me keep the money. I can tell you that it drove her mad, week in and week out, to have to give me the money when I was going for the cream. She had to, in case Uncle Jim ever took it. But he didn't. It was only thanks to Uncle Jim that I had pocket money for years.

Sometimes Uncle Jim's field was set for hay and it was always an exciting time when the hay was cut and baled. In the early years, the dried grass was stacked in haycocks and these would be pitched, with old fashioned two tined pitchforks no less, onto the horse-drawn carts to be taken to the hay barn. Later, an old round baler was the equipment of choice and the long yellow grass was bundled up into small Swiss rolls of hay that were dotted all over the field. By the time I was old enough for secondary school, it was the more modern square bale, and this baler was towed by a farm tractor. I still preferred the good old days of horses, hay stacks and round bales myself. Regardless of what form the hay was in, bringing in the hay was a big occasion, and one I looked forward to every year. I'm not sure if we kids were really helping or if we were just getting in the way but it seemed like there was always a big crowd of people around to bring in the hay. For my cousins and me, it was one of the best playtimes of the year. I remember it as hot and sweaty work on a warm summer's day though, and us kids would be up high on the top of the stack to fix the bales into position in the loft, or the barn. That was the hottest place to be, as the heat built up near the roof, and the dust from the bales was thick in the air. You could see millions of bits of hay dust particles in the air where a shaft of sunlight broke through. In addition to being hard work, you couldn't help but pick up a dozen or more sceartains (ticks) during the course make weights for fishing lines. I would make little structures with matchsticks and twigs, just to set them alight. I was burning model airplanes and my toy soldiers in simulated battles. It was all so much fun. One day, I wondered what it would be like to set Uncle Jim's field of hay on fire! I purloined my mother's box of matches and hatched a plan. I would only burn the bit next to the fence to see what it looked like and then I would put it out. I had had a lot of practice with little fires up to this point and I had no fear that I couldn't control things. Within about three seconds of starting the fire, I knew I was fucked. Holy Jaysus, the whole field was taking off. I ran screaming for my mother and between the two of us, with some combination of a panicked beating of brooms, buckets of water, and lots of yelling and screaming, the bloody thing was finally out. Thank God we had that rain barrel of water right by the corner of the house or Uncle Jim might never have spoken to me again. To be honest, I can't remember how much damage I did, and that might be a bad sign too, but I know we finally managed to put it out and I was in the dog house for the longest time afterwards. I think Ma broke her wooden spoon off my arse somewhere in the proceedings too.

Despite the terror that incident recalls for me, I still enjoy looking out over Uncle Jim's field every time I'm back home.

15 – Tribalism

I'm not sure how I earned the nickname but as a kid I was known in Marian Avenue as Paul Bull. I have no idea why I didn't like it because it sounds pretty good now, but I didn't like it much back then. If I have blanked out some negative connotation behind the nickname, I would prefer to keep it blanked out so, if you happen to know, please don't tell me. These days, however, I would happily exchange a Bull-like physique and persona for my more rotund middle-aged form. While probably not unique to Carrick, and not even to Ireland, growing up there we all belonged to tribes. Born in my Grandmother's house in Marian Avenue, that street was my first tribe, my earliest sense of belonging outside of family. The Carrick Swan Club was right across The Green beside my Grandmother's house and my grandparents had moved across from an area long since gone, the Level. Coming from The Level was a real working-class badge of honor, and it was located just at the other side of the Swan club. Though I never swung a hurley for long enough to be any good at the sport, and I can only recall going to a handful of games over the years, I was still a Swan. My Auntie Jean, on the other hand, was a devout Swan and had a bellow of support that redefined the distance implied with the phrase: being within shouting distance. Across town, the Davins had a similar support base in Treacy Park and elsewhere. While St. Molleran's were the GAA tribe across the river in Carrickbeg. The tribes were fluid and flexible in nature, with temporary alignments and truces pitting one street or neighborhood against another from time to time. The nature of the town was such that the family, our primary tribe, crossed territorial divides and that made for additional challenges of allegiance. I had family in Marian Avenue, Pearse Square, Carrickbeg, and out in the country. As time went by and family members moved around, we were randomly mottled across the whole community and beyond. That could complicate things too as blood relatives, and those connected by marriage, had varying allegiances to club, town, county and indeed country. It all made for great arguments. I'm not sure how much of this is cultural or familial but we kids took an almost malicious pleasure in arguments, especially family squabbles. We looked forward, with great anticipation to any family gathering that celebrated a holiday, a birth, a wedding, and even a death. The event didn't matter, it was the potential for a good, drink-laden, family row that had appeal.

Christmas was always a great time at our house. Despite there being some lean years, there was always a festive air about the place and the build-up to the holiday began as soon as the month of December rolled in. The crates of beer were bought well ahead of the festive season, the bottles clanking off each other in the wooden crates as my father took them from the car to the garage. Financial condition aside, we were a bit fancy and we had a garage with our house in the country. Bottles of Smithwicks and Guinness for the men, Harp and Babycham for the women. Things were openly sexist back then and nobody seemed to mind. Except for maybe my mother sometimes. Well, maybe a bit more than sometimes. Then, as now, women really ruled the roost for the most important things anyway. My grandmother, Nanny we called her, drank Guinness with impunity, for example. Half pint bottles in a half pint glass was her standard fare. There seemed to be a chronological age where women's power increased, and from my earliest memory, my skinny Nanny had that power. And woe befell those who might have questioned it along the way. My mother was her daughter and she acquired her power early on too. Even with things that she might not have understood well, she was often the driving force behind the decision-making process, nagging and goading my more languid father into action. Nobody needed goading coming up to the Christmas season though and all due diligence was given to the early preparations.

Our house had a "front room" too. Some called it a parlor or living room, and it was reserved for Christmas and special occasions. Much larger in my childhood memory than it was in adult reality, it contained a sofa and a couple of armchairs, along with a coffee table and matching end tables that my father had made. All these items somehow surrounded the white-tiled fireplace, which was then the focal point of the room. Off to one side of the fireplace was a serving hatch that could be opened to pass food and drink through from the kitchen. The fire guard was a wrought iron and copper beauty that my father had made and the metal scroll work matched the wrought iron chandelier and wall sconces that were also the products of his skills. I still have the matching fire iron set that sat beside the mantle. Early every December the first fire was lit. We used to look up the chimney to see if we could see any evidence of bird droppings or twigs, in case they had nested there and we were in danger of smoking the house out. We couldn't see up more than a foot or two but regardless, we always made the call that all was well. Along with tightly balled and twisted sheets of newspaper, we carefully placed a little white fuel-soaked "firelighter" brick in the center. We added kindling next, and then some magical combination of coal and peat briquettes. Applying the lighted matchstick to the little fringes of paper sticking out from under the black and brown tower of fossil fuels, the glow of those first flames signaled the start of the holiday season.

Over the years, along with the parties at our house, we also had family get-togethers at all the aunts and uncles. I have only the fondest memories of spending time in Carrickbeg, in Pearse Square, and with our grandparents in Marian Avenue. But there was one particular party at our house that really stands out. For the most part, these get-togethers were with one side of the family or the other, either my mother's or my father's side. But this Christmas, it was a gathering from both sides. Let me start off the recount by saying that this combining families is not always a good idea! In later years, I wondered how it was possible to get this many people into our house, let alone into the living room. Most of my uncles and aunts were there, along with my mother's parents. It must have been after Christmas Day because ham and turkey sandwiches were served, through the hatch from the kitchen, and fairly early in the evening's proceedings too. The fire was roaring up the chimney, those star-shape Christmas lights, blue and red, were sparkling and winking on the tree in the bay window at the front. The ambiance was a festive glow of fire and Christmas lights, with great storytelling in progress from the start. I took it upon myself to take the empty beer bottles out of the living room and put them in the wooden crates that were aligned along the wall in the hall for that very purpose. My father liked to dispense the new bottles to our guests but after a few pints, he was more interested in the chat so that duty then fell to me. Since this was an adult party, few if any of my cousins were around so I was happy to have a job that kept me busy and out of the way of aunts that wanted to cuddle and kiss the nephew still more as the night wore on. Somehow, we kids felt the burden of responsibility to live out the unaccomplished parts of their lives for them and they imparted those ambitions of a grander life to us with alcohol soaked embraces. We loved it all anyway and believed that somehow, we would fulfill their vicarious wishes for that wonderful life they dreamed of. Needless to say, any family member not present was discussed at great length. And they were typically reviewed with a most jaundiced eye. Friends and neighbors were all good candidates for discussion too but the best was saved for absent family. Once all those were adjudicated upon, they turned on each other. By this time, of course, everyone was sufficiently well-oiled that the truth wasn't as intimidating as it might have been only hours earlier. Though such criticisms were often introduced under the guise of being helpful to the subject under attack.

"Now why did you do …" was a common introduction to a question that, after listening to the response, was going to be followed by an explanation of why you might be have been so daft as to have done such a thing, in such a way. By the time everyone had sent a barb or two towards their favorite target of the moment, one of these little brush fires was sure to turn into a major conflagration. This was my favorite time! Now I could whisk away beer bottles that still had a bit left in the bottom and I could down that on my way to depositing the empties in the crate. It was much easier now to sneak an odd cigarette from someone's pack too. I really didn't know how to smoke then, and I couldn't inhale without choking, but the very wickedness of it all was quite a thrill. By this time, the conversation was so engaging that even my overly-loving aunts weren't seeing me wandering around in the background and, if I was out of the room often enough on my beer bottle duties, they started to forget about me. This is when the conversations got juicy. Despite my efforts to stay invisible in the early part of the evening, I could still feel a temporary hush descend whenever I came back into the room. Though I would resort to pausing, and listening, outside the door for longer and longer spells, nothing really worked better than them consuming a few more drinks. The busier I was draining beer bottles, the less I minded about what scandal I might be missing out on. I wish I could remember a little more about the content of such discussions but, for whatever reason, these stories are lost to me. At some later stage of the evening, my Aunties Edna and Jean were crying and singing Tears of a Clown, their arms around my shoulders. My mother did her rendition of Sliabh na mBan and my Aunties Edna and Shiela sang another Irish camalin that had us all with tears in our eyes. Though I had no idea what I was crying about to be honest. The men all told stories of the past, with sage expressions on their faces, while my grandmother ridiculed the whole gathering as being a bunch of drunkards with not a shred of sense amongst the lot of them. My grandmother was very insightful sometimes.

On the evening in question, my Uncle Tom was present. He was back from Australia for a visit at the time. This was the same Uncle that threw me into the fire as a baby, accidently I hope, and burned my arm. Regardless, I loved him right along with all my other aunts and uncles and it was all very exotic to us, having an uncle that lived in Australia. Anyway, he and my mother got into some kind of big fight and she was screaming at him at the top of her lungs, her words lighting up the air better than the fire. And he was screaming back, albeit a few tones lower. I think, as the youngest brother, he would have been conscious of my Da and my Uncle Pat keeping an eye on him with regards to any of the women in the family. I'm damned if I can remember what this was all about either but I was very upset by the whole affair and I must have somehow made that known. I was out on the front grass, fulminating to myself on this travesty, when my uncle came out to join me. He was trying to placate me and say it was just a grown-up family thing. I wasn't having any of it, or at least not 'til my mother and uncle made up, and I told him so. I remember going into a lengthy rant about him being away in Australia and that it just wasn't on for him to go back to Australia without having this fixed. Somehow, my mother found herself out with us on the grass too and I lectured them both about the importance of family, while the rest of the clans gathered on the front steps to watch the proceedings. By some manipulative set of childish techniques, and after about ten minutes of childish negotiation, though it seemed like much longer at the time, I had the two of them hug and make up. Then they both hugged me and it was back to the steps for the biggest family hugging session I ever partook in. God almighty, the things a kid had to do sometimes.

Anywhere but Ireland, that might have signaled an end to the night's festivities. In our house, however, it was just an interesting pause in the proceedings and I was hiding outside the door listening to them all talk about how grown up I was for a little fella and them all quoting the "from the mouth of babes" line. While I basked in the glory of it all, it didn't last very long. I'm sure it was within mere minutes that they were all back to bashing those absent again. In even shorter time than before, they were back to bashing those present and your typical Irish family gathering was back in full swing. Next up on the fight card for the night was Ma and her sister, my Auntie Edna. They were at it hammer and tongs.

"Ah, fuck it!", said I to myself, and I grabbed a bottle of Harp and a smoke before heading down to the sand pile behind the garage. They were both local, let them fix it themselves this time.

PS – They weren't talking for about three weeks after than night but they all enjoyed the gatherings at Aunite Edna's on a Saturday night too much to let it go on longer than that!

16 - Kilkieran

It's nice to know where you're going to wind up. Though it probably won't matter much at that point, there is a sense of completeness, of the roundness of life, to having a known destination in mind when the day of reckoning comes. I'll have to get my facts straight on this next time I'm home but I think I'll be part of the 5th generation of the Walshs to be buried up in Kilkieran Cemetery. Regardless of how many generations are in there, my father and mother, my grandfather and grandmother, along with his forebears and many of my uncles and aunts, are all in the family crypt at Kilkieran. Strange as it might seem to some, I have the fondest memories of family funerals at Kilkieran. I feel so connected to the place that it was important to bring back our Canadian-born children, as babies, to have them photographed next to the family tomb. I have no idea if I've damaged them for life, or if I have sown the seeds of connection to the place, but I can only hope it is the latter. It's kind of warming to think that we'll all be carrying on the party on the hill above Skough, surrounded by family, friends and neighbors, for the rest of time.

Kilkieran is a beautiful setting, perched on the side of a hill overlooking the Suir valley, as it is. It's also a designated historical site so it's not uncommon to see tourists sauntering through the headstones when I go home to visit the folks. Proud as I am of it, I am tempted to regale them with stories of the funerals I have attended here. But I resist. Knowing they would probably be alarmed were I to do so. You have to grow up with this weirdness to appreciate it. Along with the ancient high crosses, the cemetery is home to St. Kieran's Holy Well. Drinking water from the Holy Well is said to be a cure for headaches. Ma always thought that it was a cure for other head ailments too and she could occasionally be heard recommending that this or that person might benefit from downing, or dowsing with, a drop or two of the blessed liquid. I never had a headache when I drank from its crystal coldness so I can't confirm its curative properties but it is clear, cold and refreshing. And you won't be struck by lightning for imbibing with the sole purpose of slaking a thirst. Off to one side is Stranger's Corner. This if flagged by a small stone marker, and it commemorates those who were buried without a friend or family member to bid them farewell.

Our family tomb is right beside one of the High Crosses, surrounded by an aged wrought iron railing. One day we'll have to catch up on the inscriptions, my own parents aren't noted there yet, for example. Hopefully we can do that without doing any damage to the original blue-grey stone. It would be nice if we are all remembered to those who come behind us. The stone monument, surrounded by the railings, sits atop a chamber where we are each in turn, laid to rest. It's a very eco-friendly method of burial and, as each one of us is interred, we get an update on the condition of the previous and most recent occupants. So long as we pace ourselves, the ebb and flow of the seasons, the rains and what have you, all take care of the process of assimilation, so that there is always room for those of us to follow. Believe me, I know how strange this all sounds but there is a kind of comfort in knowing that we are all blending together in the earth that is our home, for eternity. In preparation for a burial, our neighbors remove the soil from outside the railing, to reveal the slabs that cover the steps to the underground chamber. With the slabs out of the way, the steps to the underground chamber and the entryway are revealed. While we all take pride in carrying the coffins of our forebears, as I did with Ma first, and then Da some years later, we only take the coffin to the top of the steps. The story goes that it's bad luck for any male member of the Walsh family to enter the underground chamber and so, we don't. Responsibility for the few remaining steps downward are handled by friends and neighbors.

There is no more beautifully melancholic a setting for a funeral than a grey, rainy day on the hill above Skough. I'm not sure if I should ask for a piper to bid me farewell when my turn comes, or if I should have one of the lads blasting some rock anthem through a Bluetooth speaker for me. Or I could do something drastic and have a hot Latin number belting it out over the valley. And maybe everyone should have a glass in their hand!

The old way was, and may even still be, that the men remain resolutely stoic and tear-free on such occasions. While the girls are allowed to release their emotions. I was in Canada when I got the call that my mother had cancer. She had never been sick a day in her life and we always just expected her to outlive my father by decades. Perhaps she'd even outlive me. I really couldn't handle it when I first got the news and, for reasons that I'm not sure I can even now put into words, I didn't jump on a plane to go see her. I know I didn't want to accept that this could happen to Ma. Some few months later, the news came that she was gone. I didn't want to go home for the funeral. If I didn't go, she wouldn't be gone. Somehow, the girls managed to talk me into getting on a plane. I hadn't seen her in decline and beautiful though the presentation was, what with the weight loss of cancer and the preparation for presentation, I almost didn't recognize her laid out in the funeral home in New Street. I was with my sisters as we walked in. My chest was hurting, and the first words out of my mouth when I saw her were:

"That's not my Ma!"

It was a beautiful residue of her but to me, it wasn't her. I never knew her without the fire in her eyes. Through times thick and thin, she was a pocket-sized container of an immense lifeforce. In times of pain or pleasure, regardless of the dearth or excesses of daily life, she was always a force. Within a couple of minutes, I felt a sense of calmness. She was probably out there somewhere, still a lifeforce for me.

On the day we buried Ma, it was a typical Irish day, four kinds of weather every hour. Very suitable for the occasion that was in it. I did my stoic duty, carrying her coffin to the top of the steps and passing on that duty to a kindly neighbor to take her down those few remaining steps. Standing with my sisters, I only half listened to the prayers and intonations. Surrounded by the sobs of those in attendance, I can remember deeply breathing in the fresh mountain air. I would fly back to Canada and Ma would still be making tea in our house down the road. I did not shed a tear. The great thing about Kilkieran is that it's only a short walk from Willie Maloney's pub, at the cross of Skough. Ma had helped him out when Willie took over the pub from his two old aunts so they would have known each other well. He hosted one of the best post-funeral get togethers that I have ever attended. Surrounded by friends and family, we remembered and celebrated a life quenched all too soon. My Auntie Jean was one of my mother's chief cheerleaders in her absence. While they might have killed each other from time to time, she added my mother's energy to her own on that day, and she shed enough tears to cover my lack. I think I stopped drinking after a while, knowing my father would probably need a bit of support later on. This was not the way he expected things to go. Despite the misty muddiness of the memories surrounding that day, I look back with fondness on the celebration of her life, and on the equivocal emptiness that would be mine going forward.

Later, back in Canada once again, I found myself feeling guilty that I hadn't cried on the day. What was wrong with me? There was no doubt that my mother and I had clashed over the years but I never had any doubt that she loved me with a fierceness that was reassuring and comforting, even in the worst of times. And didn't I love her or what? Of course, I did. It may have been a couple of years before we returned to Ireland and I found myself driving up to Kilkieran, alone, one morning. I sauntered down the hill and over the stile, into the graveyard. I had the place to myself. With my arms folded on the railing, I rested my chin on my arm and stared at the stone. I'm not sure how long I rested in that position but then I saw drops rolling from my cheek and onto the sleeve of my coat. I wondered if it was the rain. For a while, I thought I was crying because I hadn't been able to cry on the day of her funeral. This day, there was no amount of mental steel. stoicism or resolve that could stop it though, I really missed my Ma.

There is one funny thing about our tomb. It has the Walsh coat of arms on one end. The Walsh crest has a shield with three pheons or arrowheads, separated by a chevron, above which sits a swan atop an armet, or helmet. The swan is pierced through the body with an arrow. The motto below this is ...

Dum Spiro Spero (So long as we breathe, we hope)

I am not sure if this is peculiar to our particular line of the Walshs or if it was the penchant or ignorance of an ancestor, since the Walsh motto is generally thought to be ...

Transfixus Sed Non Mortuus (Transfixed but not dead)

The former, I believe, is the motto of the Cotter family so I'm not sure how it found its way onto a Walsh crest. It's an interesting family history anomaly and another point of conversation at every funeral. I sometimes wonder what any Cotters visiting Kilkieran might make of it all.

Another great thing to come out of Ma's funeral was the Walsh Family Tree. Imelda, daughter of my grandfather's sister, Ettie, presented me with a cardboard tube, right beside the crypt, in Kilkieran. Inside was an old, old handwritten document. It was done by my great grandfather and it recounted our family's existence since 1169. It was a lengthy piece of paper and transcribing it by hand was going to be difficult, especially given the typical post-funeral socialization that is the norm in Ireland. Instead, I came back to Canada with a series of poorly transcribed paper scrolls, and several cans of film with snapshots of its many tree limbs. While I researched around the periphery of it, Imelda had already done most of the work. It can only be validated back to 1644 and I'm guessing that my great grandfather could have been a little loose in directly connecting us to the original invader, Haylen (this is my preferred version, he was also known as Hayle or Howel) Walsh. He was a knight and baron, reputedly a descendant of David, King of South Wales. The original Walshs came to Ireland, among the group leading the Norman invasion. Despite the tenuousness of the connection, I have made a few pilgrimages to Castlehale (originally Castle Howel), to see the stones that are supposed to have come from the original Walsh castle in Kilkenny. Cromwell, the bastard, killed all the Walshs in Castlehale and sacked the castle. With that little snippet, you'll see why I'm uncertain about how my great grandfather might have connected the dots back as far as he did. That said, there are reports of a few of them having been elsewhere during the sacking so maybe it's true, it really doesn't matter that much. Nonetheless, I still have a small etching of Cromwell that I hang on my wall at home, close to the floor, and upside down, typically near the boot tray. Don't let anyone tell you the Irish have short memories!

The color in the family tree was fantastic and, spread all over the kitchen table, it was a great distraction from the sadness surrounding Ma's funeral. One of the Walshs, Antoine, had built the boat that carried Bonnie Prince Charlie to Scotland for a journey that would culminate in his ill-fated battle at Culloden. One of the ladies was reputed to have had an entanglement with the last Duke of Buckingham. I think it was one of my Grandfather's aunts that was a sister to Michael Flatley's grandmother or great grandmother. During the early part of his career, I always thought Flatley was a bit of a blowhard and a braggard but as soon as I knew he was related, I realized that it was just the natural family pride in his genes bursting through. And I immediately became a huge fan! If my grandfather had taken the road not taken and gone to his family in Chicago as a young man, I might have grown up fluting around, boxing and dancing with Flatley. Do you think I might have missed a bit of an opportunity there? One day, I'll have to get around to getting that family tree pulled together in a digital format, it's just too bloody big for paper. I'm sure there is a "factional" story or two amongst the ranks of my ancestors that will be worth embellishing. That reminds me, there is this great story about the two towers on either side of Belline House, near Piltown and once a Walsh home. The story was that the couple living there, my great great grandparents, I think, didn't get on very well so they built these two towers on either side of the big house. At night, after supper, yer man would go to one tower while yer wan would go to the other.

"A load of bollocks!", claimed my father.

"Where did the feckin' seven children and all of us come from then?", he'd demand. He's probably right. And the ancestors in question are in the tomb too so I may get the rest of the story one day.

Back to funerals in Kilkieran. Some year's later, I went through a similar routine for Da's funeral. Somehow, it was a bit easier with him, as I'd had the practice run with Ma. After my experience with her, I managed to talk myself into getting home to see Da before he went. It was cancer again, and we all knew he was on the final steps of his journey when I visited. Neither my parents, nor my aunts and uncles over recent years, have any legend on the tomb stone to note their lives. There's a marble slab on top of the tomb to add some space for some of the departed. Though my Grandad and his brothers are on it, and I'm glad they're being remembered, I never quite liked the look of it. It took from the clean lines of the original structure and it's more exposed to the elements so it probably won't endure the test of time as well as the original sheltered words on the sides. That's just a bit of family rumpus bait there but you have to throw the cat amongst the pigeons every now and again, don't you! The reality is though, that there isn't enough space for all of us to be inscribed on the sides, so I understand why it was done. We do want our folk to be remembered. We want to be remembered. There needs to be some little residue of our lives that will remind folk that we once walked the surface of this earth. And while I haven't come up with a better way to create more space on the family tomb, perhaps this little story will help.

And I really do need to get around to doing something with that family tree but in the meantime, and for the record …

We are the Walshs of Belline, Fanningstown and Ballycastlane. And of Carrick, Piltown and Skough, and we are all buried here, with our family, in Kilkieran. R.I.P. Hopefully it'll be a while yet before a Canadian Walsh comes to join them!

Drop by and say hello if you're passing, there's always a party in Kilkieran.

17 – Segs

Being cool in a small country town was never easy and practicing the art of cool demanded that you endure periods of ridicule, along with the few successes that you might garner along the way. If you persisted though, you could manage enough episodes of cool to build up the self-confidence necessary to explore boundaries outside of Carrick. Where we usually discovered that we weren't that cool and had to start all over again.

I don't recall having too many pairs of shoes as I grew up and that may account for the fact that my shoe collection today outnumbers my wife's count by about four to one. And she really likes shoes! It may have been the shoe scarcity in my younger years that prompts today's excesses but the bottom line is that I love shoes. As a child though, buying a pair of shoes was an event. We could spend weeks in advance of the big purchase discussing when we might go to Meany's shoe shop, on the Main Street. Ma always insisted on Blackthorn leather loafers and I was just fine with that. They looked almost cool and, with their leather soles, they sounded even cooler. Ma didn't like the price but they lasted forever and she liked that. I spent half my childhood wearing shoes that were too small because the bloody things lasted so long. They usually were resoled a couple or three times before the uppers gave out and I could finally get a new pair. The best pair I ever had were a gorgeous light tan in color. They blew me away the first time I caught a glimpse of them. We went to Meany's this one time and I had already tried on about half a dozen pairs. They were all black or stodgy brown in color, and none were impressing me that much. Then the girl brought out the next box. As soon as she lifted the lid off, my eyes were drawn to the flash of tan leather that glanced out between the light sheets of tissue paper protecting the shoes. I didn't care if they fit, nor whether or not they hurt. Once I saw them, I wanted them. Fortunately, the first shoe passed muster and I pulled on the second. Aided by Ma and the girl in the shop, both of them were wielding shoe horns. It was very important in those days to protect the integrity of the newness of the shoes in case we didn't take them. Once these babies were on my feet though, I knew they weren't coming off. They were a bit more expensive than the stodgy pairs I had already tried on but I wanted these tan beauties and that was that. I knew Ma would be too embarrassed to argue with me, in public, about the price of them so I pushed it. I pushed very carefully, cautiously and gently though. Pushing too hard could see her snap, box my ears, and frog-march me out of the shop. The added humiliation of me making her do that would have her grinding me for days and I didn't need that kind of aggravation in my life. And I really wanted those shoes.

I have no idea how I got away with it but it worked, and I got to keep the tan loafers. We marched out of the shop with my new shoes on. Since the old ones were worn to the point of utter uselessness, they went into the box and the new shoes remained my feet. Another miracle, the other pair were so worn that I didn't even have to save the new ones for months as my Sunday shoes. As I walked, my head remained bowed, my eyes drawn down by the lovely leather, as it flashed back and forth below. I continued talking to Ma.

"I need the segs, Ma!", I begged.

"To make sure my new shoes won't wear out too soon, Ma.", I whined.

Blakey's is a UK company that has been around since the 1800's making shoe protectors, and the little corner heel segs were the in-thing for us then. Some of the country kids used to put things that looked like horseshoes on the heels of their boots but that was way too uncool for a hybrid townie-country boy like myself! You could get little ones that you nailed in yourself but they weren't as good as the heavy-duty heel segs that the shoemaker fitted. Off we marched down the Main Street and I kept talking to Ma. Somehow, I justified the added protection for these very expensive shoes to her, and down we went to Mackie's, the shoemaker. I didn't see another thing on the way down, my eyes were still locked on my new shoes. If Ma wasn't holding my hand and dragging me along, I could have spent the rest of the day like a stringless puppet. Head bowed, staring at my new shoes, in the middle of the Main Street. Anyway, we wound up at the counter in Mackie's and I told the man what I wanted. Ma had some conversation about the price of the different segs but the man agreed with me, you needed the heavy duty segs to protect such a fine pair of shoes. He had to grind off the leather on the outside corner of the heel and I was scared shitless that he might abrade the leather on the wrong part of the shoe with that bloody spinning grinding wheel. My heart was in my mouth the whole time he was working on them. It didn't take long before he was offering up the seg to the first one, making sure the cut was perfectly matched to the shape and depth of the iron seg. Once he was happy with the cut, he positioned the seg and nailed it in place. One done. God, this was torture. I stood, in stockinged feet, while he worked on the other one. Finally ... finished! They looked feckin' great. I tried them on and banged my heel off the floor to test them out. Jaysus, they sounded great too!

The shoe polish was kept in the lower left cupboard of our back kitchen at home and we had black, brown and oxblood polish, along with a set of application and finishing brushes for each color. None of these could be used on my new tan shoes so we got a tin of neutral polish, just for them. I wanted new brushes too ... sure, wouldn't I have to look after these new dear (expensive) shoes too, Ma? Yer man in Mackie's had these lovely soft finishing cloths as well but I must have pushed it too far because Ma boxed me around the ears when I started keenter-cauling about needing one of those.

"You can use one of the old nappies!", she proclaimed, meaning one of the old cotton diapers that were relegated to polishing duty after the absorbency had deteriorated too much to serve their original purpose. Ah well, I got most of what I wanted. Now to be fair to Ma, I had never polished a pair of shoes in my life so her expectations were justifiably low that this might change, fancy new shoes or not. She went off out through the West Gate to bring the old shoes down to the car. Da's workshop was down the back, by the Ormond Hall, and she didn't want to have to carry an old pair of shoes around while doing the rest of her shopping. With a final admonition that if I scuffed the new shoes, she'd box my ears, again, she was off. And so was I, the look and the sound off these new shoes was just brilliant. It was difficult to adjust my gait to that of a hard heel-walker but I persisted and the sound of the iron seg hitting the concrete pavement was nothing short of magical music to my ears. I lengthened my stride and pounded the pavement with glee. It was the coolest I'd felt in a long time. I strutted down the Main Street, desperate to run into some of the gang, who would truly appreciate these new shoes. I had the only pair of tan shoes on the whole of the Main Street that day and there were none that had the sound of new segs on board either.

Ma was very big on us going to mass every Sunday and while I'd typically be trying to figure out ways to get out of going, that wasn't the case this next Sunday. These new shoes were special. And they needed a special introduction. I decided I was going to Carrick to the big chapel for mass, and not to our local church in Faugheen. Fortunately, the whole family was going to mass in Carrick that weekend so I didn't need to destroy the lovely leather soles on my new shoes walking the road to town. Unusually for us, on this occasion we were early but I didn't want to go in right away. I wound up arguing the point with Ma outside the main gates at St. Nick's. She thought I was trying to ditch mass again and I reassured her by telling her that I was just waiting for the lads and that I would soon be marching right up to the front pew so she could see me. With a look of total disbelief on her face, she finally bought it and said there would be hell to pay if I didn't. A few of the lads arrived and wanted to go in but we wound up in an argument about where we'd go in the church. We usually stood around with the auld fellas just inside the doors, so we could leave with the confusion of communion time. Back then the churches were packed and most people went to communion so it was easy to dart out with the all the drama and traffic of people going up to receive the holy sacrament.

"I can't!", said I to the lads, "I told Ma I'd go up to the front and if I don't, she'll kill me!"

Mass had just started and only one or two decided to take the long walk to the front with me. Father Kelleher was saying mass and most people feared him. I loved him though, he had baptized me and I was an altar boy in Faugheen with him. I thought he was a tough but funny man, especially for a priest. He even married Ma and Da too. Anyway, Fr. Kelleher was doing the opening lines while I made my way through the standing crowd at the back of the church. Once through, I began my heel-first, striding walk, right down the tiled middle aisle of the big church. The segs were only feckin' wicked! The iron-heeled clash of metal on tile echoed throughout the hallowed high halls of the church and brought total silence to the throng within. Even Father Kelleher stopped speaking and stared. It was only magic, Ma would know I was going to mass now!

St. Nick's is a fairly big church but on that day, it seemed like a mile from the back to the front. The two lads with me were tucked in behind, trying to hide from the stare that Father Kelleher was laser-beaming down the center aisle at us. By the time I was half way down, my confidence was restored and my audible stride had everyone in the church turning around in their seats to see who was coming. I loved it! Head high, I continued my cacophonous march. By now Father Kelleher had recognized me and I think there was the hint of a smile under the scathing demeanor. He remained silent, interrupting the progression of the mass, 'til we made it all the way to the less sparsely populated front pews. We excused ourselves past the few parishioners who were daring enough to choose these pews and I did an up and down walk, one foot on the wooden kneeler board, the other on the tiled floor, to make an alternating wood-tile seg sound as the finale for my grand entrance! I wish I could remember his exact words but Father Kelleher passed some comment about this being a bit different to being disturbed by the usual gaggle of high-heeled ladies shoes. Much to the mirth of the gathered assembly. Despite the entertainment value and the ensuing outburst of laughter, Ma still boxed my ears later, for embarrassing her in public. Some things are just worth the pain though!

18 – The Haircut

Getting a haircut in Carrick was great. It was such a memorable experience from my childhood that I wound up marrying a hair dresser. I don't think I worried too much about my appearance as a child but I do recall fighting with my mother every time she called on me to go to the barber's shop. That resistance may just have been part of my ongoing commitment to thwart my mother's every wish, and just because. The reality was that I enjoyed going to Paddy Carroll's Barber Shop on the Main Street. The style, if you can call it that, for all young boys at the time was a straight forward short back and sides. I know I had a pretty shaggy mop ahead of these infrequent visits to Paddy's barber shop, and it was pretty much shorn to the skull every time I climbed down from the big leather chair.

Contrary to the almost military style cuts sported by all the boys of the day, my sisters were treated totally differently. Ma often spent hours doing pigtails, or curls, or some other fancy hair-do, and I just couldn't understand the logic behind it all. Cut the hair off and be done with it seemed like a far easier approach to me. The groans and cries of my sisters as the ribbons were cinched tight around a pigtail or a pony tail were all too big a price to pay, no matter how good you thought you looked like at the end of it. Even when Ma was brushing their hair, it was a cacophony of agony. The squealing and moaning that accompanied each tangled brush stroke was too much for me and I'd have to leave the room. Now washing hair in our house was a bit of challenge in those days too. We didn't have a proper shower. Somewhere along the way, we reached a consensus that rinsing hair in "dirty" bathwater wasn't the best approach. This pink rubbery hose contraption appeared in our house one day. And, while I've managed to wear the odd ludicrous pink shirt over the years, that tepid pink color was so distasteful that I would cross the road to avoid it. This contraption was a Y-shaped rubber hose, with two bell-shaped cups on the short arms of the Y. The long leg of the Y had the spray nozzle. When the thing was new, the rubber was resilient and you had an awful time trying to get those bloody cups up onto the big taps on our bath. As the rubber aged and petrified, the bloody cups would then fall off one tap or the other and you'd be either scalded or frozen as the water came onto your head from only one side.

One time, I went through a phase where I was a bit of a germaphobe. I tied a piece of string around my own personal cup, for example, so that I always had my cup of tea from the same cup and no one else was allowed to drink from that cup. I remember it well, it was an ochre yellow mug, and a bit ugly I'll admit. But it only had my own personal germs on it and that was important to me. I had one blue willow patterned plate, it was the only one from an old set, and that's what I used for my dinner. Along with my own knife and fork too. It didn't strike me 'til now but I never minded what I ate from, or with, while at anyone else's house. Regardless, I religiously drank my tea from this one mug. It also never struck me at the time to wash all the fruit and veggies I was eating, bird shit and all, from the garden. And all the wild stuff I ate from around the fields, who knows what was on them. However, I had some additional logic attached to my germophobic approach when it came to the bathing process. The thinking was that if you were going to waste time getting yourself clean, then you should get clean and not be rinsing your hair in water that was after removing a week's worth of dirt and scum from your body. Despite the ugliness of the pink rubber thing, it did provide a fresh stream of clean water to rinse off the shampoo. I thought I was very clever when I realized that I could use this hose and nozzle thing to rinse off the rest of my body too. That was to become an integral part of my bathing routine. I would diligently rinse out every last molecule of shampoo from my hair and then I would stand up in the bath and pull the plug. While the water was draining out, I would be spraying my body with the wand. I'd keep spraying until the bath was completely drained and then I would rinse off the bath and, finally, my feet. That was just perfect. Except for the fact that the bathroom floor would be flooded by then. Of course, that was my mother's problem so I didn't mind.

What I did mind was how bloody cold that bathroom could be in winter. Or even in summer, depending on the day that was in it. The bathroom was probably pretty art-deco cool looking in its day but in addition to whatever the temperature was, the black and white theme gave it a psychological coldness that had you feeling cold even when you were sweating. The bath, sink and throne were all white and the cistern, toilet seat and lid were jet black. The floor tiles, a thin vinyl layer laid on concrete, were a chequered black and white pattern. The porcelain wall tiles were a shiny black and white backdrop around the bath tub and sink. The sink was where we had to wash our hair, if we weren't taking a bath. That was bloody awful. You'd be banging your head off the sharp edges of the taps when you dipped your head in the shallow sink. I finally got around to using the pink rubber contraption on the sink too. Jaysus, you wouldn't believe the amount of water on the floor after that. You nearly got a free foot bath at the same time! I remember having my hair washed in the kitchen sink a few times too. We had one of those big, white, rectangular, porcelain sinks in the scullery. I don't know why I did this but I know if you open your mouth on the edge of this sink, and if you bang your teeth on it, it hurts a lot.

Back in Paddy Carroll's, on the other hand, you had the comfort of his big leather barber's chairs. It was always warm in there, I think there was one of those old electric bar heaters back in the corner by the door. Paddy didn't wash our hair, mind, but after he had shorn off my golden locks he put vinegar on what remained. Well, it wasn't really vinegar, but it was some kind of blue colored lotion or potion. I used to think it was hair fertilizer so that you'd have to come back again soon. But it was in the same kind of fat-bottomed bottle that Mary Heffernan had her vinegar in, round at the fish 'n' chip shop. It even had the same pointy cap with the hole. Paddy would be buzzing away on my head for ages. Then he'd trim here, do an edge there, and tweak it all with the little scissors he had. After a quick brush with that big soft brush of his, to remove the fallen hair around your neck, he'd start tapping and slapping the head around for a bit, adjusting little things here and there. Finally, he'd be happy. Then he'd take the vinegar bottle and shake it all over your head. He'd be chatting with Da all the time but you'd see him squinting in concentration, eyes totally focused on the head, every step of the way. Once the hair was soaked with this blue lotion, he'd whip out the metal comb from his top pocket. This was the grand finale, the coup de grace. With a flourish, he'd be waving that comb around; combing, tucking, tricking, and parting the hair with a precision that I knew Da only loved. I, on the other hand, loved the sensation of the cold blue stuff going on my head. And by the time Paddy was finished his hairstyling symphony with the comb, your whole head of hair would be starting to stiffen up. That blue vinegar would lock the hair into the perfect shape he was after by the time you had to climb down from the chair. It was like some kind of special barber's super-glue, it was. Da and himself would chat for a few minutes more, while Da paid him, and then I'd be out on the town sporting my new stiff haircut. You'd feel absolutely frozen when you stepped outside the door. What with all the hair being gone and the coldness of the blue stuff, you'd nearly be shivering, even if it wasn't a cold day. And often it was a cold day too. I used to walk along the Main Street, looking at myself in the shop windows. I'd be shaking my head so as to watch the solid spears of hair wiggling back and forth on my head. It was great having the hair cut in Paddy Carroll's.

Despite having the service available on-demand at home now, every now and again, I'm tempted to go out and find an old-fashioned barber. One that has that blue hair fertilizer, dispensed from a vinegar bottle!

19 – The Seamstress

When we were little we called our mothers Mammy. If you had English cousins that visited from time to time, like I had, it was somehow very embarrassing to be going "Mammy this" and "Mammy that" while the cousins were doing this sophisticated "Mum" thing in their fancy English accents. I could never bring myself to call my Mammy Mum but as I got older, I thought it was a bit more cool and laid back to refer to her as "Ma". As much as we were embarrassments to our mothers growing up in Ireland, I don't think Ma had any idea how big of an embarrassment she was to me on many an occasion. My cousin and I were walking out to our house in Skough one day, for example, and we borrowed a high nelly bicycle we found lying against the ditch down near the gates at Ballycastlane. We had walked all the way from town and we thought the bicycle was just the thing to get us home quicker for that last half mile. We just left it up against the wall outside our house. Later on my father's cousin, Lar, showed up to claim the bicycle. There was a ten minute conversation that ensued, with lots of adult nodding, proclamations and gesticulations during the course of it. After which Ma came charging back in like a bull gone mad. We had stolen the bicycle according to her!

"No, we only borrowed it!", said I, proclaiming my innocence while my cousin, Pa, stood off to the side with a grin on his face. He knew I was getting the brunt of this and he wasn't about to say a word that might see him get caught in the crossfire.

Of course, it was all my fault. I was the thief and the miscreant and the indignity of being tongue lashed in front of my cousin was surely an indignity the equal of my mother's misplaced belief that she was raising some kind of thief and blaggard. For Jaysus sake, I left the thing out by the front wall so the owner could pick it up, what else did she want! The big thing for my mother was what the neighbors might think and this event was right up there with all the things they might think the worst of.

My mother thought the neighbors were very sensitive to religious matters too so it was very important to be dressed up for mass on a Sunday morning, and to go to confession every week to confess your sins and what have you. Living the righteous life that she expected of us, it would be hard to imagine that we had a load of sins to confess every week but, nonetheless, we were all frog-marched off to confession with a regularity that would shame a metronome. We were very near the church in Faugheen but the congregation was much smaller at this little country church. So I complained to Ma that the priest would know who I was and that I didn't want to confess all my sins to him. Jaysus, I might even run into him in the street afterwards and I'd be very embarrassed. She tried to pry out of me what I had to be embarrassed about but I claimed the Godly fifth on that one. I made the argument that my sins were only between God and me, it said so in our catechism book and I showed it to her. It must have been a good argument because she had no answer to that one!

After several months of bartering and conversation, I finally managed to convince her that I was better off going to Carrick for my weekly Act of Contrition.

"What's the difference?", she asked, "It's still the same priests."

"There's a bigger crowd there.", I explained, "And I'll get lost in the crowd."

I have a sneaking suspicion that she might have used that strategy herself along the way so she looked on that argument more kindly than she might otherwise have. I did wonder from time to time what she had to confess: was she bad mouthing her sisters behind their backs? Maybe she was gossiping about the neighbors. And what about all the abuse she subjected me to? A lot of my sins were relating to how I wasn't respecting my parents the way I should but I doubt she had that problem, no one messed with Nanny. I got into a big row with Nanny one time and we were effin' and blindin' one another and when I got so carried away that I spat in her direction. She chased me out of the house brandishing a carving knife. Good job I was fit, I cleared the front gate in Marian Avenue in a single leap and stood across the street glaring back at her. She knew she couldn't catch me so she lit the street on fire with her words for a few more minutes before going back inside. All the way muttering still more threats about what she'd do to me when she caught me. I'm sure I caught the start of a grin on her face as she turned though. Nanny was great!

The first time Ma let me go to confession in Carrick, alone, I followed the letter of the law. I went in to the church early to contemplate my sins, though I skipped over the bad thoughts I was having about the future sins I was imminently hoping to commit. I looked around the church to take in which station of the cross was nearest the confessional I was going into. I noted who else was in the church that I knew and I took careful note of who I spoke to outside the church, on the way in and on the way out. I knew from the rumbling of the voice in the box, dispensing forgiveness and penance, that it was Fr. Kelleher in residence. God, he was everywhere. And that was good and bad. The good was that Fr. Kelleher was Ma's favorite priest but the bad was that he was tough dishing out the penance so I'd be longer doing my penance in the church afterwards. Only God remembers what sins I recounted that day but when I finally got home from Carrick, after playing with my friends the rest of the day, I was subjected to the inquisition. I knew this would happen and I was well prepared. It all went exactly as planned. I had run into one of her friends on the way into confession and one of my aunts, her sister, on the way out. She had all the witnesses she needed to confirm that everything I was saying was true. I didn't use the bit about which station of the cross was closest to the confessional, I thought that much detail might suggest that I was setting something up. Ma was a human lie detector so, from an early age, I had to become very adept at exactly how much to skew the truth to get one over on her.

For the next few weeks I followed the same pattern, refining my strategy to perfection. I'm sure God knew what I was up to but I hadn't received any divine signs yet so I thought I was on the right path. Once I felt comfortable, I started skipping confession. I would always walk up to the church though, to see if I could see anyone I knew or, more importantly, someone my mother knew. Then I'd walk in one door of the church, quickly check which priest was hearing confession, and then go straight out the other. One fine day I did just that and I walked straight into my mother's glowering face! The abuse I got was just ungodly. And it must have lasted half an hour because half the town came in and out of the church during that episode and I was mortified, twice over, by the indignity of it all. To make matters worse, I was marched into the church, my mother leading me by the ear, and I had to confess everything to Fr. Kelleher in the box. Including lying to Ma about going to confession when I didn't.

It wasn't only religion that caused all the early embarrassments in my young life, my mother's ability as a seamstress brings back some of my most horrid memories. The woman could sew and she had an old flywheel Singer machine that was in constant production. She made curtains for every room in the house, along with net curtains, or sheers, for every window you could look through. She loved to take the bus up to Dublin to visit Guiney's and she often came back with a swatch of floral print material that would get turned into dresses for my sisters. She even came back with this heavy green stuff one time and re-covered the entire living room suite with it. It was amazing what she could do but I was horrified this one time when she came back from a clearance sale with a big swatch of bright red corduroy cloth. She said was going to make this luminous thing into a pair of jeans for me! Now I admit to being in a silly phase where I had her doing some funny colored patches and inserts for my blue jeans but this was something else again. A little v-shaped thing at the bottom seams of the pant legs was one thing but all-over, completely bright red jeans? Not even the girls would wear something this color and my sisters were having a high old time of it, laughing at me all the way, while this electric pair of jeans were in production. Ma had procured one of those tissue paper patterns for some jeans from God knows where and she was full tilt into making this abomination for me. I had no idea how to handle this one. Did I say aloud what I was thinking to her? Or should I just wait and rip the shit out of them on a thorny bush the first time I wore them? I decided to hint around the problem I was having but that didn't work. I wound up trying on the jeans a few times, as they were progressed towards a finish. They were even worse than I could ever possibly have imagined. It was one thing wearing ill-fitting blue jeans but this thing was like a beacon when I tried it on. I was going to be an absolute laughing stock.

The first day I had to wear them into the real world, I picked my longest jumper (sweater) to cover up as much of the red as I could. I decided to wear my wellies with them too, so that I could tuck the red swishing flares into the rubber boots. It didn't matter what I did, there was just too much, all-too-bright red showing in between. Ah well, sometimes you just have to do things for your Ma so off I went to school. The ridicule was worse than I expected. I had twenty questions before I even made it across the playground to the door. I had been hoping to get the red tucked under the school desk before anyone took notice but it was not to be. I was so flustered that I blurted out that my mother had made them and that was the end of any hope of anonymity I might have harbored. I was the talk of the school for the entire day and we weren't always that kind to each other in those days. If you did something ridiculous, you were ridiculed, get on with it. Now there were a couple of things I think I learned from those years and the first one was that God must've been Irish because of the wicked sense of humor he displayed on occasion. The second was that, despite the ongoing embarrassments she caused me, I must've loved my Ma to have worn those red jeans for her.

I'm not sure exactly how long I had to endure the red jeans for before I got to retire them. But I do remember making serious efforts to subject them to some hard wear and tear to expedite the process. Suffice it to say that when she turned up with a swatch of green corduroy cloth from the next sale, I was almost relieved!

20 – The Businessman

As good a seamstress as Ma was, Da was the businessman, of sorts, in our house. I'm not sure he ever intended to be a businessman but when he got laid off from Miloko, the chocolate crumb factory we called it, he decided he was going to do his own thing with the redundancy money. We were sickened that he was leaving Miloko because that meant we'd have no more chocolate crumb. If you never had a chance to try this stuff, you missed out. It came in hard and soft versions. You could get the hard crumb in a white chocolate version and in a version that had a very light chocolate colored hue to it. The soft stuff only came in a darker chocolate color and when you cut it with the carving knife, you understood what the word "decadent" meant. You could only cut it slowly, there was no rushing the job. You had to put pressure on both ends of the carving knife and wait, patiently, as you rocked the knife back and forth, all the way through to the bottom. It was heavy but so soft that if you cut a thin enough slice, it would fall over slowly under its own weight. It had a similar effect on the stomach if you ate too much of it! Sometimes, I liked the hard chocolate stuff best myself, not the white one though. You couldn't chew your way through a knob of the hard chocolate crumb over the course of an entire film down at the Castle Cinema on a Saturday afternoon. Da was a fitter welder at Miloko. My Uncle Pat was a fitter turner there. And my Grandad worked there too so there was no shortage of chocolate crumb amongst our clan. When the layoffs came along, half the family was all out of work all at the one time. My Da's ambitions were probably more fueled by my mother's aspirations than his own but, after the layoffs, he didn't think much of having someone else in control of his life. This is when he thought he'd start his own company. Many nights, and many pots of tea, were consumed in the planning stages, as company names were bandied about and plans were made for what machines and equipment had to be purchased. It was a great time, we were driving all over the place, up to Clonmel and down to Waterford, to check out the steel suppliers. We were in Kilkenny checking out welding equipment. We even had a trip or two to Dublin on the back of getting this business up and running. Precision Engineering Company Limited was the name that finally came out on top and Da was in business. While Ma was all anxious, in a positive way, about him becoming a big businessman, she also spent weeks prodding and poking him about getting a job before all the redundancy money ran out. What did the woman want? He couldn't do both things at once but it certainly motivated him to get up and running, and to get out of the house, sooner rather than later.

Despite my young age, or perhaps because of it, I was very confident in Da's ability to get this business off the ground. He was great with his hands. He had started out his working life as a mechanic in the Royal Electrical and Mechanical Engineers, in England. Later, he worked on heavy vehicles for the local council in Hammersmith before finally coming back to Ireland. In those days, they really fixed things. Rather than just throwing out the suspect part and sticking in a new one. I'm not sure if he switched to the fitter welder trade in England first, or if that happened after he came back to Ireland, but in any case, there wasn't much he couldn't make from scratch. And he could fix anything. He might have been a bit too rigid to be an artist, though some of his work came pretty close to being artistic. After calling out for my Mammy and for food, I think the first words I learned as a baby were: measure twice, cut once! There was almost nothing around our house that he hadn't made or at least tried to make at one time or another. The kitchen cabinets and counters in our house were his handiwork. A dresser cabinet, coffee and end tables. There was metalwork everywhere. As a child, I had a galvanized steel "rocking horse", that more resembled a tank than a horse. I think it might still be around with some later generation of the family to this day. One of my Christmas pressies in the early years was a fort, with ramparts and doors that opened. It was made out of chipboard and painted in camouflage greens and tans. It was awesome and I conducted many a battle with that over the years. My Auntie Jean worked in the tannery and Da asked her to buy him a cowhide, a rich burgundy colored hide of leather it was. It was really thick, and roughly the shape of a cow that had been splayed out and flattened by a steam roller. The kitchen was like a factory for months after that and we had leather objects being produced for all sorts of uses. My pride and joy was a burgundy leather school bag. It was held together by steel rivets along the seams, and given structure by a formed brazing rod along the back and sides. The buckles that secured its two straps were steel. It was a mighty bag, indestructible, and I had it all through primary and secondary school. It was still capable of doing the job but I didn't think it cool enough for university so it found its way to the attic. Da was able to take any raw material and turn it into something else, something of use. While his mastery was over metal, that didn't stop him going to work on any other material that came to hand, be it wood, leather, plastic or any other substance that cut be cut, formed, joined or beaten into its intended shape. My mother didn't always like the outcome when it came to projects related to the home but that was all part of the fun of growing up in Skough too.

Da's first workshop was in the back yard of Mulcahy's, down by the Ormonde Hall. It was a great spot, with a big steel mesh gate that had to be unlocked and slid sideways to gain access to the yard. While his was the only business in the yard to begin with, later on he moved to the big corrugated steel shed at the back and Martin took over his old place to fix cars. Later still Tony had a tire shop there, and still later, Peter had one. Somehow, the assumption was made that I would be spending my Saturdays at the workshop. In the beginning, it was great. However, it didn't take long for me to realize that I was the dogsbody in this two-man organization. The full complement of shite jobs all fell into my area of responsibility. I had to wire brush all the rust off the metal, scale the welds, paint all the finished metal with the red oxide paint, sweep and bin the swarf, and other jobs like that. I was only about nine or ten at the start of it all. I was coached on how to hold the pieces steady while my father welded, I was warned about not rocking the bar while the saw cut through, and so on. There was a little bit of a bedding-in period but, eventually, it became apparent that one of my big advantages in the workshop was that I was lazy! The lazy guy will always find the easy way to do everything and, if you have half a brain, you'll figure out how to do it right, and to only do it once. My laziness used to drive him crazy in the beginning though. I'd have to have a crate to sit on to hold something for him, for example, I couldn't just stand there for ages. He'd be standing at the drill press, ready to go, and I'd be off hunting for my crate. It used to drive him mental. But soon, and for the most part, he learned to shut his mouth and let me do my thing because many times my lazy methodology was working. Along the way, we found the balance between his way and mine, and I continued to go to the workshop with him on Saturdays and during school holidays. Bit by bit, I got coached on using the saws, the drills, the lathe and the welders. Bit by bit, I got to do real work and I began making my own things from scrap metal. I was sporting copper rings on my fingers during one phase. I drove my mother mad filling the house with my metal sculptures during another. But all the time, I was learning and getting better. Naturally, I got the low-end real jobs for a while too. I was cutting all the bars to length while my father did the more sophisticated bending, forming and welding. Eventually, though, I almost became the real thing. And I was doing real work. Looking back, I might have been nothing more than cheap child labor but I have to say, I enjoyed it!

One of the great things about doing this kind of thing in a small town was that, sooner or later, nearly everyone, from every walk of life came into the workshop. Whether it was something new to be made or something broken to be repaired, we got to see so many interesting things and meet so many interesting people that I almost couldn't bear to miss a Saturday at the workshop. Not that I wanted to spend all day there either, mind you, so I often took off for a stroll along the main street in my overalls.

One of my father's first customers was Joe Mulcahy, son of the very man who's yard the workshop was in. Joe was a prominent businessman in the town and he had a haulage business. His trucks always needed some kind of repair or modification so he was always down talking to Da about some job or other. We made rotating license plates for the big trailers since, in Ireland, they had to have the same number as the truck or tractor that was pulling them. This rotating box meant that any time you switched cabs, you had four trucks covered at one time. All you had to do was rotate the box to match the license plate of the cab that was about to haul it away. Joe was one of my favorite customers, he always had great stories and he was always doing exciting things. He brought us all out on his boat to fish for mackerel off Helvic Head one time. It was a stormy day, with big waves, rain and all kinds of danger. We saw a shark and I was in fear of my life, my mother was worse, but I carried on throwing out the lead weighted fishing line anyway. Regardless of whatever sea monsters that might be there, I was hauling up the mackerel, three or four, sometimes half a dozen, at a time. When we got back to shore, we made a fire and cooked the mackerel on the spot. You have not eaten mackerel 'til you've eaten one this fresh. No wonder I loved it when Joe came to the yard.

Joe must have been a better businessman than my father because he kept getting more and more trucks. He also showed up more often, bringing more work in for Da. The trailers were constantly being repaired and upgraded and, on one of them, we had to replace the beat-up wooden floor with a new steel floor. It was an unusually hot and sunny week when we were doing that job and good thing too, since it was so big that we had to do it outside. I was stripped to the waist, welding the seams between the sheet steel that was to become the new floor. I didn't realize how badly sunburned I was 'til I couldn't sit back against the car seat on the way home. Worse, my stomach and chest were roasted too. The bloody UV light coming off the arc welder had fried my front worse than the sun had done in my back. The welding mask had protected my face and neck so I looked like some kind of weird Irish panda for a few days with my white face and piebald red torso. While the trailers were fun, it wasn't until Joe brought a big container into the yard that things got really exciting. By this time, Joe was an antique car collector and inside the container was a 1919 Delage that had been raced at Le Mans back in the day. It needed a part that couldn't be found anywhere and my father had to make it from scratch. He had the existing, but broken, part as a model for the one he was about to make. It took a bit of doing but eventually, the part was finished and installed. We awaited Joe's return to see if the beast would fire up. Joe came in on the Saturday morning and, with a hefty turn of the crank, the Delage grunted to life. With barely any hesitation, I might add, to differentiate it from our own Austin A40 that wasn't always so co-operative. Upon reversing the stately looking machine out of the container, Joe asked us if we wanted to go for a spin. Was he serious? I was sitting high and proud in the front seat of the Delage that day, smiling at everyone as we rumbled down the Main Street. I didn't even mind that I was wearing my blue coveralls.

I loved it when Franco came to town. He came from somewhere in Italy, he had the accent and everything, and he was like an international mystery man when he arrived to open up his fish 'n' chip shop and restaurant in Carrick. He was always in and out to Da's workshop, getting things repaired and having new brackets and things made. Franco loved speed. Cars, boats, anything with an engine, he loved them all to go fast. He had an Escort that he used to rally and the way he tuned the engine had it going so fast that it used to shake. He had Da make a special set of struts to stabilize the thing for when he was racing. He had all sorts of other fancy cars along the way but my favorite was his bright yellow De Tomaso Pantera. I loved it when he showed up at that shop in that one. The big stone wall that enclosed the workshop yard had ivy growing all over it. It grew up over the top and hung three quarters of the way down the wall on the outside. One time Franco asked me if I wanted to drive the Pantera in the car park (parking lot). Does a fish want to swim! It was early in the day and there was nothing going on in the Ormonde Hall so the car park was empty. I reversed it out of the yard slowly and, even if you only gently feathered the pedal, you could feel the thing wanting to go. I backed it up against the ivy-covered stone wall and sank my foot. I was hardly after hitting the pedal when this huge machinegun-like noise was deafening me. I nearly shit myself it was so loud and I jumped on the brakes. Good job too because I barely stopped the beast before the wall at the other side of the car park got in the way! The brakes were awesome too but the surface of the car park was all gravel and I nearly slid into the wall at the other side. After I recovered a bit, and Franco was laughing at me, I motored around the place with a little more care and caution. When I turned around and saw the wall, it looked like someone had shot two big holes in the ivy and there was a big mound of ivy leaves and stems on the ground by the base of the wall. The machinegun sounds had been the result of the rear wheels spitting the gravel against the wall. Best hedge trimmer I ever saw, that Pantera, and I think that day was one of the highlights that made for great job satisfaction at the shop.

One of the things I loved to watch Da do was age the metal work he had done. He made big decorative hinges for castle doors, for example. These he would make with all the usual care and precision but then he'd heat them up, hold them on the anvil, and give them a bit of a beating with some of his old forge hammers. It gave them the look of old forge work and they looked both old and fantastic. We got to visit some amazing places when he was supplying work to old manse and castle restoration projects. One of them was a castle being restored by an American millionaire. The castle was built on the edge of a cliff and there was a big red rock in the river that flowed by the base of the cliff. The story goes that it was red from the blood of a priest that had been thrown from the cliff, centuries before, and during a time of persecution. And God knows, our history books were filled with stories of persecution. It really was fantastic stuff to see when you consider the humble nature of Da's shop. If I had been a little wiser, I might have paid more attention at the time but the memories of some of the antics are great nonetheless. Eventually, I was combining what Da was teaching me with what I was learning in school. I remember the first time I calculated an angle for him in about 30 seconds; it took him about 10 minutes to figure it out his old-fashioned way and at the end of it, he went:

"Holy God, you were right!"

Of course I was but he claimed all the credit anyway, since he was feeding and clothing me while I was going to school. That might have been my only technical victory over the years but I think I was the better businessman.

Along with all the fun stuff that went on at the workshop, the business side of things had to be taken care of too. My Da fixed a lot of those little aluminium (sorry, have to stick with the English spelling for this one!) baby strollers for the mothers of the town.

They always broke where the rivets passed through the point where the two folding tubes crossed. This riveted section allowed the stroller to collapse for storage. It was an obvious weak point in the design and my father believed it was intentional on the part of the manufacturer. So they could sell more of them, you see. They were otherwise decent but they always failed at this spot, on one or the other of the handles. My father used to only charge a pound or two for a stroller repair in the early days. And not too much more than that as the years went by. Light gauge aluminium was a bitch to work with, and it was very fragile under the heat of the oxy-acetylene flame. For this kind of repair, he needed to build up the metal thickness in the area around the pin so that it wouldn't break again. Sometimes, and especially on the cheap models, the tubing was so light that it was a nightmare to rebuild and he would take ages doing the job. He would then take the time to file and emery paper the joint to blend it better with the narrow tube so that it looked decent for the woman. He would still only charge the woman the same low amount. One time, he totally dismantled the thing and put a metal tube insert inside. It took him about two or three hours and he still only asked for a little more than his usual fee. I can't remember the hourly rate he charged back then but I knew he was losing money on these jobs, especially on this one, and I asked him what he thought he was playing at!

"Ah the poor woman doesn't have it.", he'd say.

"Nor do we, Da!", was my retort.

Though I was glad to learn that he had a bit of heart too. Still, even with all of that, you'd have the odd one that would think they were being overcharged. What can you do sometimes! The more I worked with Da over the years, the more I realized that my father was a sometimes-gruff, but essentially a nice man. However, I was beginning to think that he might not have the strongest instincts when it came to business. Or maybe his way was the right way, I don't know anymore. It wasn't that he was in any way clueless but he was certainly a little less interested in running the business than he was chatting with his customers. He liked making and fixing things too but the business side just wasn't his favorite kind of work. His overdue payment system was pretty unique. If someone paid him cash, that was great, and that usually went to my mother for the weekly shopping and what have you. If someone was picking up a job and offered to pay him by cheque, he would often just say:

"Ah, don't mind it now. Just whenever you get round to it."

He knew they'd need an invoice and he wouldn't want to go get the book, do the calculations, and write up the invoice for them. He'd be more interested in getting back to finish up a job that someone else was coming to collect later. He didn't want to let anyone down. Some wouldn't offer to pay on the day and they'd just ask him to send them an invoice. Now there were a few scurrilous rascals that knew this might buy them 2, 3 or even 6 months' worth of free credit and they'd do this deliberately, the bastards. His more regular and bigger customers would just accumulate a load of work so he could bill them for all those jobs at one time. These were typically gentlemen, and women, of character as they sometimes came back to visit him for no other reason than to harass him for the invoices so they could pay him. Da's collections trigger though, was a combination of my mother and the bank manager! Ma was constantly on his back because the kids were going back to school, someone needed clothes, or some new thing for the house had to be bought and paid for. For the most part, that was all water off the duck's back to Da. When the bank manager joined the party though, Ma would go to town on him. She wouldn't want to have the bank manager looking down on us because our account was overdrawn. The bank manager knew my father well and, to my knowledge, he never actually stopped his credit. Though I'm sure he had to threaten him from time to time. Sometimes, the bank manager would even drop into the yard to have a chat with Da about getting on with collecting some money to fill up the bank account again.

Eventually, Da would have to give in to the pressure and then he'd have to stay at home for a week to prepare everything. Despite the collections activity being ignored, he always kept excellent records of the time and materials for each and every job. He had these carbon copy books, with Precision Engineering Company Limited printed across the top of each page, that detailed every little thing. He would slowly and carefully handwrite out each individual invoice, in his very elegant sloped script. He would fold the top copy of each one and put it in a brown envelope, the meticulously hand-written name and address of the customer appearing in the window. I'm not sure what he did when I wasn't around but by the time I turned sixteen, I was his delivery boy. And his collections agent. My Grandfather, in London, had brought me home a 50cc Raleigh Runabout moped the summer before. I'd stuff all the envelopes into one of my father's old army satchels and set off to deliver invoices and bring home cheques. Riding around the town and country on my moped was great. I loved this job, especially during the summer holidays. And Ma loved when I started doing it and the money was being collected. Most people realized that they were well overdue to pay and immediately wrote a cheque. I'd stuff that into my satchel and move onto the next one. There were always the few that said the boss was out for lunch so I'd tell them that I'd be back later, if they could please have the cheque ready. And I'd keep coming back, sometimes three or four times in one day. Some others might say the boss was on holiday, or out sick, or whatever so I'd ask when was a suitable time to come back to collect. Then I'd come back the next day, and the next, until they finally got rid of me by having the cheque ready. Maybe I wasn't quite as brave as I remember being in the collections game but my mother thought I was and I was certainly better than Da at it! Though I sometimes hated being trapped in the workshop on Saturdays, when everyone else was up wandering around the Main Street, I have to say the memories are great. And despite any criticisms that might be levelled at Da's business acumen, he did manage to get us all educated and out the door. I think he might have recognized that I had a little business acumen along the way though, even at that early age.

Though he was a bit mystified when the first business I started, with my wife, was a hairdressing salon. I remember going home for the weekend one time and Da was in the midst of taking a few days off to get the invoicing all done. I was laughing at him having to do it all himself now, without me around to do the collections run on the moped for him. He saw the funny side of it alright but Ma was wishing even more that I was there for that part of the job, she wanted grocery money. I used to put the rolls of cash from the salon in my coat pocket every evening and I didn't have the chance to deposit them before going home to Skough that weekend. I pulled out a roll and peeled off a few hundred pounds for Ma, for the shopping. I knew it'd be another week before Da had things squared away. Da was looking at me wide-eyed.

"What, in the name of Jaysus, is that?", says he to me, a look of shock on his face.

"Just the takings from the salon.", says I, "I didn't have a chance to do the bank run before we came down.", I finished.

"How much have you going around in your coast pocket?", he wanted to know, flabbergasted.

Ma was killin' herself laughing and I couldn't help it, I burst out laughing myself. Da was after working his fingers to the bone all his life and here was this little slip of a blonde thing, my wife, able to generate rolls of cash in the hair business. He couldn't fathom it at all and he took off to pour himself a fresh cup of tea. You could hear him mumbling, muttering and swearing to himself as he went out to the back kitchen to get the milk from the fridge. I don't think he meant to kick the dog along the way!

21 – Uncle Davy

My Uncle Davy was a bachelor who rode a bicycle around town. On an odd occasion, he might be drunk while riding his bicycle and that might have been the cause of a few cuts and bruises that he picked up from time to time. He got up to all sorts of embarrassing antics over the years. They weren't very embarrassing to me but I somehow knew that he was a bit of a family embarrassment because of the way the conversations between my mother and her sisters, and their mother, were conducted. Because of this, I felt I needed to be embarrassed about it all too but, for the most part, I thought Uncle Davy was hilarious. He always had a stutter (that word wasn't politically incorrect then and that's what we called it) and it got worse when he drank. He was at his most entertaining when he began pontificating on the rights and wrongs of life while in that condition. From time to time, he managed to hold down a job for a while but, as often as not, he was on the dole. I think there was one time he had a girlfriend but he never managed to hang on to her long enough to get married. He did try to dry out every now and again too though. But he was a more morose human being during those times, to the point that I was almost happy for him when he fell off the wagon. What use is a life of misery after all.

He could expound on politics, religion and far deeper things while drunk. If you could get him to repeat things enough times to understand him, a lot of what he said even made sense. Since Uncle Davy lived his whole life in Nanny's house, we saw him regularly, as a visit to see my grandmother mostly involved seeing Davy too. Even after I had grown up and moved away, I always went in to see Nanny when I returned home. When I was dating the girl I later married, I had to bring her in to meet Nanny during one of my return visits home. It would probably be a little egotistically chauvinistic of me to think I was bringing this "absolute babe" to town to meet the family but, regrettably, that was the case. I was very proud of having this good-looking blonde on my arm so we headed into Carrick one Saturday morning so I could introduce her to Nanny. My girlfriend's family was a little more restrained than some members of mine. I don't think my father-in-law ever took a drop in his life and a couple of sherries a year would be going overboard for my mother-in-law. Accordingly, I had given her fair warning that if Uncle Davy was in residence, he might be indulging, even though it was only shortly after lunch time. I didn't spend too much time preparing her to meet Uncle Davy, as words could do little justice to his antics sometimes. That was to prove prophetic.

There weren't too many cars in Marian Avenue then so I got parked right in front of Nanny's gate. The little dog came flying down the front steps barking his head off in greeting. He was frenziedly wagging his stubby tail in anticipation, though the stupid thing really had no idea who we were. It was one of a procession of small dogs that lived in my grandmother's house over the years. There were three of four doggie names that were recycled for most of the dogs that lived there and they were mostly names like Bonzo, Blackie or Spot. Nanny always referred to them as pups, even when they were wizened and grey. Uncle Davy used to take them off on his country walks to go hunting and though the stories were always great, I didn't ever see a rabbit in the pot over the years. My grandfather and, later doing his turn, my Uncle Davy were often to be seen circling the park at the end of our street. With the dog du jour, of course. The men would meander their way slowly along the paths of the park but the dog did a quickstep, dancing from tree to tree and rushing around their master's legs the whole way around. Though in fairness, Uncle Davy's walks were at a far brisker pace than Grandad's, one that would almost put you in mind of a man with some serious intent on healing his body through exercise. Both are long gone now but I still have the habit of checking the park as a I drive by to see if I can spot them walking the dog.

I'm wandering now, let's get back to introducing the girlfriend to the family! Once she realized that that dog wasn't going to chew the heels off her shoes, we pushed the metal gate inward and checked out the spuds Uncle Davy had growing in the garden at the side of the house. He also had rows of onions, carrots and who knows what else on the go. He was always great with the garden and he had it producing way more vegetables than you'd ever imagine such a small plot could produce. The rows were very straight and organized, the hedges surrounding the plot manicured and laser edged. A small insight to the mind of the man he might have been had he not been afflicted with a weakness for the drink. Sure enough, once we got inside, there was Nanny at the stove, moving pots around the range for the right degree of heat, while my Uncle Davy was at the kitchen table with a bottle of stout in front of him. I was mentally preparing for the worst; would she be totally embarrassed about becoming part of this family and leave me on the spot or what? I was inclined to be a bit dramatic in those days! Nanny smiled her way through the introductions and Davy giddily came upright to shake her hand and was stammering his way through his introduction. For the most part, I knew she hadn't a clue what he was saying. However, the word "lovely" came through often enough for her to realize that it was all very complimentary and she managed to smile her way through the whole process until Uncle Davy decided he'd been sufficiently complimentary enough to sit back down at the kitchen table, in his favored spot by the widow. A little while later, when she excused herself and asked directions to the bathroom, Uncle Davy was back on topic with me. I'm paraphrasing and translating into single, non-repeating-word sentences here, by way of clearer understanding, but essentially what he said was ….

"Jaysus, boy, fuckin' beautiful. Fuckin' beautiful girl. You better get her married and pregnant quick or she'll be gone on you."

Repeating this exhortation was interspersed with cajolements to "Chain her to the feckin' kitchen sink with babies, boy.", and other such advice, which led me to believe that Uncle Davy was quite taken with the girl I had brought home to meet the family. He wouldn't let up until I committed to him that she'd be pregnant going to the altar to take her marriage vows. I was going to work on it right away, I assured him. Just for the record, she wasn't! But I did wonder in later years what prompted that extraordinary degree of encouragement from Uncle Davy. Would that lost love in his past have changed everything for him?

In later years, after Nanny was gone, the sisters all rallied around to make sure their brother was okay. Or at least as okay as was possible for such a great character, living alone. They took turns visiting during the week. They would check the fridge to see if he had spent his dole money on food or on drink. If it proved to be the latter, they typically filled up the fridge with the basics; some milk, butter and bread. Other times they'd get him meat, potatoes and onions, sometimes just rashers, sausages and eggs. Things they knew he'd manage to concoct a meal from, regardless of his state. Sometimes they might cook something for him or bring him a casserole or a stew but otherwise, he had built a rhythm of his own for this colorful path he'd chosen. He turned his gardening skills into a sporadically thriving garden maintenance business. Though he probably remained on the dole right the way through! He had a little garden tool kit and a pair of garden clippers that he tied onto the carrier, over the rear wheel of his bicycle, and he would cycle far and wide taking care of grass cutting, hedge trimming and pruning for people. He had regulars where he would go to tidy things up in spring and autumn. His demons were always snapping at his heels though and,

For a Man or a Dog

in between sober periods of gardening, he would succumb to the them.

In memory of my mother, and long after I'd moved away from Carrick, I would sometimes visit Uncle Davy when I returned to town. Even when he wasn't there, the front door was always open so I went in and checked the fridge, throwing in a few bags of groceries in case he needed something later. One time I remember thinking that this wasn't enough and that I should be doing something more. I came up with what I thought was a great idea one time and I bought him a petrol (gas) powered hedge trimmer. It took him way too long to cut hedges with his clippers and I thought if he could get them done more efficiently during his gardening phases, he could pick up more jobs. That would help him make a bit more money to take him through the other times. I showed up with this lovely red hedge trimming tool on the next visit and Uncle Davy was only delighted. He was in the middle of a gardening phase and he was grinning from ear to ear, as he held the tool at arm's length to admire it. And he even hugged me, I couldn't believe it. And all this in a stone cold sober state. That was a first and I think I felt as good about the whole thing as he did that sunny morning. In fact, he had a job on for tomorrow, doing the gardens at a big house up the Cregg Road, and he invite me to come along to see his new baby in action. I did, and I brought my camera. There was Uncle Davy, his glasses halfway down his nose, whacking his way through this huge laurel hedge at high speed. He loved his new hedge trimmer, and the big, wide grin on his face radiated that. I stood at the end of the driveway for a few minutes, just watching him, bobbing up and down in his knitted red and white cap and sharing in his joy in a second-hand way, before I finally called out to him. He went into rapturous utterances of gratitude and exultations of how great this thing was, not a single stammered word through the whole thing. He was going to have a job that would've taken a couple of days done by lunchtime. After a few minutes, I let him get on with his work, and I stood back to fire off a few more shots with the camera. Later, I was checking the photographs on the computer. I thought Ma would have been proud of me and that it was a pity she wasn't around to see the photographs.

Some months later I was back in Carrick and someone, can't remember if it was my aunt or my sister, told me that Uncle Davy had later sold the trimmer to buy drink. That's my Uncle Davy. Sorry, Ma!

22 – Gone to the Dogs

"Gone to the dogs" was one of my mother's favorite phrases to describe someone or something that had deteriorated past the point of no return. To emphasize that, it was often accompanied by a further description that someone or something was "gone beyond it". I don't know what the dogs ever did to anyone that would warrant them being analogized in such a negative way because we always had dogs growing up and we all liked dogs. In fact, just about everyone had dogs in those days and they wandered freely in yards, gardens, and around the streets. Maybe I didn't pay attention to such things back then but there were no poop and scoop rules either. Though I take a dim view of abandoned poop now, myself, it didn't seem too a big deal back then. Maybe we were so used to it that we were on autopilot and able to dance around poop all the time, I don't know. The first dog I remember in our house was Lassie. I know, not very original, and our Lassie wasn't even a sheepdog. She was a far smaller mongrel terrier. I was so young that I can only vaguely recall the sadness surrounding Lassie's passing on to the doggie afterworld. Though I do recall having one memorable nightmare around that time too. This might be my earliest memory of a dream and it must have been significant because I can still picture it, clearly, today. I don't think it was ever my room but I awakened to a strange purple glow in the front bedroom. Instead of a bulb, there was one of those purple carpenter's pencils hanging from the light socket by a short piece of string. The lavender hued glow in the room matched the color of the pencil's exterior. Immediately, I knew something was wrong because my mother was wailing outside the bedroom window. I had to climb up on the dresser to see out the window and to find out why Ma was bawling. There, lying in my mother's flower bed, were a pair of tiny dead doggies, one black and one white. Little Scotties, they were, like those on the bottle of scotch my father had. Ma was standing on the path, crying, with her hands on her face, as she stared down at the two little dead dogs. I started crying too. Then I woke up. I was saddened and confused. We only had one dog, where did that second dog come from? And besides, Lassie was neither black nor white. The poor dead doggies of my nightmare looked nothing like Lassie anyway but there you have it. Lassie was dead and I was having nightmares.

It wasn't long after that when I got MY first dog and we called him Fritz. He was a German Shepherd, though we typically referred to dogs of the breed as Alsatians. I was so young when we got Fritz that he used to guard me in my pram. My pram was a big heavy metal thing, with big wheels and metal springs. These behemoths were like battle tanks, there were no lightweight strollers around then. Fritz was big but still not much more than a pup when we got him so we grew up together. I dragged on his ears and his tail, I stuck my hand in his mouth to pull his bone out and I did all sorts of whacky things to him, and with him. Things that would have paralyzed me with fear were I ever to have seen my own children interacting with a dog in such a way. But Fritz never bit me. He had a big square proud head and huge paws. I know I tried to ride him like a pony on a few occasions but I never stayed on board for very long. He was instinctively a great guard dog, growling with all the ferocity of the demons of hell whenever anyone he didn't know approached the front gate. The snarling muzzle and dripping spit were enough to intimidate anyone who didn't know him.

We often had travelling people going up and down the road in front of our house. It was always a colorful procession, as they passed in their canvas covered, horse drawn carts. Locally known as caravans, the green canvas covers were supported and surrounded by woodwork painted with bright reds, yellows and greens. I didn't know that this term was used disparagingly as a child, but back then, we sometimes called the travelling people "tinkers". I thought it was only because they made things out of tin: metal cups, buckets and so on. The travelling people were also stereotyped by the settled community as being the type of people that would steal the eye out of your head and it'd be gone without you knowing it. As is often the case, ignorance fueled such thinking but in those days, most settled people were a little leery of them coming around. Anyway, back then the travelling people would sometimes come to the door asking for a little help for the "babbie". Usually it would be a mother and child doing the asking. Mother would have her shawl draped over her own shoulders, and around her arms so as to keep her and the baby protected from the wind and the rain.

It must have been the next summer after we got Fritz that I was out playing on the front steps and I noticed the first of the caravans coming around the corner at the end of the road. Their coming announced by the slow clip-clop of the horses iron shod feet on the road. I loved it when the caravans passed by. I dashed round the back and into the garage. From here, I could watch the caravans passing by through the hole in the garage door. Da was in the garage at the time and he went to the other hole to see what was happening. I whispered to him:

"The tinkers are coming!"

Despite my mother having a little trepidation about the travelling people, she usually felt for the children and she often gave them something. Maybe only a bottle of milk, a loaf of bread and a can of beans or some such things, but that meant we were a regular stop for them on their travels. As the first of the caravans made it to the road in front of our house, a young lad jumped off the first caravan and came across to our gate. I watched as he clanked the latch and pushing the opening section of the heavy metal gate inward. It was painted a puce green, to match our roof, and the hinges squeaked as it drifted inward. The young lad carefully closed and latched the gate behind him. He had loped his way about half way up the driveway when an older man leaned out of the following caravan and yelled:

"No Seanie, ger ourra dere quick, dere's a big fuckin' dog in dere now!"

Seanie stopped dead in his tracks, a look of confusion on his face. While he was still trying to work out the older man's warning in his head, Fritz came barreling around the corner of the garage at high speed. The dog's demeanor was only demonic looking and the snarl had him spraying spittle as he hurtled towards Seanie. As his big paws sought purchase, the sound of his claws grating on the concrete surface added to the possessed look and sound of it all. Seanie was quick to react, I'll give him that. He spun and started heading back towards the gate at high speed himself. I knew Fritz would get him before he managed to open the gate but fear gave Seanie the ability to grab the top of the gate and heave himself over it in a single bound, just as Fritz arrived and slammed up against the metal. Fritz was only the merest of moments behind Seanie's leap, and he crashed right into the space Seanie had just vacated. Ma would probably have thought that I was making it all up but, as it happens, with Da in the garage that day, he saw the whole thing too. Or at least right up to the point where he realized Fritz was on the loose and he went rushing off, screaming at the top of his lungs, to try and stop him getting a hold of Seanie. When Ma heard all the commotion, she was more worried about the poor woman that she'd gotten to know not getting anything so she ran to the fridge to round up a few bits and pieces and went running out the front door with her arms full.

For years afterwards, I was trying to clear the front gate like Seanie did that day but I never managed it. I don't know if Seanie was just a great athlete or if I just needed the kind of motivation he had that day. In one of those wonderful twists of life, I have a friend in Canada who is the granddaughter of a traveller. She happens to have a PhD and does systems engineering applications for leading edge educational programs in the medical field. We laugh at the funny paths and intersections that life brings our way sometimes. And we wonder if her grandmother ever passed by my front door in Skough?

Fritz was a really big part of my life growing up but, as with all such great things, the day came when he died. We buried him in the back garden, just down from my bedroom window. My bedroom was at the back of the house and I wanted to be able to see where Fritz was from my window. In earlier years, I used to pull him up by the paws and into my bedroom through that window and it just somehow seemed better if I could see where he was sleeping. We planted a cedar tree over where he lay and it later became part of a cedar tree hedge that surrounded our gardens. It's still there today and so is Fritz.

I often found stray dogs along the way to and from school back in those days and they all followed me home! My mother used to go mental when I showed up with another dog. I think she must have loved Fritz as much as I did but she wasn't as keen to replace him with another dog as I was. I didn't see them replacing Fritz, it was just a whole 'nother dog to me. Mostly the dogs I found weren't real strays, they would have just left their homes and were wandering around the countryside having a good old time of it. Ma would tie them to the front gate on a long leash and very often the owners would show up looking for them. Or one of the neighbors might recognize who might own the dog and let them know. There was a lovely black and white collie, Ringo I called him, that came home with me one day. He was out by the front gate for a week and no one claimed him. Ringo was a bundle of energy and I loved playing with him. Unfortunately, our Uncle Jim was looking for a good farm dog around that time and Ringo went to Uncle Jim. I don't know how long I was ranting on about needing another dog but our cousins, the Coakleys, were visiting us from Cork this one time and they knew of someone who had Alsatian pups that were looking for a home. They were lovely black pups our cousins told us and I was mesmerized with the thought of a dog like Fritz that would be all black. Off we went to Cork that weekend and we came home with Duke and Dutch. As it turned out, they were a cross between a Black Lab and a German Shepherd so they never got to be as big a Fritz was but by the time we figured that out we already loved them, and they became part of the family anyway. Duke was the more sober and sensible of the two while Dutch was a lunatic. He bit my cousin, Joe, one time and was nearly put down for it. Poor Joe, poor Dutch, it was all a big mess. He wasn't put down but we were always more careful about him around people after that. I was riding a motorcycle by then and one time I opened the door to the back kitchen, where the dogs usually hung out if we didn't want them under our feet. I still had my helmet on and Dutch didn't know who this helmet-clad human was so he attacked! I immediately knew what was happening and whipped back, slamming the door shut at the same time. My bloody big helmet got stuck between the door and the jamb and Dutch nearly, and literally, had me by the balls! Fortunately, I was quick enough to yank my head back fully on the second attempt and to get the door closed in his face. I took the helmet off and then opened the door to a now confused Dutch, who was trying to rationalize me, with the helmet now in my hand. He calmed down quickly though and the tails were wagging within seconds. Dutch was what you might call a dangerous dog, but he was probably the best guard dog we ever had. Duke was a far more sober-sided animal, with a very calm temperament. Good thing too, as that was probably a calming influence on his wilder brother. Between them, they made it to a good old age and I was already on my own way in the world as they moved on.

Fritz must have made a great impression on me though, as I went on to own two more German Shepherds. And one very pugnacious and mischievous Kerry Blue, but that's another story. While I can say, with hand on heart, that I loved all my cats and dogs along the way, Fritz will always be just a little bit special. Gone to the dogs will never be a bad expression in my mind.

23 – Big Game Hunters

Hunting was very much a part of casual conversation during my early years in Carrick but I was never much of a hunter. There were farmers with shotguns for hunting ducks, pheasants and rabbits. And, of course, they might protect their chickens, lambs and calves from foxes, stray dogs, and what have you too. The lads in town often went off out to the country with their terriers, to hunt rabbits and badgers. I have no idea why they hunted badgers, nobody ate badger meat that I ever knew of, and I didn't see any women walking around town with badger coats or anything. Despite my dual town and country life, I never got into hunting. I think I was traumatized by some early cruelty that put me off killing things.

My cousin, Jim, who lived across the road from Nanny's house, was older than me and he always had something going on with animals; it might be dogs or birds. One time he had a baby jackdaw that he hand-raised and he was hoping it would fly around and steal rings off the kitchen windows of the women who had taken them off to wash the dishes! I don't know if it ever managed to get any rings for him but it was a very entertaining bird, and he was teaching it to talk. I couldn't understand what it was saying but Jim used to have conversations with him and it certainly sounded like they were talking to each other. While I enjoyed having it sit on my shoulder or on my outstretched hand, every now and again, I was a bit scared of it in case it went mad like those birds in the Hitchcock film. One time, when I was even younger, Jim came up to me in the street and asked me if I wanted a baby Blue Tit. He had his big hands cupped and said there was a baby Blue Tin in the pocket between his fingers and palms. I didn't believe him so he asked me to move closer and that he'd show me. As I craned forward, Jim made to open a crack between his thumb on one hand and the base of his palm on the other. As I got closer, his hands flew towards my face and he yelled Boo. I nearly shit myself! It took him ten minutes to talk me into to getting close again but I really did want to see if he had a baby Blue Tit so I did. And he did have a baby Blue Tit! It was the cutest little thing. It had fallen from the nest and he wasn't able to get back up the tree to put it back. He said it would die if I didn't take it but I was frightened to touch it in case it pecked me. Jim mustn't have had much patience with me that day because he said if I didn't take it, he'd have to break its neck rather than leave it on the ground for a cat or a dog to tear it apart while it was still alive. Jaysus, now I was under serious pressure. I wasn't feeling too rushed though, Jim was always playing with animals and I knew he would never do that. But I took too long to muster up the courage to take the little bird and he did. I bawled my eyes out and went flying back to Nanny's to tell her what Jim had done.

For us kids growing up in Carrick, we learned early how to make our own tools and weapons. Down the back of the castle was the Sally Island, a wet and swampy patch of land on the banks of the river that supported a little forest of "sally trees". These were willows that were planted for the wattles needed for basket weaving and for securing thatched roofs. I can still smell the damp "salliness" of the sap that soaked into our hands as we peeled the bark off the young wattles. The sally trees were our supply of wood for making bows and arrows. A thicker bough, the longer the better, was strung for the bow. We would peel off all the bark, save for about six or eight inches in the center where the hand held the bow, and then we attached the string to one end. A combination of a notch and multiple, tight winds ensured it stayed put. A thick, strong, waxed string worked best, like the string the butchers used to tie up a parcel of meat. Pushing the strung end into the ground, you had to lean on the other end to bend the bow and then you tied the string to the other end in the same manner. Under pressure, we would thread it through the second notch, then wrap it with multiple turns and finally, tie it off at the end. When finished, peeled and strung tight to a delightfully taut twang, it was a thing of beauty. The arrows were made from the younger, straighter and more slender wattles of the same tree. We peeled these too, leaving an inch or so of bark at the top. Here we wound a tight coil of disassembled chicken wire to add weight the head. A few quick taps of the tip created a mushroom of wood at the top and this would prevent the wire coming off as the arrow hit its target. These were beautiful looking things, the white of the peeled wood contrasting with the darker green of the remaining bark. And they worked. The bows were capable of sending the arrows to immense heights, and across great distances, with simply elegant trajectories. While it's probably politically incorrect today, playing cowboys and Indians was the norm for us back then. Despite the Indians (with apologies to First Nations peoples everywhere) always losing in the films we took in at the Castle Cinema, we all wanted to be Indians so we could use our bows and arrows. And because of that, we made the Indians out to be the good guys. Considering how protective our mothers were of us, I just can't imagine why we were allowed to "play" with these things. They really were quite deadly but we loved them. My cousin, Davy, was nearly a gonner because of these bloody things. Though he ran into the back end of an arrow that was stuck in the ground, nobody hit him with one. That said, these things really were a bit mad to be considered a child's toy. I'm told they only make selfie sticks with the sallies these days and that's probably a far safer use!

The other weapon of choice back then was the gallibandy or gallybander. While we called it a gallibandy, I think gallybander is the more correct variation. Regardless of what you called it, these were homemade and handheld catapults or slingshots. All you needed was a "Y" shaped branch from a tree or a bush to make the frame and handle. You could also make a gallibandy from a piece of strong wire, by bending it with a pair of pliers. The wooden version was just cut to size, while the wire version required the that the wire was bent into a "Y" shape, with a small loop at the top of each of the arms of the "Y". A rectangular piece of bicycle tube rubber, or better yet a piece of soft leather from the local tannery, was pierced on each of the short sides to make the projectile pouch. The heaviest elastic or rubber bands you could find were looped into the holes on either side of the leather pouch and the other end of the bands were attached to the tips of the Y-shaped frame. Sometimes we used long strips of the tube rubber instead of elastic bands but this was often for a bigger model, one designed to kill big birds and things. Once the manufacturing work was done, there was nothing like the buzz you got when the first shot went catapulting off into the air at high speed. These gallybanders were real weapons and you could do some serious damage to windows, birds, cats, dogs, and humans too. The stones from the road were the most frequently used ammunition, since they were readily available, and free. Because of their symmetry, marbles and ball bearings were the premium ammunition for accuracy, distance and projectile speed. Of course, they cost money or were difficult to come by so we used those only sparingly. Mostly we shot cans, though exploding bottles and any available glassware were far more fun. Sometimes we shot projectiles at each other. The expression "take your eye out" was often heard during gallybander fights, to encourage the more lunatic among us to aim low. We did try to soften the release when firing at each other but every now and again, you got hit with a shot that bloody hurt.

I had never fired at an animal with intent 'til that one time up in the graveyard of the protestant church. Now beautifully restored, maintained, and used as the local Heritage Centre, the abandoned protestant church was one of our favorite playgrounds. We did wonder, from time to time, about the lives of those buried there and we hoped they enjoyed watching us play. Besides they were only protestants so it wasn't the same as playing on catholic graves, we reasoned. For the most part though, the gravestones, along with the overgrown trees and shrubs, were great cover from enemy projectiles, as we waged war on each other in the grounds. I guess this was the precursor to paintball games, which are a far safer way to play nowadays. In any case, on this particular day, my cousin and I were wandering the grounds in search of prey. I spotted a robin sitting atop a headstone, twittering and tweeting his little heart out. I was still a fair distance away but I didn't want to scare him off by moving closer. By feel, I selected the roundest stone in my pocket and slowly loaded my gallybander. I raised it up so slowly that I felt for sure he'd be gone before I aimed. But he wasn't! I took aim and let fly. Got him, dead center. Down he went behind the gravestone and I was stunned. Then I burst out crying. Aw Jaysus, I'd killed a harmless little robin, for feck's sake!

I was inconsolable, I couldn't believe that I'd killed a little bird for nothing. Fortunately, when I went over to check out the scene of the crime, he was still alive and shuffling around in the grass, trying to dust himself off. A few minutes later, he had recovered enough to gather his wits and fly away, alive and well. I was so relieved. I promised God and myself that I'd never deliberately aim at another animal again. And I didn't. Though there was that one time that I fired my father's pellet gun into the air and hit a crow flying overhead right in the arse! I swear, it's true, I just took quick aim upward and fired from the hip, with really no chance of hitting anything. But the crow's arse whipped upward for a second and a few feathers came flying out. Fortunately, he kept on flying and there I was again, thanking God and promising that I would never aim a pellet gun at any living thing ever again. You can probably tell by now that I wasn't cut out to be a hunter ... but my mother was!

I have no idea if she planned this from the start or what but we had this lovely cock pheasant that my mother used to feed raisins to. He was out in Uncle Jim's field and my mother started putting out raisins for him, right along by the barbed-wire fence. The pheasant came up daily for his little feast of raisins. My mother must have thought that I was too young to handle the stress and cruelty of this story at the time, because the truth, or some semblance of that, only came out, bit by bit, over time. I loved climbing up on the seat by the window to watch this beautiful bird eat the raisins every day but then one day he wasn't there. I'm not sure how long after the pheasant's disappearance I learned of this but we had apparently had had him for Sunday dinner some time before. At first the story was that my mother caught him with a raisin tied to a piece of string. That didn't work too well for me, I was very troubled thinking about the string choking the poor bird to death and I couldn't possibly imagine my mother wringing the poor creature's neck after reeling him in at the end of a piece of string. Later it turned out that she shot him through the eye with Da's pellet gun. I was horrified, mortified and distraught that we had eaten my pet pheasant, albeit verbally disguised as chicken at the time. And worse yet was the thought that my mother had shot him herself. I'm not sure if this was an additional fabrication or not but the story was subsequently expanded to explain that she had to do it as one of the neighbors was down around the fields looking to shoot him for their Sunday dinner. Since Ma had been feeding him, she reasoned, it was better that we ate him rather than he go to someone else's table. Ah, well, I guess Ma was the hunter in our house!

24 – Paddington Station

For me, as a kid, Paddington Station was a destination as exotic as the North Pole or the Amazon rainforest. The mere mention of its name still sends shivers up and down my spine. Paddington had the smells of machine oil and diesel, surrounded by the sounds of hissing steam and grinding metal. And all were made more vibrant by the tremors of rolling stock. The noise of the crowds, with the musicality of an array of accents from England, Scotland, Wales, Ireland and beyond, was an aural symphony of diversity. The whole place was a delight to the ear. And it all heralded the start of my summer holidays in London. The variety of dress was astounding to a child only familiar with the more limited fashions on display in small town Ireland. Though why anyone would want to wear one of those silly bowler hats was beyond the comprehension of my young mind, impressive and dapper though the wearers otherwise were. There must have been mischief afoot too, since there were always some London Police about the place. The bobbies were tall and made taller still by the peaked helmets atop their dark uniforms, and this contrasted by the glint of their silver buttons and epaulettes. It made them look almost like supermen, and evoked images of still further parts of the realm, even India. Though I might look down on it now, back then a simple ham sandwich here was the first taste of England for me. It was the signal that another wonderful summer of fun and adventure was about to begin. Paddington was a huge, hustling and bustling center of travel activity and it was the end of a long journey from Carrick to London. The sights, smells and sounds of Paddington Station all served to prove that I had arrived in London, a place where I spent many happy summers with my Grandparents. Granny was a little woman, and she sported a shock of neatly arranged grey hair from my earliest memories of her. Though small, she commanded space and was very easy to spot among the crowds on the platform. My lasting impression of my arrivals in England is of her smiling widely and waving enthusiastically in my direction as I walked the platform towards her. After a big warm hug, and the required exchange about how the family were doing back in Ireland, Granny took out a little nail scissors from her bag and cut the label off my arm. Say what!

In those times, I'm not sure that I knew of anyone in Carrick who didn't have some family member living in England. And London was one of the most popular destinations for those seeking work outside of our own small town. You may argue the history and politics of this most peculiar relationship between the countries of the British Isles 'til the cows come home but, regardless of how you might feel about it, there are a lot of Irish in the UK. Regardless of conflicting opinions over the course of history, these countries have been, and are still, bound together for better or worse. For me, it's mostly on the better side of the line. London was my childhood summer home and I really looked forward to meeting all my English relatives. So many of my aunts and uncles were there, along with my legion of cousins. My English friends in East Acton were all locals and Londoners, though of mixed heritage. Being this close to Shepherd's Bush, the local lads were Queens Park Rangers supporters and therefore I was too. Indeed, it was probably fated to be this way, since my mother once had a part time job at The White Horse, on the Uxbridge Road. This pub is just down the way from the QPR stadium, at Loftus Road. It was a local watering hole for the QPR supporters on match day and I think she was pregnant with me while working there. So, and despite the masochism that, by necessity, goes along with being a QPR supporter, how could I possibly be anything else!

Anyway, the journey begins at the other end, in our lovely little railway station in Carrick. Though I vaguely remember the GWR, or the Great Western Railway, I think the rail system in Ireland back then was already the CIE, or in Irish: Córas Iompair Éireann. Don't bother trying to pronounce it if you didn't grow up learning Irish, stick with the acronym. The big black and orange trains were the epitome of adventure; they looked like big, bad, bumble bees that could take you off into the sunset. This was a time when not everyone had a car and rail transportation was an important means of travel. Trains spelled adventure, whether it be for a shopping trip in Waterford, or a major adventure to the Big Smoke: Dublin. For me though, the most adventurous run of all was from Carrick to Rosslare, where the ferry awaited to take those lucky enough to make the trip to Fishguard, in Wales. We all knew the ferry as the mail boat. I guess there were a lot of letters being written between Ireland and England in those days. Husbands might, for example, be sending money back home to their wives in Ireland to take care of their families. Though some were reputed to be drinking their weekly wage and leaving their families high and dry, while they were being soused in the pubs of England. All the boats were named after saints and I think I was on the St. Patrick and the St. David for most of my journeys. The time aboard the boat was the best. It was usually a night crossing and always dark as we travelled across the Irish Sea. I loved to tuck my coat up around my neck and find the part of the metal wall that was warm from the heat of the smoke stack. I would huddle there, wild wind and salty mist whipping into my face, and stare into the dark distance ahead, pondering the adventures to come. Every now and again, I would go back inside to warm up. And to watch the crowds chatting, the men downing bottles of porter and laughing, while the women herded swarms of kids. It was a man's world back then but, on a few family trips, I think I discovered that my Ma was a bit of a feminist. In fact, Ma was probably more a suffragette, meaning that if she was going to suffer, Da was going to suffer too! It was a great education for me though, I didn't want my Ma to suffer and her quiet, but furious, distain for male chauvinism imparted a healthy respect for women in me. Not that I'm claiming any moral high ground here, I'm just knowledgeably fearful of the consequences of a woman's wrath.

At the end of the sea crossing was Fishguard, in south Wales. We eagerly went down the gangplank to board the British Rail train that would take us to Paddington Station. I loved the different look of the British Rail trains. I knew I was in the UK then but this part of the journey was long. I would have benefitted from going asleep but I didn't want to miss anything along the way, no matter how little I could see in the dark. I spent much of the journey in the small space between carriages so I could have the window down and breathe the different air of the towns and countryside we passed through. As the dawn broke, we were getting nearer to London and the satellite towns and cities were coming awake. You could get that London smell quite a few miles away from Paddington, it was special.

One of the unique things about that era was the embarrassing label that was tied around my arm, just above the elbow. I think I was nine or ten years old when I travelled to London, alone, for the first time. I felt all grown up. Unfortunately, the label gave me away as being nothing but a child. The label and string were like those used by the butcher's shops. It was a dun colored card, with a reinforced hole at the tapered end. On one side of it, my mother had written my name and home address. On the other was my grandmother's name, along with her address and phone number in London. I don't think we had a phone then. The string was the unbreakable wax style string that, once tied, couldn't be removed without cutting. When I was being shipped over to my grandmother for the summer, Ma would carefully write the label and attach it to my arm. The railway station was always very busy with so many people travelling back and forth in those days. Once we arrived at the Carrick station, Ma would look around for a trustworthy adult going to London. She would then ask them to keep an eye on me for the journey. If you can believe it, that really is how it all worked, and kids were essentially "mailed" across the Irish Sea to their family members in the UK.

The good old days!

25 – Minnie

It was a big event when my grandparents came home from London for the summer. Not only did they bring us suitcases that disgorged strange and wonderful English sweets and biscuits (those'd be candies and cookies on the other side of the pond) but there were always new adventures that surrounded their visits to Ireland. There were old friends and relatives to reconnect with. We had to visit a series of family graves. Pubs, naturally, had to be frequented. And, best of all, I had to go on walks with my Grandfather, where he recounted the wild tales of his youth. There was one time I dropped my new car over the wall down by Barry's Mill. I'm not sure if it was a Matchbox or a Dinky but we called them all dinkies. My toy narrowly avoided going into the Lingaun river. The car was a new one, a duck egg blue Ford Anglia, and it sat on the narrow verge, between the high stone wall and the river. The only way I could see to get at it was by going back to the bridge, crossing over and going down through the field, and then wading across the river. Grandad, on the other hand, thought we could get down to it from the road side. But only if we had a rope. This all sounded very exciting, my Da would never have come up with this approach!

Back up to the house we went to get a rope from the garage. When we returned to the scene of the crime with that, Grandad uncoiled a length of the rope and tossed it over the wall.

"Up you go there now.", said he to me, as he coiled a length of the rope around his leg and waist. He stood on the remainder of the coil. So as to not drop me into the river as well.

I couldn't believe it, he was letting me climb down to the river on the rope. That was just great. I jumped up on the wall. Grabbed hold of rope and bounced my way down to the narrow ledge, where the car was nestled beside a clump of dandelions. There wasn't much room and I hung onto the rope so as not to fall into the water. Once I pocketed the car, I put both hands back on the rope and walked up the wall. There was no fear of the rope slipping or anything like that, Grandad was a big man. Further down the wall, right in front of the gates into Barry's mill, we went down to the stile, a rocky stone gap in the wall. A stile was a common sight in a stone wall. It allowed a man to step up and through to the other side but animals couldn't get out through it. The stile here was special though, because it had my Grandad's hand prints in the concrete on either side. When he was a young man, they had just refinished the stile when Grandad ran up, put his hands on each side so he could swing his legs through the gap to the other side. For whatever reason, at that time, nobody bothered to fix it again so my Grandad's handprints were a more permanent reminder of his youthful exuberance. Over the years, even after I left home, I always tested my hands in Grandad's prints when I came back. Mine never quite got as big as his. There was no further adventure by the river that day as we were going to visit relations "up the country". These were Grandad's cousins, and they were farmers up in the Brown Mountain.

This was one of the regular visits on the schedule when my grandparents came back to Ireland and I loved going there. They had an old thatched cottage for a house, with a real flagstone floor in the kitchen. The place was warmed by a big, open hearth fire, winter or summer. There was an iron bar across the width of it that always had a back kettle hanging off to the side. I know there was a big three-legged pot that they used for boiling spuds and what have you too but I remember this mainly sitting on the hearth. The chimney was big enough that you could nearly drive a Morris Minor up it and I always wondered what happened when it rained. Did the fire go out or what? It was never raining any time I was there so I never found out. When I was small, it seemed like all the relations that Granny and Grandad visited were old and they all lived in an old thatched cottage. We used to go to Neary's house, on the hill just above the church in Owning too. That was a farm with yet another old white-washed cottage, and again it had a thatched roof. Grandad used to do a bit of work up there every time he came home and I always went along so that I could use dangerous implements that Ma would kill me for touching otherwise. We used to get out the big scythes and sharpen them with a stone for half an hour. Then we'd go out into the fields to top the buachalán buí, the yellow ragwort. I don't know why it was important to top the buachaláns, maybe they poisoned the animals if they ate them or something. You'd think a cow wouldn't eat it again if it got sick the first time, wouldn't you? Maybe it made the milk yellow? I grew up in the country but we didn't have a farm so I didn't know as much as I liked to pretend I did when I was talking to townies. When I go back to Ireland these days, I still like to visit our family there. Kitty and Michael have this lovely cottage half way up the boreen to Neary's and we usually take a little walk up the road to where the old cottage once stood in the sunshine. Though last time I went there it was raining. Anyway, the fun of the scythe was that, once sharpened, you could cut buachaláns by the score with the heft of the scythe flying around your body. It was great. One time, I made too big a swing with the scythe and it unbalance me. The bloody thing came too close to my ankle at the end of the stroke and it frightened the bejaysus out of me so I was a bit more careful from then on. Despite being in all these old cottages with Grandad over the years, I never once saw a pig in the kitchen. But I did see a sheep!

When we went to the Brown Mountain this day, there was the usual long-lost relative shenanigans. Hugs, back-slapping, along with some male greetings that sounded more like grunts of disgust than of welcome. That was the Irish way back then: you knew everybody loved everybody but you wouldn't be caught dead saying such muck. If you were a child, as I was then, you had to put up with sloppy wet cheek kisses from these auld wans and it was only disgusting. It was okay for women to display affection to each other and to kids but men stood aloof from all that stuff. And sure, wasn't I nearly a man now? I tried to hang back far enough, and for long enough, that I might be overlooked in the whole process but, as usual, it didn't work and I was plastered with love anyway.

"Isn't he getting so big now!", they'd exclaim, and on and on it would go for far too long for comfort.

Once inside, a few bottles of porter would appear and the kettle would go on for tea. This time though, I was in for a surprise. Amongst the dogs and cats that bounded around in all the commotion, there was a little while lamb! I swear to Jaysus, it's true. There was a lamb bouncing around with the dogs. I think the thing thought it was a dog and it would come hopping over to be petted and then it'd dash off again, just like the sheep dogs. The lamb's name was Minnie. I was over the moon. This would be a great story to tell the lads when I got back to Carrick. I fell in love with this stupid little sheep and I had the best day ever in the Brown Mountain.

The following year, I was really looking forward to Gran and Grandad's return. Not only was I looking forward to whatever English treats they might bring us but I wanted to go back to the Brown Mountain again to see Minnie. They came and it all happened. Just as I imagined it would. Yes, we had all the usual greeting fluff again and I couldn't wait to get through it all. It seemed like it went on for an eternity before we went through the front door. I'm not sure if the doorway was really this low but let's not ruin a good story with facts: my recollection was that Grandad had to stoop to go through it. The dogs came bounding over to see what the commotion was all about and yes, Minnie came bounding over too. This time, however, Minnie was a full-grown sheep! She had grown far more than I had so when she bounced in close to get petted, she knocked me off my feet and I was on my arse on the floor with this big bloody sheep nuzzling me in the face. It was great! I had the best day ever. We went out into the garden and I tried to ride Minnie around the yard. She wasn't having it though, so I was black with dirt after a few tries, and falls, of trying to get on her back. Minnie was having a great time too. She was mostly sitting by the fire with the dogs when she was with all the old people so having a kid to play with made it all as much fun for Minnie as it was for me. The dogs would get jealous every now and again so I had to divide my time up between the dogs and the sheep so they were all happy. I can't remember much about anything else that happened that day, it was all about Minnie and me.

The following summer couldn't come around fast enough but finally it did. Granny and Grandad arrived and I could barely wait to get through all the usual introductory nonsense before asking if we were going to Brown Mountain again this year. And, fortunately, we were. Thank God. You could never tell what was going to happen with the grown-ups, someone might have fallen out with someone, or maybe somebody died or got sick. You'd never know what might change that could ruin a good adventure in those days. Nothing bad had happened though and we were off to Brown Mountain that following Saturday. Now I had shot up a bit over the course of that past year so I figured that I'd be riding Minnie around like a race horse during this trip. I was so wrapped up in the adventures I was about to have that I don't remember a single thing about the drive. Nor do I remember anything about the meet and greet nonsense that would have followed our arrival. When I entered the cottage though, I was devastated to find that Minnie wasn't there. I was absolutely wrecked, where was she? The adults went on with a lot of that adult kind of whispering they engage in when they don't want the child to know what's going on. I threw a bit of a tantrum but it didn't get me anywhere and things weren't getting any clearer. I disconsolately played with the dogs and I went out to the fields to see if Minnie was out there. There were lots of sheep, and plenty of new lambs, but no Minnie. The lambs in the field weren't any good. They would run away when you ran after them and they wouldn't play with you like Minnie used to. There was no consoling me. I was moody for the rest of the day and I really wasn't happy at all. As usual, we all sat down for dinner at the end of the day. There was a little wooden table for the kids, with little log seats to sit on. I always enjoyed my food in Brown Mountain and this time was no different. We had a great mutton stew with floury boiled spuds, in their skins, covered in butter. After that, we went home, and I still wonder what happened to Minnie to this very day. I never did find out what all the whispering was about when we arrived. And nobody ever told me the contents of the furtive adult conversations that happened when we were all having that lovely mutton stew. Some things are just fated to remain a mystery!

26 – Playing with Fire

Me and Gerry, who lived up the road, wanted to make some new lead weights for our fishing rods one time. We lived close and we used to fish the Lingaun together a fair bit. Mostly we bought our hooks, fishing line and lead weights in O'Keeffe's, in Carrick. We were always very creative though, and if we could find a cheaper way to do something, or a way to do something a bit different just for fun, then we did it. Particularly if the process involved doing something we knew we shouldn't be doing. One of the best things to play with in those days was fire. Gerry found this cast iron ladle somewhere and his Da had told him that it came from a blacksmith's forge. Right away, we made the connection to fire. I can't remember if it was Gerry or me that had it but, between us, we also had a small sheet of lead. In Carrick circles, it was common to think of lead as coming from church roofs! Now, I can tell you that neither of us had ever been up on a church roof so, with total honesty, I can say that I have no idea of the origins of this particular piece of lead. Lead was certainly a tradeable item among the children of the town so we may have come by it that way. Mostly we'd just cut off little rectangles of the pliable metal and fold it around the fishing line, a foot or two up from the hook. Then we'd bite down on it with our teeth to clamp it in place. That was right up there, in the child toy safety stakes, with the little plastic box of mercury I used to play with in my bare hands. Anyway, we had much grander ideas for this little sheet of lead. We were going to make little plumb weights, just the ones you could buy in O'Keeffe's. We made a circle of rocks out the back of Gerry's house and we built a fire. The ladle got plonked on top early in the process so as to warm it up. As the fire matured into a lovely bed of embers, the flames died down and you'd swear the ladle was nearly glowing when we started cutting up the lead sheet into smaller pieces. We began tossing the little pieces into the ladle and, while we waited for the lead to melt, we cut some pieces of wire into short lengths. These we bent into a "U" shape and we tightened up the curve at the end with a pair of pliers. These would become the "eye" of the weight. We were a bit stuck for a mold for the whole process. We had nothing that could tolerate the temperature of the molten lead and if we were going to all this effort, we wanted a nice shape on the finished product too. We hunted around the garage until we found this small piece of metal rod with a lovely rounded end on it. This was Ireland now, so the ground was already damp, and we tamped down a bit of bare earth with our feet. Once the ground underfoot was good and solid, we poked a hole in it with the round end of the little bar. We had to have a few tries before we were happy with the condition of the hole. By then the lead was a silvery liquid in the ladle. There was a bit of dross on the top and we skimmed that off with a stick before pouring a little of the liquid into the hole. This was just a test run so we didn't bother with the eye wire yet. There was a bit of hissing and sizzling as the hot lead drove out the moisture from the ground surrounding the hole. We poked our first attempt out of the ground and inspected it. It wasn't bad at all, though maybe a bit too small. For the next attempt, we decided to wiggle the rod so as to make the base of the hole bigger and a bit more round. That would give us a bottom-heavy weight, exactly what we wanted. This time, I held the piece of wire with a pliers, while Gerry poured the molten lead in. I had enough time to straighten up the wire, after Gerry took away the ladle, and while the metal was still molten. Jaysus, the little weight we dug out of the ground was only gorgeous! We took turns pouring and holding, experimenting with a few different sizes of weight. By the time we had enough weights made to keep us fishing the Lingaun for the rest of the year, we decided to make a couple of big ones to use up the last of the hot lead. It took a fair bit of wiggling with the little iron bar before we were happy we'd made a big enough hole. I was on wire holding duty for this one. Now, we had taken some safety precautions, using Gerry's Ma's kitchen gloves for protection against the heat, for example. Unfortunately, it didn't help in this instance. When Gerry began the pour, there was a big spluttering explosion of hot lead out of the hole and a bit caught me in the eye. Jaysus, I was stunned and it bloody hurt. I was screaming like a mad thing and Gerry's Ma came flying out to see what was the matter. It all got a bit chaotic for a few minutes then, with Gerry's Ma chasing Gerry around the yard for him trying to blind me and what have you. That must have entertained me enough for the shock of the hot lead in the eye to wear off because I don't remember too much excitement after that. I think Gerry's Ma may have dragged me back home then because I have a vague recollection of my own Ma doing some histrionics around the whole affair too. I'll have to ask Gerry one time if he remembers any more about the event but it was certainly one more memorable day in a whole series of good fishing stories over the years.

Most of our fire activities were a bit more harmless. As a child around Carrick, fire lighters were one of the first things you learned to play with. These little white bricks were soaked in something that smelled a bit like petrol or lighter fluid. They sold these in Bennett's supermarket and anywhere else you might go shopping, since everyone needed to light the fire at home. The bricks were soft enough that you could break them up with your fingers so as to extend the play time by having more pieces. We used to light them and throw them at each other. The flames weren't that big and they didn't last that long so you'd aim for the other fella's hair, thinking you'd have some chance of doing a bit of damage that way. If you got a burning bit stuck in your hair, you'd have to beat the head off yourself to put it out before the whole head of hair took off. We used to juggle the burning pieces in the air with our bare hands too. It was great. Sometimes though, when there was enough of the juice on your hands, you'd set your own hands on fire. Then you'd have to beat your hands on something to put out the flames before you got burned. The easiest way was to clamp the burning hands between your legs but, if you weren't wearing long pants on the day, you could be in trouble. You might wind up with burning hands and legs. Me and Gerry raided the fridges in both our houses one day and went off across the fields, along with a few fire lighters, to have a picnic. It was a drizzly auld day but we set the fire under the trees and it took off with the fire lighters. We had the best rashers and sausages you ever tasted.

One of my favorite fire toys in those days was flaming torches. We used to head off out towards Tybroughney, along the railway tracks. There was a great swampy area out that way, where the bulrushes grew. We would cut the stalks with the biggest, most solid, heads. You could buy petrol in a gallon can at any of the filling stations. We would soak the head of the bulrush in petrol and set light to it. They flamed and smoked like nothing you've ever seen, they were great. We used to run around The Green at night with these things and we'd have flaming sword fights and what have you. I got a belt of a flaming torch in the face one night from Johnny, my cousin across the road, we had a great time. Plastic light sabers, my arse, this was the way to play! Where we played on the Green was just behind the Guards Barracks but I don't ever remember the police doing anything to stop us. Though I'm sure they kept an eye on us just the same. We used to have big bonfires on the Green too. There was always someone getting burned at those events though, what with us all trying to jump over and through the flames. Someone always went home burned and crying from such events.

One of the good things about living in the country was that you knew plenty of farmers and you could buy, or trade for, a few crow bangers from the lads that grew up on a farm. A crow banger was a rope with little sticks of dynamite hanging off it every few inches. The farmers used them to frighten off the crows so they wouldn't eat their crops. You lit the big rope and, as it slowly burned down, it would light the fuse on each little fire cracker that it caught up to along the length of the rope. If you went into Dowley's in town, they wouldn't sell them to you. You had to be a farmer and they knew us kids would be up to no good with them. The kids would cut off all the bangers off the rope so they could be used one at a time. There were all kinds of horror stories about what could happen when you were messing with crow bangers. You'd hear stories of fellas blowing their fingers off or, horror of horrors, having one going off in the pocket next to the family jewels! In the main, we lit them for our own entertainment. Watching them explode in the dark of night was great. The big bang seemed way louder at night too. Some would go a bit too far and shove them in through the letter boxes in people's front doors. It would frighten the shit out of everyone inside the house and one time, I heard a story about someone's letters going on fire inside the front door.

If you didn't have anything else, you couldn't go wrong with a big nut, a couple of big bolts and a roll of caps. We used to buy the rolls of caps for our cap guns. The roll of paper had these little pockets of sulphur or some kind of stuff that would spark and bang when the hammer of the toy gun would strike it. That was all fine and well for a little while but it wasn't all that exciting and we tried to figure out other ways to amuse ourselves with the caps. We'd spark them with our nails and try not to burn our fingers off at the same time. We'd put down a whole roll of caps and hit it with a rock so the whole roll would explode at once. The best trick though, was the bolts and nut. You'd screw one of the bolts part way into the nut and then drop the roll of caps into the still-open side of the nut. Then you'd screw the second bolt into the other side of the nut, torqueing it down as tight as you could. Sometimes, the bloody caps would go off while you were tightening the bolt and it would nearly blow the hand off you. Once you had everything together, the idea was to fling the thing as high as you possibly could into the air. Then you'd step back and wait for it to come sailing down and hit the concrete. When it did, there was the mightiest of explosions, a huge flash, and the bolts and nut would go flying in all directions. Woe betide the poor bastard who go hit with one of those things flying through the air. If you only had a small set of bolts and a nut, you could do the same thing but you could only use a little strip of the cap roll. It was all very entertaining stuff but it's a wonder half of us weren't blinded and maimed by such activities.

The very best fires I ever saw though, came about when Mrs. Gorman's nephew, from England, came to visit her. Mrs. Gorman lived in a lovely little cottage next door to us. I used to visit regularly because she knew stuff that nobody else knew. She had a sand pit in the lean-to by the shed that she stored vegetables in. She would put her bottle of milk in the sand to keep it cool and fresh before everyone had a fridge. The woman was a genius and she was nice. Her nephew was a grown man when I first met him and I was only a little kid. His job had something to do with all this kind of burning and explosion stuff. He got paid for blowing shit up, would you believe it! He used to mix fertilizer and sugar and then he'd put on the most magical displays. They were far better than fireworks because the explosions were bigger, brighter and louder than you could imagine. He used to have all these metal tubes and things that he would pack with the fertilizer mix and then he would run little threads of the powder back a safe distance. All the threads would come together at his feet and he would light that little mound. We would watch, rapt, as the smoking fizz raced off towards whatever he had set up at the other end. And then there would be a series of mighty flashes and bangs as the whole thing erupted. There were geyser-like spews of flame and sparks soaring into the sky, flaming trails, loud explosions, bits and pieces flying in all directions. It was all just amazing. I just had to get my hands on some of that fertilizer. This was even tougher to come by than the crow bangers but every now and again, you'd get lucky. Fertilizer was one of the most prized things back in the day. You'd have an entourage a mile long if you were heading out to play with that stuff. This one did terrify us though, thank God, and we were far more careful with fertilizer than with any other fire making toys that we played with. My displays were never as good as those done by the English lad but I would probably still go out of my way to watch a fertilizer firework display today.

Looking back, it's hard to imagine that any of these insane things were considered toys. And I really don't know how so many of us got away with it but I'm glad to have survived. Apologies to my own kids for my overly-protective tendencies as you grew up. I probably figured that you had my insanity gene and that you needed it!

27 – Tick Tock

The death of a parent is a big thing. Much to our surprise, of our parents, my mother was the first to go. She had never been sick a day in her life but the big C snuck up on her and took her out. Quickly. That event left us surprised, shocked and saddened. My father was never quite the same afterwards and it wasn't too many years later that he followed her. I didn't want to remember my mother sick and dying but I've always regretted not making a better effort to get back home to see her before she went. Funny enough, I think she was of a similar mindset. During our last phone conversation, and she was already getting close to her departure day, she was encouraging me not to bother coming home and that everything would be grand. It would be just like my mother to think that she wouldn't want me to see her, and to remember her, sick like that. Somehow, that's how it worked out and I didn't get to say goodbye face to face. I sometimes regret that I didn't overcome both our feelings on the topic and go back home to see her anyway. I did manage to get back to see my father before he went. Though in this case, it didn't work out quite so well. He was a smidgen more obstreperous in his later years and we clashed a little bit more than was the norm over most of our lives together. That said, I was still glad I'd made the trip. It rained the entire week that I returned to Ireland for my mother's funeral. Very fitting. Aside from the party at Moloney's pub after the funeral, most of the week was spent at the kitchen table. We drank tea, he drank the odd glass of Jameson between cups of tea, and we chatted. Aside from immediate family, there was a constant flow of family, friends and neighbors visiting. It wasn't unusual to hear the front door opening past midnight, as someone spotted the light on and came in for a chat. Despite the melancholy surrounding the whole affair, it was nice to see. I knew when I left that there would be people calling on my father to help him through the whole grieving process. I knew I'd be going back to Canada and that I would be living a life where I could almost imagine Ma still doing her thing in the kitchen back in Skough. I did make a couple of visits back up to Kilkieran to chat with Ma during the week. It's a great place to spend time in the rain. It wasn't until my next visit to Ireland that I managed to cry for what was lost.

Ma had this cute little pair of earrings, little gold boots, that she'd always loved. That was all I wanted of hers. Sure, there were a few things around the house that I might pick up and see value in but one of my earliest memories of my mother was of her wearing those earrings. My sisters let me have them. Though I also have a tiny gold teapot that was permanently shuffled around the shelves in the corner on the kitchen. It went from a little jewelry tray, to a clean ashtray, to being lost in the corner behind last week's mail. The little teapot, a bracelet charm most likely, reminded me of Ma and her tea. The biggest regret I have about my mother going early was that she never got to visit Canada. We were to have brought her out that summer. She died never having flown. And that may not only apply to getting on an airplane.

There's a whole other story about Da's passing but I'd spent most of my life learning from him and going to him in times of trouble. My first car was a little, well-used, Chrysler Sunbeam. I thought I was hot shit driving around in that. Of course, I'd had to give up my trusty old green Honda CB250 G5 to get that. And only because my then girlfriend, now wife, wouldn't get up on it after her first ride as a pillion passenger. I had to replace a cog in the gearbox of the old bike one time and, much to my amazement, it worked when I was finished. The car was a whole other problem though. When the clutch started to fail, I needed Da's help so I headed back down to Skough. We had a pit in the garage and we dropped out the transmission to stick in a new clutch plate. Wouldn't have tried that one on my own. My biggest problem with Da was that he moved in Da time. I think my mother used to have the same problem. His to-do list never seemed to get acted upon and it drove her up the wall. I might have picked up my attitude towards Da from her. Even his story telling used to drive her crazy. Me too! He'd wander off topic and spend so long telling some other incidental story that you'd forget what the original story was all about until he surprised you by swinging back on track. Good God, is that where I get it from! Anyway, Da was born in the UK. He was a child in London at the start of World War II but his parents, my grandparents, were planning on sending him back to Ireland to avoid the ravages of the blitz. There was a story about his younger brother, asleep in his crib, when a bomb came through the roof and landed in the baby's room. Amazingly, and fortunately, it was a dud and it never exploded. Apparently, Uncle Tom stayed asleep thorough the whole process but that was the last straw, the kids were being shipped off to family in Ireland.

Shortly after this event Da was out playing in the streets of London when he was approached by this lady. She was one of the neighbors and he knew her by sight. It's unfortunate but I no longer remember her name. She had heard my Dad and his brothers and sisters were going to Ireland for safety and she wanted to speak to him about that. Da added some of the content and context of this exchange to his telling but I don't recall the details with sufficient clarity to share them. Pity that, I would like to have known more of the background. But then this is why I write down such stories for my kids. At the end of the conversation, she handed my Dad a silver pocket watch and told him to take it to Ireland with him. It was her husband's and he was off fighting the war. The feeling I still retain from this tale was that she didn't think her husband was coming back from the war and that she was quite uncertain that she, herself, would survive the blitz. Somehow, my Dad taking the watch to Ireland was taking a little of them there too. My father spoke fondly, and with sadness, of his exchange with this brave lady. Sad that but nice too.

Da felt connected to that watch and was quite proud of it. It occasionally came out for review, and as the focal point for some storytelling, when we had visitors to our house over the years. Some weird combination of that prized possession being a watch, along with Da's excruciating and meandering storytelling, made that watch epitomize my father, for me. It really was the only thing of his that I wanted when he moved on. Again, my sisters were tolerant and allowed me to have it. There were a few lessons that I later realized were to be learned from all this. It's an old adage that time and tide waits for no man, or woman, but I haven't always lived my life by that dictum. The old pocket watch, and my folks' early departures, remind me of that from time to time.

28 – Chocolate Crumb

I don't want to ruin a good story by checking the facts first. I probably could talk to my brother-in-law about the history of this place but the mere mention of the name "Miloko" brings on gustatory memories of orgasmic proportions for me. The ring of the name has an onomatopoeic echo on the tongue, driving a burst of anticipatory saliva, that can nevermore be satisfied. I would expect the same to be true for anyone of my generation that grew up in Carrick. Miloko ... a strange name, to be sure, and one that I find difficult to imagine any Celtic origins for. It sounds tropical and chocolatey to me and, indeed, that's what it's famous for: a strange and wonderful collection of products we knew as chocolate crumb. My father, my grandfather, my uncle and a variety of other family members worked in the Miloko factory over the years. Now, this wasn't your actual chocolate for eating but rather a set of chocolate ingredients that were used in the confectionary industry to make chocolatey products that eventually found their way on to supermarket shelves.

There were three types of crumb that passed my lips over the years. The first types were hard crumb, one a light milk-chocolate color, the other the color of white chocolate. A lump of either was as hard as the hobs of hell. Like a brick it was. If you had a big lump of hard chocolate crumb, it could last you for days. When I got my hands on a knob, I used to go around with it in a plastic bag in my pocket. You could take it out for a gnaw and put it back a hundred times before it'd be small enough to put the whole thing in your mouth at once. I'm sure this stuff was what started my dental problems. The gnawing was the thing though. You'd be grinding away at it in the Castle Cinema on a Saturday afternoon and, during a quiet spell in the film, everyone would be screaming at you to stop making the noise. Everyone in Carrick knew what it was you were doing. It was a great movie snack if you didn't have the money for sweets. It would last the length of the short film, the long film, and would then go back in the plastic bag for later. Fortunately, we mostly went to films with Bruce Lee, Audie Murphy, and the like, so you wouldn't have too many quite spots. Though Audie used to be making up to women every now and again and the girls used to love those bits. There were times where you might get a bit impatient with not having enough small chocolatey bits in your mouth to chew on all at once so you'd have to take a tool to it and smash up enough to fill your mouth with crumbs of crumb. I used to get the ballpeen hammer and pound the shit out of it to get a fistful of crumbs and dust. The best way to do it was to put it inside two, maybe even three, plastic bags. They you'd get a nappy (diaper), one of the old cloth ones, and fold that across itself two or three times. Once that was wrapped around the plastic bags, with the knob of crumb in the middle of the package, you could pound away on it and not worry about losing any of the dust. You wouldn't want to lose a spec of this stuff, so precious was it. The smashed mess was then poured from the bag next to the crumb, into the next outer one, and finally to the last one. If you did it all the right way, with just the right amount of force on each tap, only the inner bags would have been perforated by the sharp edges of the crumb as you beat the livin' daylights out of it. Then you would tap all the crumbs and dust into the corner of the last bag and upend the whole lot into your mouth. I can assure you that the explosion of flavor, combined with the sharp resistance of the larger pieces between your teeth, is not matched by anything you can buy in a sweet shop or candy store today. These days, the mammies would probably get mad if their kids were eating anything like this but, if it came on the market, I'd be the first to line up to buy it! We used to eat the white stuff the same way. It was just as hard as the chocolate colored crumb but it had the flavor you would expect from a white chocolate.

Now the soft crumb was a whole other story. This stuff was dense. Heavy duty. It had mass. I swear to God, it felt way heavier than it looked, like the lead version of chocolate. If you had a slab of this stuff, you would cut off slices to eat. Using the biggest carving knife in the drawer, you would have to center the blade of the knife over the slab. Much like you might cut off a slice of cheese, you would have one hand on the handle of the knife, while the other would be at the end near the tip of the blade. With heavy pressure, a gentle rocking back and forth would eventually free up a slice of this heavenly treat. While the soft crumb was indeed soft, it was so firm that you might imagine cutting a block of old cheddar that had four or five times the resistance to being cut. This stuff was so precious that the Mammies and Daddies would be hiding it in all the best hiding places. For fear that if the kids found it, they would devour it all in one sitting and be as sick as dogs. If you thought the hard crumb had flavor, even when crushed, you just can't imagine the flavor of this stuff. There's no doubt that if you ate a ton of it, you felt it. It would be sitting in your belly like a slab of lead. But you wouldn't care, you'd do it anyway so delicious was it. The soft crumb never lasted as long as the hard stuff but to delay and prolong the pleasure, you would have to park a big lump of it in your mouth and not chew. Never. Not one chew. If you couldn't answer a question in the cinema, the other kids knew you had a gobfull of the soft chocolate crumb and then they'd all want some. You just had to lie and say that was the only piece you had. Usually done by a shoulder shrug, with the hands upraised, to indicate that was your very last bit! Much as I loved the hard crumb, soft chocolate crumb was my favorite. Or was it? That hard stuff was great and it lasted so long. Whichever, I loved them both and I must admit to sometimes being a secret chocolate crumb devourer. So as not to have to share.

Nowadays, the Miloko name lives on in Carrick. It is a Glanbia plant that produces other dairy products entirely. I, however, will always remember the name on my tongue as the place that made chocolate crumb.

I have no idea if these kinds of chocolate products are produced anywhere now but if you know of any such thing, don't keep it a secret, I want some crumb!

29 – The Big Fish

Fishing was a part of all our lives growing up in Carrick. A walk along the quays of the Suir could take hours if you stopped for a word with everyone that was casting a line. For some it was done just for fun, but for most of us it was done for the food too. Trout were the primary preoccupation amongst the casual anglers. Though you might also hook an eel or a fluke. On rarer occasions, maybe even a salmon. Carrick was famous for its cots. Little flat-bottomed boats that have been used by the local snap-net fishermen for generations. We spent hours watching the fisherman with their nets, slowly moving along the river. To be honest, I was never sure of how the whole fishing license thing worked but sometimes I think there were as many "pooched" (poached … but not in the cooking sense!) salmon, as there were legal. Da showed up once or twice with a salmon that he got from one of the lads and it was like a spy movie, with the way he would furtively get the fish from the car to the kitchen. Our house was out in the country, who did he think was watching? Despite all the hours I spent by the Suir, I never once fished it. In Skough, the Lingaun flowed, on its way down towards the Suir, about one hundred yards from my front door. And that was where I honed my fishing skills.

I'm not sure what age I was, but I would have been very young when I got my first fishing rod. It was a little blue fiberglass thing, a single piece, with a spinning reel. Truth be told, it was a bit of an embarrassment, it was that small. I added the line and a lead weight, but no hook yet, so that I could practice my casting skills in the grass of the front garden. I don't ever remember using this rod to actually fish and my real interest in fishing only launched when I got my first three-piece fly rod. This was a long, slender, supple thing, so fine at the tip you could imagine it breaking with a fish of any decent size on the end of the line. It never did though. From years of listening to my father, my grandfather and the uncles, all singing the praises of fly fishing, I knew I was in the big leagues now. I spent hours in O'Keeffe's, in town, browsing the selection of flies. An Olive Drab was my first purchase. This was followed by a Greenwells Glory but only after several more visits for appropriately serious deliberations. What those poor people in that shop had to put up with from us kids. I was ready to fish. But now that I had them, these flies were such beautiful little works of art that it seemed a shame to drop them on the water. My grandfather, who I'm not sure fished a day in his life, told me that real fishermen tied their own flies so I headed off to the library to find out how that was done. I only read a couple of chapters before I felt like I had the idea and off I went to buy some bare hooks. I set myself up in the garage, my first hook mounted on the vice, and I was ready to go to work. I went off out into the fields, looking for dead birds. Well, where else would you think you might get feathers back then?

A few weeks later, after patrolling the local hills and monitoring our cats hunting activities, I had a great collection of feathers, harvested from dead birds of all kinds and colors. I had feathers of every hue, blue, red, orange, green, grey, brown and black. All donated by an assortment of dead finches, tits, robins and wagtails. I knew I was supposed to mimic the shapes and colors of the real flies that you might find on the river but the real flies were all a bit earthy and boring and, somehow, mine all turned out to be highly colorful. More like the little works of art you could buy in the shop than anything resembling a real fly but I liked them. Rather than doing any fishing, making flies became the hobby for a while. Sooner or later, I had to get around to the real thing though. When that finally happened, I just couldn't use my own flies. I had put so much into making these lovely little things, I couldn't stand the thought of tossing them in the water either. Back to the Olive Drab and the

Greenwells Glory. My first fly fishing adventure was a total disaster and I lost all my flies in the overhanging branches within the first hour. Fly-fishing, my arse, enough of that shite, I was off to get some Three Counties!

Back then, the fishing lure of choice around Carrick was Three Counties cheese. I think it came from Mitchelstown Creameries, in the County Cork. The little triangular cheeses came in a flat, round box, with six, foil-wrapped segments of cheese in each. It was a semi-spreadable white cheese so you peeled the foil off the tip of the triangle and a gentle squeeze would emit a small gob of cheese at the opening. You could then manipulate and mold that piece into a little ball around a treble hook. If you kept the triangle in your pocket, it would stay warm and then it would be easier to squeeze out just the right amount that you needed. Once the soft cheese hit the cold water, it firmed up and was a good reliable bait for several casts. Now, according to my father, my grandfather and an assortment of uncles, this wasn't real fishing. But what did they know? The only time I ever saw them going off fishing, they came back soaking wet and all they caught was a bat. Fishing at night? Were they stupid or what! The Lingaun is a small river and it is lined by trees, bushes and what have you for virtually the whole length of its banks. You would find an odd opening here and here, often because the farmer might have removed the trees and foliage to make his field a bit bigger or to give the cows access to the river for a drink of water. Other openings gave access to swimming holes or little picnic spots that had been more slowly eroded by human intervention over the years. You could probably catch a fish anywhere in the river but we like to imagine that there were some whoppers in the slower-moving, deeper and darker spots up and down its length. The Turn Hole was our favorite swimming spot so often that would be the final destination on a fishing expedition. If we caught nothing, and if it was a sunny day, we could always go swimming. We usually stopped for a few casts under the Faugheen Bridge before climbing over the stile into Tommy's and Willie's field. Checking that the big bull wasn't there first, of course. What with the traffic going over the bridge, we never held out much hope for catching anything there but, over the years, I think the best fish I ever caught came from my first cast under the bridge one day. More often than not though, it was just an easy place to get into the way of casting the line. You might need a bit of practice before getting into the more challenging spots, where you had to wiggle the tip of the rod through tree branches. And then you'd have to do some country fishing gymnastics to lob the line in just the right spot, without getting the bloody line stuck in the trees. I lost a fair few hooks and weights over the years, while learning the art of fishing the Lingaun. I used to go fishing with Gerry, from up the road, sometimes. Other times it might be with one of the lads from school. There were a few occasions where my cousins, from Carrick, would come out and we'd head off for a bit of fishing. It was always a bit of a fiasco with the townies. They were used to fishing the Suir from the quays and all you had to do there was hoik the rod back over your shoulder and then whip it, as hard as you could, in the direction you wanted to cast in. The Suir was a much bigger river and you wanted to lash your hook out as far as you could towards the middle of the river. These particular skills did not work well on the Lingaun. Here, you needed a light and gentle touch. A series of soft swings, with ever-increasing but with slow momentum gains, were what was required. The boys would be whipping the rods around like lunatics and very often lost a weeks' worth of hooks in the first twenty minutes. Then they'd just be jumping around, shouting and screaming, frightening all the fish, so there would be no good fishing left in a day like that. And that was probably why I spent more of my hours fishing the Lingaun alone.

I knew I was a social being from the start but there were two things best done alone: reading and fishing. I probably spent way more hours fishing alone than with company. I still don't know how my mother thought that wandering the banks of a river, alone, was okay. And that going to Carrick to hang out with the lads wasn't. On one particularly nice day, I was fishing alone. I had my few casts at the bridge but lost patience quickly. The swimming hole for the little kids, those just learning to swim, was about fifty yards further upstream. You could get at it from where we went in to swim but then the fish would see you so I went a little further up. Here you hand to wiggle your way through the brambles and the trees but then you had them for camouflage. No luck at this spot either and I was a bit impatient on the day so I soon left, going further upstream, to the Turn Hole. I think this hole came about because they redirected the river way back. We called it the Turn Hole because it made a ninety degree bend and there was no mountain or rock that would make that a natural thing. This was where we big kids swam. Whether they dug this hole deep when they changed the flow or maybe the sharp turn caused eddy currents that made it deeper, I'm not sure. But it was dark and deep and it earned its name because of that. I don't know exactly how deep it was but we couldn't see the bottom and we weren't inclined to swim down to the bottom to check it out either. Who knew what river monsters might be lurking down there. Somehow though, we felt fine about swimming in the Turn Hole. As it happened, no luck here either. I mused over a few final casts as to where I might try next and I decided to give the Black Hole a go. Now this is the most feared spot on the river. It is bigger, longer, deeper and darker than the Turn Hole. There is a bit of a stone weir at the end of it, allowing the river to return to its clear and rocky turbulence, but the Black Hole was ... well ... the Black Hole. So frightened were we of what might be at the bottom of its murky waters, we only ever dared to attempt swimming here a couple of times in all those years. We didn't last long and we were relieved when someone chickened out and suggested we go back to the Turn Hole. I'm pretty sure it wasn't me that chickened out first!

I took a few casts at the upstream end and I got a bite or two. You can beat the feeling of the rod twitching, and tickling the muscles in your forearms when the fish try to get that cheese. I struck but didn't hook anything. Clever little bastards, these Lingaun trout. At last, though, a challenge! I tried a few more casts and there was nothing. I had probably frightened them off but it felt like there was a big one there so I went downstream and positioned myself right by the weir. Now I was casting back upstream, hoping the fish had all moved to this end. I was up to their tricks today. It didn't take long before I got another tug on the line. Jaysus, I knew it, there was a big fella in there. The great thing about fishing alone was that you had this running conversation going on in your head, with what I just knew were the smartest fish in the world. You could burn up an hour, no problem, talking to them at each spot along the way. No wonder I often came back after a day's fishing with my mother screaming about "where was I" and giving out about long I was gone. I'm not sure how long I was engaged in this practice that day, and I was very focused now, but out of the corner of my eye, I saw a flash of silver.

"What in the name of Jaysus was that?", thought I. To myself.

Now I was torn between watching the surface of the water for any movement of the line, along with keeping half an eye in the direction of the silver flash.

"Jaysus, there it is again!", as the glint happened again, and just off to my right. And right in front of the weir where I was standing on the rocks.

I stopped worrying about the line and turned my full attention to the weir. Not long after, I was rewarded. There was a bloody salmon trying to get up the weir! We just didn't have salmon in the Lingaun so I was completed mesmerized and gobsmacked. I stood like a statue while the bloody salmon tried again to make it up the weir.

"Holy shit!", said I. Again to myself … "I want that feckin' fish!"

Right about then, I got another strike. I was so distracted by the antics of the salmon that the strike on the line threw me for a loop and I stumbled and fell, arse first into the river.

"Fuck the trout, I want the salmon!", I thought.

But there was no way that a salmon was going to forget about jumping the weir and spend any time admiring my bit of Three Counties cheese. What should I do? I needed a spear! I had a fish on the line so I put a rock on top of the handle of the fishing rod and I took off like a scalded cat, heading for home. I was a decent distance runner as a kid but I was all the way up at the Black Hole so the distance home made it more of an endurance sprint. I was hatching my plan as I ran. I was going to tie the carving knife onto the handle of the sweeping brush. I was gasping when I ran in the back door and grabbed the sweeping brush from the back kitchen and the carving knife from the drawer. Ma ran after me as I raced to the garage for a bit of baling twine to lash the two together. I gasped … "Salmon!" … "Weir" … "Black Hole" … and who knows what else but it must have made enough sense to her because Ma went back to whatever she was doing in the kitchen. I was still tying off the knots on the twine as I flew out the front gate. I leaped over the stile at the bridge and pounded my way up through the fields. I was totally winded, maybe beyond repair, by the time I made it back to the Black Hole. I barged down to the water's edge and stood, poised, spear at the ready. I poised some more. And then some more.

"Where was that little shagger!?!?!"

Actually, he was a big shagger and that's what made this so

important. I would be a legend. A salmon! In the Lingaun! And I was going to catch him. I'm not sure how long I stood there but it eventually came to rest in my mind that he was gone. I paced, and cursed, and threw rocks into the river in the hopes of getting a jump out of it but I finally had to accept that the salmon might be gone. I was devastated. I put down my spear and went over to get my fishing rod. At least I had a trout at the end of that. The bloody rod was in the water and I had to get wet, again, going out to retrieve it. Obviously, the fish was big enough that he dragged it out from under the rock so maybe the day wasn't lost. Soaking wet, I reached down to get the rod from the river bed. When I started reeling it in, I knew there wasn't even a dead trout at the end of it.

Saddened. Morose. Dejected. I squished my way back home. No fish. Still, I had a great story to tell and I told it to everyone who might listen. Nobody ever believed me about there being a salmon trying to swim upstream in the Lingaun. But I swear, on my mother's grave, there was.

30 – The Bone Setter

Sometimes I think I must have spent my childhood dreaming. Some of the stories of traditional Irish cures are the stuff of legends and fairy tales. Most of the half-remembered stories in my head today can't possibly be true and if they are, it's amazing that someone didn't bottle or patent them. Any of them would have made you millions. My Uncle Eddie was my Grand Uncle but we all called him Uncle Eddie because that's what Da called him. He lived up in Ballinacroney and he used to keep bees in the orchard. He had hives all over the place, like little cottages, arranged amongst the apple trees. I went up to him and Auntie Peg a few times but now, with the foggy clarity of hindsight, I wish I had done it more often. He was amazing with the bees. I don't remember half the stories he told me because I was often shaking in anticipation of going out to the orchard to "play" with the bees. I know he had all sorts of gloves, nets, head gear, and all kinds of tools and gadgets for when he worked on the hives but any time he took me out there, it seemed like we didn't wear anything. I was quaking in my boots the first time. No, I was quaking every time he brought me out there. I was expecting to be stung alive and it was quite the rush to come back from the orchard in one piece, with honey dribbling down the sides of my mouth. You just wouldn't believe the taste of Uncle Eddie's honey. Once you were done spitting out hard bits of the honeycomb wax, you realized that it was way more delicious than the honey in the jars from the supermarket. Uncle Eddie would be talking in that calm way he had when we were among the hives. He had a bee smoker but it mostly sat on the ground. He'd be waving his hand, gently, this way and that, as he told me all about the secrets of bee keeping. I don't remember a thing about it though, my eyes were riveted on the bees as he lifted the top off the hive. He would put his hand in amongst the bees and withdraw it with a mass of bees all over it, sometimes they were halfway up his arm. It was like a velvet glove of bees. Then he'd have me put my hand into the bees or he's wipe some of them off his hand and onto mine. He was like a bee whisperer, and they never stung him. Better still, they never stung me either! I wouldn't have dared go anywhere near them if Uncle Eddie wasn't around.

Uncle Eddie was famous in our family for one other thing: he had a cure for burns and we called it Black Plaster. A "plaster", in the vernacular, was what we called the adhesive bandages that you put on a cut or a burn. Uncle Eddie's burn plaster, however, was more akin to the plaster you might finish a wall with, it was that thick. Ma always had a little jar of it in the cupboard, along with her little tin of liver salts and her tablets for the odd headache she might have. One time I remember getting a bad burn on my hand. It might have been when I set Uncle Jim's hay field on fire. Anyway, I got burned and Ma put a big dab of Uncle Eddie's burn cure on it. It was dark in color, goopy, and it had a strong smell to it. I was convinced it had some of Uncle Eddie's honey in it. Regardless of the ingredients, my memory of it was that the burning feeling went away almost immediately. And that the burn healed up quicker than if it was no more than a cigarette burn. I often wondered if it had some of those big yellow flowers in it too. We used to let the back-garden fallow, in between harvesting and then planting the vegetables again in the spring. All around the outside of the garden, the weeds would leap out of the ground. One of these weeds had this tall shoot in the center, taller than a man, and the tip would be covered in yellow flowers. The leaves were large and plentiful, growing in a big cluster, down close to the ground. They had a silvery fur all over them. My mother used to let them grow tall and then hack them out with a bill hook. I always thought they looked nicer than half the flowers in the flower beds. Maybe that's why she let them grow first, before taking the slasher to them. There was one time Uncle Eddie came in on his way home from Miloko and he asked her if he could take a few of them. That's when I wondered if they went into his burn plaster concoction. Now that these weeds were a valuable plant, Ma left them all grow until Uncle Eddie came in to harvest whatever he needed. Next thing you know there's another neighbor coming in to ask Ma if he could take some. There were plenty, and Uncle Eddie already had what he needed, so Ma told him to go ahead. This fella was making a cure for bronchitis, or colds, or some such human ailments but he also said it made a cure for some kind of disease that cows had from time to time. Ma was gobsmacked. She was still a bit of a townie though so not too surprising that. In any case, she thought this was amazing: weeds were now great. Years later, I looked it up and I think this particular weed is a type of Verbascum. Nowadays it seems to be a legitimate garden flower so Ma might have been on the bleeding edge of gardening with this one!

I was used to all this mystical and magical stuff. Everyone at school had stories about this and that cure, for this and that ailment. We were taught all about miracles in catechism class and sure these cures were only minor little miracles by comparison. Throw in a few stories about Gaoithe Sidhe, the Fairy Wind, tossing the haystacks around the field and the notion of curing all sorts of ailments with a natural, and even the odd supernatural, remedy wasn't much of a stretch. I don't think Ma ever became a true believer though. Until that time when Mary, from up the road, came in to tell her that her father, my Grandad, had died that day. Ma kept looking out the window throughout the afternoon and she kept saying: I thought I heard my father calling me. I was there, I saw her and I heard her doing just that, not a word of a lie. At times, she'd hand me her wedding ring to make three signs of the cross on the odd sty I might get in my eye. It worked every time. To this day, I like to mess with my friends in North America when I tell them about this one. I tell them that it must be the wedding band of an honest and faithfully married woman. Sometimes I think there might be a bit of reluctance to volunteer the ring! Ma gave me a great cure for a wart too. You get a little pebble and make three signs of the cross on the wart with it. Then you put it inside a sweet paper (a candy wrapper) and throw it away. Like magic, the wart disappears in a few days. Maybe it'd take a week if you weren't going to confession. I was always worried about what would happen if another child found it and thought it was a sweet. Would they get the wart transferred to them if they opened it?

While we would never admit to believing in leprechauns, or anything like that, we had no bother believing in all these aul' cures. There was one that frightened me a bit though, and that was the use of Cahill's blood to cure wildfire, or shingles. After a few Saturday matinee performances of Dracula, that one sent a shiver up the spine so I'm glad I never had to find a Cahill to help out with such conditions. From what I understood, the member of the Cahill family would prick their finger, and then rub the blood over the affected area. Within a few days, the problem was gone. One of the best local cures that I ever received myself though was the result of a visit to a bonesetter.

Paddy Bolger was a farmer, I think he lived up by Sliabh na mBan (Slievenamon in English, it means the Mountain of the Women), and he had a great reputation as a bone setter around Carrick. I was heading out from Marian Avenue one day, down by the park. I was probably going up the Main Street to see if any of the lads were around. Anyway, the sidewalk there had a great tall curb to it and it was great to run as fast as you could, with one foot high on the sidewalk, the other one low on the road. The difference in height had you bouncing up and down like a mad thing as you flew along by the Forrester's Hall, towards the Guards Barracks. I was in great form and I was at full tilt when I turned my bloody ankle. The one on the road went from under me and, since that was the lower one, my full weight bore down on the ankle when it was turned and I fell in a heap on the road. I remember a guard poking his head over the wall at the pitch of the scream I let out. I went down like a sack of spuds and I had to drag myself back up, arse first, onto the curb. There was no one around to help so I had to get up on my good leg and hop all the way back to Nanny's house. I can't remember what happened in between but somehow, I wound up at the hospital with Ma. Now I didn't have very fond memories of the hospital.

When I was little, my Auntie Jean had me on the back of her bike. We were riding around Carrick like mad things. We were with one of the Smiths, our cousins across the road from Nanny's, and I was loving every minute of it. There weren't the same rules and regulations then so I was sitting on the metal carrier, over the back wheel, no helmet, nor any of the other modern safety accessories you might have to wear today. Not that they would have helped in this situation. Anyway, I had on those horrible plastic sandals they made us wear as kids and the hard plastic sole made a great clicking sound if you positioned your foot just right, just up against the spinning spokes. We went all over town and were going down the Main Street when Jean decided we'd go down to the river. She was pedaling down the hill towards the quays so fast that I thought we'd wind up swimming in the Suir and I was screaming with the thrill of it all. Unfortunately, I was trying to make my plastic sandals clack louder on the spokes and my bloody foot went in between the metal stem and the spokes. I swear to God that the anguish of the flesh being peeled of my foot with each passing spoke abrading as it passed is as real to me now as it was on that day. I was being tortured in real time and the spokes were flaying my leg alive as the wheel rotated at high speed down the hill. I was screaming like a demented thing for her to stop but it took so long for the squealing brakes to work that my foot was totally fucked by the time she came to a halt. The two girls were trying to hold me and the bike upright while at the same time trying to extricate my mangled and bloody foot from the spokes. The sandal was gone and I couldn't see my foot for the flood of blood on it. My Auntie Jean was always one for drama and at the young age she was then, her cries could be heard the length of the Main Street. It wasn't long before some passers-by came to lend a hand and I must have blanked out the memory of what happened for a bit because the next thing I remember is being wheeled through the hospital, still screaming. They got me up on a table and I have this mental image of this wicked looking auld nun coming at me with a gas mask connected to the end of a big pipe. God wasn't I already tortured enough? The smell of the stuff in the pipe was only obnoxious and I didn't want that big mask smothering me along with all the other trauma I was enduring. I screamed even louder and that was probably a good thing because a gulp or two of gas later, I was out for the count. I have no recollection of the immediate aftermath but I do recall being brought back to the hospital in a baby stroller, for weeks afterwards. Can you imagine the sheer indignity of it all? They had to replace the bandages every week. The bandages became embedded in the oozing mess of flesh and scab that was my foot and I almost wished that the horrible nun would come gas me again it was so painful. Amazingly, I have no external scars to show for this traumatic event but I can tell you that I have a few mental scars that I'll carry all the way to the grave. Anyway, with a permanent imprint of all that terror in my mind, I did not want to go to the bloody hospital again. And especially not with another foot problem. But Ma said I had to so I went.

This time, with a turned ankle, there was no blood but I was keeping an eye out for the evil nun anyway. Fortunately, it was a white-coated doctor and a nurse that come to look at me. My foot, by then, had swollen up to the size of a soccer ball. They looked at my foot, at me, at my mother, and at each other. I couldn't have been much more than 8 or 9 at the time but I was old enough to realize, by the looks on all their faces, that they hadn't a clue what to do next. Uh oh! After much adult musing and hand-over-mouth whispering, the doctor pronounced that I should be taken to Paddy Bolger, the bone setter. By now my father had arrived on the scene and it was decided we should head off to Slievenamon to track down this bone setter. Other than the pain and throbbing in my foot, and since I couldn't walk and play now anyway, I was all on for a drive in the country. Maybe they'd buy me a bag of chips or an ice cream along the way somewhere. I remember we went by Kilcash castle on the way and I was reciting the Irish poem about the place. This is a lament so it was very fitting for the occasion as I was lamenting the condition of the swollen orb that was now my foot. Past Kilcash though, Da started to slow down. We were in our old gray Austin A40 and that old wagon wasn't very fast at the best of times. To Ma, and to me, it was obvious that he hadn't a clue where he was going but we couldn't say anything. After going down a boreen or two that turned into dead ends, you could tell there might be a bit of frustration building. As we meandered further up the mountain, Ma started humming one of her favorite songs, and if you're Irish you can guess this one, it was Slievenamon! I think it was Ma's way of biting her lip. And you could see the furrows on Da's brow as we went further into the wilderness, totally clueless. Fortunately, down the road a bit was an old man with a walking stick. The sense of relief was palpable. As Da cruised to a stop beside him, Ma stopped humming.

"Good day to you, sir.", said Da, "Would you have any notion of how to get to Paddy Bolger's house?"

"Paddy Bolger's house!", mused the old man, as he removed his cap and bent over to rest his elbow on the car door.

"Paddy Bolger's house!", he went again, staring up the road, into the distance. With a wistful look on his face.

"Paddy Bolger's house!", he went for the third time. And I could tell my father was wondering if he shouldn't just drive on. But he couldn't with the old man resting on the car door.

"Well now.", said the old man, beating his cap off the knee of his trousers, "Paddy Bolger's house!"

Aw Jaysus! I was beside myself because I knew Da was already under pressure here. Ma, to her credit, was sitting tight-lipped and saying nothing.

"Do you see that telephone pole right there?", said the man, pointing with his walking stick at the pole not ten feet from the car.

"I do.", says Da.

"Well now.", and he paused here again, "If you follow the poles 'til there's only one wire on it …"

"Yes.", nodded Da, hoping to encourage the completion of the sentence.

"Keep an eye on that last wire …" he paused again, to introduce himself and everyone had to shake hands and what have you. We were going to be here all day at this rate.

"If you keep going to the last telephone pole …", another pause, "and you follow that last wire to the house at the end of it …", yet another pause.

"That will be Paddy Bolger's house!", he finished with a flourish.

Jaysus, you couldn't beat that with a big stick for directions, could you! There's no north and south directions in Ireland because all the roads back then went wherever the sheep and goats used to go in times past but I thought that was the best directions I ever heard anyone give. Fortunately, so did Da and there was an immediate improvement in his countenance and his outlook improved no end. I could see the relief on Ma's face too. A few more minutes of chit-chat, the old man wanted to know why we were going to see Paddy, and I had to lift up my globular foot to show him. More drivel about the weather and what have you, and we were finally on our way.

As we drove up towards the house, a few dogs came bounding out, barking and wagging their tails. Paddy himself came in their wake, to see what the commotion was all about. Paddy was a stout man, old by my young perceptions, with a brimmed hat and he too had a walking stick. Though he didn't seem to need it. The usual Irish rigmarole ensued, about the weather, the livestock, the dogs and all of that. Finally, we got around to what brought us up to Slievenamon, my foot. With the back door open, I extended my football foot for Paddy to review. He had big, beefy hands with strong fingers that looked like Denny's sausages that lifted weights. He held my heel in one hand while the fingers of the other gently probed around the swollen foot. As Paddy was casually asking me what I had done, and without any warning, he suddenly pressed hard with his thumb and there was a big snap sound. It probably wasn't as loud as I remember it but it sure felt like it was loud. The amazing thing was that I immediately knew he had fixed it. It just felt fixed. It was still all swollen but Paddy said that would be gone in a day or two and that I'd be right as rain.

Ma and Da were delighted. I was delighted. Paddy was just great. While I petted the dogs by the open door, Ma and Da were now out standing by Paddy, and Ma was telling him about this problem she had with her hand. This was some old problem that she'd had for a few years and Paddy, saying nothing, took her hand in his. Same thing again, a quick snap of his thumb on the offending bone and she was beaming. Da then got into the traditional Irish thing about paying for Paddy's services and Paddy was resisting. I'm not sure if there was some kind of tradition about not accepting payment or what but finally, timing it to the end of the thanks and farewell part of the conversation, Da stuffed a note into the top pocket of Paddy's tweed jacket and bolted for the car. We were still waving and calling our goodbyes out the open windows as we headed back down towards the road for the trip home.

That Paddy Bolger was some man. And I got chips and ice cream on the way home. We were all very happy that day.

31 – A Carrick Emigrant

I have to force myself to focus on these memories now, in order to bring back the feelings, but there really was an existential angst that surrounded growing up in Carrick. Sure, times could be lean and you might have to wait for another Christmas to get the bicycle you wanted so badly but, by and large, most of us didn't suffer too much. We always had food on the table, we always had friends and family to hang out with, and there always seemed to be enough money, though sometimes barely, for the necessities of life. Money wasn't the only issue, it seemed more like, somehow, the location was the problem. Do all teenagers feel this way? Regardless of where they live? Or was the problem just me? For this, and for whatever other reasons that circled my head from time to time, I wanted to know what was around the next corner, over the next hill, and at the other sides of the seas and oceans that surrounded our fair isle. There were at least a few more like me, kindred spirits, who shared this angst. We'd spend our mornings, sitting on the steps of the Main Street, chatting about what we'd do when we grew up and it seems like such conversations were always focused on getting out of town. Sure, we talked about owning this car, and that motorcycle, and living some mythical Hollywood lifestyle, but there was a repeated theme of shaking the dust of Carrick off our shoes as we headed out into the great big world. We were going in search of adventure, fulfillment, and who knows what else. With fleeting thought, it would be easy to dismiss it all as teenage angst. But that may not be the full story.

There is a thing about small towns that can make it challenging for some to find their way to adulthood. I was one of those. Not everyone was that way, some could see their way, clearly, into how their lives would work out over the years, right there, at home. For them, Carrick wasn't a place to escape from, it was where they would build and live their lives. For others, like me, there was a yearning for so many things. There was despair and longing for I'm not sure what sometimes. And yes, adventure and exploration was part of it. This wasn't just a blind faith in faraway hills being greener, there were some real things too. We needed to leave behind the embarrassments of childhood. We had to get away from the watchful eye of parents. Parents who were supported by an army of relatives and friends who were only too happy to report any misbehaviors that might be observed, as we practiced growing up in our little town. All the usual challenges of childhood were present and it was as much those we needed to escape as it was our home town. On the positive side, most of us were born into a series of networks in Carrick. Big families were common so you had an immediate social support network. If you had a father or mother that worked at one of the few factories in town, you had another network. The social and athletic clubs provided another avenue. The street you lived on played a part. We all attended church, well mostly anyway, so that was another layer. While these structures provided support, they also imposed limitations. The first thing I noticed when I finally left Carrick was that all of this, the good and the bad, disappeared!

That meant a couple of things could happen. You might go a little crazy with the freedom of escape, for example, but you might also wind up crying in your tea cup of an evening. Of course, I did both. Despite practicing freedom at boarding school and university, I still knew where home was and it was close by. My first job was in Scotland and I found some temporary accommodations in an apartment with a group of Irish guys. There is a funny element to a group of Irish guys being in an apartment over a pub, isn't there! The reality was that we didn't spend very much time in that particular pub and, besides, I was highly motivated to find my own place, if only to get away from the uncomfortable couch I was sleeping on. Along with the couch, there were a few other problems. Some of the lads eagerly went to pick up their letters every day, hoping for a note from the Mammy, or the latest edition of the local newspaper from back home. Some of these lads had been in Edinburgh for a couple of years and they were still, in a spiritual sense, in Ireland. I couldn't handle that. If I felt like that was going to be me in two years' time, I'd have headed for the airport and gone home that same day. I'm not saying their approach was wrong, and certainly not for them, but I felt that you had to give your new life a fighting chance. And I didn't think this was the way to do it. I wound up in a weekly-rate B and B for a few months before teaming up with a couple of my new colleagues to hunt down an apartment. One of them proved to be a great friend, 'til the day he died. Once we secured our own apartment, it became party central. If my liver was ever under threat, it was during those first couple of years away from home. We drank and danced our way through a couple of great years and I was happy that I had committed to my new life! There are a couple of great stories contained within those years but for now, suffice it to say that I left Edinburgh loving it. And I then went back to … wait for it … Ireland! It wasn't that I was homesick or anything but the job opportunities there were just so much better at the time. Besides, I was going to work for an American company and that was going to help me get my first trip to America. Probably considered the ultimate emigration destination for most Irish kids at the time. I went back to a job in Dublin with an American company and they did send me to America.

America was all I dreamed it could be. I was staying at an apartment complex that had a pool, a party area with a barbeque, and there were a lot of other young graduates starting out there too. This was California in the early 80s, a boom time in the tech industries. Guys my own age were earning double and triple what I was back in

Ireland. They were driving convertible sports cars and they were living where I was staying for my month-long trip. I had a whole two-bedroom apartment to myself. Each bedroom had its own balcony and bathroom. And the sunshine! Where did it all come from? For crying' out loud, this was what life was all about. They were all cruisin' the highways in their convertibles, with cute blondes to keep them company. I might have been more jealous if it weren't for me having my own cute blonde back in Dublin. The whole experience messed me up a little bit and the emigration bug was biting, again. Even Dublin was too small to hold me now. I couldn't stop talking about the place when I got back. In that short month in California, I had stuffed in more exciting new experiences than I had in the previous two years. I'd driven a Mustang with a growling V8 Windsor engine, one of my American colleagues had me over to eat, drink and shoot guns at his house. The guy had a gun range in his house! I'd eaten Mexican food for the first time. And this gorgeous Latin beauty had given me the eye. The bedroom closet in the apartment I'd stayed in was as big as my entire bedsit back in Terenure. Everything really was bigger in America. Who knew!

After my second visit to the US plant, I got a couple of job offers to relocate. Since it's not the point of the story, I'll skip all the melodrama that saw that stopped at the 11th hour but my head had picked up the travel bug again and I was going to move somewhere. Anywhere. And fortunately, my wife was ready to come along for the ride. When we finally got around to it, we discussed Germany but she didn't want to handle the language issue. I didn't speak German either but I just didn't give a shit. Oops, sorry, but I didn't. This country had BMWs, Audis and Mercedes, along with great football, beer and sausages. What else could you want? I figured I'd work it all out along the way and that I'd be writing German poetry within about six months. The boss won, however, so it's fortunate that we also looked longingly at Australia and Canada. Off went our visa applications, with such a precision of timing that we wound up getting the medicals for both countries with one doctor, who just happened to be on the approved list of both embassies. This multi-pronged emigration approach was paying off already. We sold our first house, in Rathfarnham, to a young guy who was just kicking his career into gear in the big smoke. We were selling everything. And I mean everything. If it couldn't fit it a suitcase, it was included with the house. He had sheets and blankets on the bed, towels in the hot water closet, knives & forks in the drawer. Everything was going with the house. He drew the line when I tried to include our two dogs, an Alsatian and a Kerry Blue! They wound up going to the Ma, back in Skough, and only under a modicum of protest.

In Dublin, things were going great for us at the time but once that over the hill and far away thing strikes, there's just no resisting the urge. The Ma went mental, alternately yelling at me and then bawling her eyes out.

"How could you leave your lovely new house, Paul!", she'd exclaim between sobs.

"Aw Jaysus, Ma.", said I, "Will ya give it a bit of a rest!"

"Sure we'll send you the tickets to come out and see us within the year.", I assured her.

We didn't, but that's a whole other story. We took off to Australia first. Both visas had a one-year expiry date so you had to land, as an immigrant, before that deadline. We figured that we'd love Australia but that it'd be a bit far, and a bit costly, for most of the family to come out too often. We thought we'd be exhausted from picking up all the gold bars laying around the streets and that we'd probably need a holiday back in Ireland every year to recover. Things didn't quite work out on that front either. There's another long story in this but the short version is that the original plan to spend ten or eleven months in Australia was cut short when my uncle connected me to one of his friends and I landed a job. They were going to pay me a ton of money compared to what I'd been earning back home. It was just stupid, I thought at the time, but it fit right in with the gold bricks lying on the street concept and I was good with it. Unfortunately, that catholic upbringing can be a bit of a curse at times and it only took a day or two for the guilt to set in.

How could I possibly take a job and then abandon them just when I would be coming up to speed?

I couldn't and so I declined the job and we booked our tickets for Toronto, allowing for another month of exploring Australia. On the way to Canada, we dropped off in Hawaii for a week. You might as well, if you're passing, eh? And as we circled the airport in Vancouver, we were very impressed by the sight of the mountains, the oceans, and all the houses that had swimming pools. It took nearly two hours to go through the emigration process as a landed immigrant and myself and herself spend the whole time discussing staying in Vancouver. Instead of sticking to the original plan of hitting Toronto. What with all the money on offer in Australia, all the houses with swimming pools in Vancouver, Toronto would only blow them all away, wouldn't it? We landed in Toronto, in a blizzard, and herself was only bawling her eyes out on the taxi ride from the airport to the hotel.

"Did we do the right thing, Paul?", she sobbed. And further remarking that the shorts and t-shirts we wore on Bondi Beach last week wouldn't be much good at -12°C with the snow flying. Jaysus, I didn't know, did I? But I reassured her we had anyway, and that all would be well.

In Canada, it took me ten years to get within an ass's roar of the kind of money they had offered me in Australia. Some other bastards must've already picked up all the gold bricks in Toronto because there were none of them around either. After a spell working in Canada's first indoor mall, to stop the financial hemorrhaging, we took off for my first real job in Montreal. There are a whole bunch of fun immigrant stories from our years in Canada but the upshot of the whole thing is that we spent five years in Montreal before moving back to a small town in Ontario. A small town not too dissimilar to Carrick-on-Suir!

And that, right there, is the rub. I never minded leaving the bright lights of Edinburgh, Dublin and London behind but I must have still missed Carrick. Homesickness is a real thing for the average emigrant and, despite owning my first house in Dublin, Carrick was home and that's where I missed. I had a very good friend in Canada warn me that if things got too bad, to take the "six-week cure". This is the same friend that I had shared my first real apartment with back in Edinburgh. He had emigrated to Canada a few years ahead of us going and he had seen a few people abandon their emigration plans, only to regret the move home within a few months. He said that going home for a two or three-week holiday was no good. Everyone loved you, was delighted to see you, and they would all go to the pub with you every night. But that would only be true for about three weeks. You had to stay for six weeks so that everyone would get fed up with you again and leave you to your own devices. Only then could experience what life back home was really like again. And with that, you could then make a better decision on what was right for you.

As it happens, we never had to take the six-week cure and so ... what's the point of all this then? The point is that you have teenage angst when you're a teenager. You have adult angst when you're an adult. And it doesn't matter where you are, or who you're with, or where you decide to travel, sometimes angst just comes along for the ride. I think there were forty four thousand Irish who left Ireland the year we did, a record at the time. The Celtic Tiger was yet to roar, and fade, and with that exodus, a few from Carrick joined the throng. Including me. Would I do it all again? Yes, I think I would. With hindsight, I know that angst and adventure are all part of the package. Would I advise anyone else to do it? Not a chance! That's one of those calls we all have to make for ourselves but this story is for those who might be contemplating a bit of adventure. Regardless of where you might wander, if you came from Carrick, chances are you'll still call Carrick home.

32 – An Unfinished Story

One day, me and a bunch of the lads were heading up to Kilonerry ...

Ah sure, I haven't the time now. It's a story about how I saved the life of one of the lads one time but I'll have to come back to it later.

33 – A Carrick Haiku

The back deck, raining.
Sometimes, what I write is shite.
Now, I think I'll stop!

Notes

You probably won't be surprised to find that I'm pretty proud of my little home town. There's plenty of info online if you want to learn more, or in case you are lucky enough to be planning a visit. Below are a few examples of local items and places that you might like to check out.

FaceBook page: Things I Miss about Carrick-on-Suir
https://www.facebook.com/groups/656396771067851/

Follow the Mixed Race Irish project created by my cousin, Lol. She's on FaceBook, Instagram and Twitter.
https://www.facebook.com/Iamblirish/

Once you get to town, and now that you know a little more about the history of the place, start with Carrick-on-Suir Heritage Centre (http://www.carrickonsuirheritagecentre.com/)

Surely you'll go visit the ancient high crosses in Kilkieran. And if you do, be sure to say hello to my Ma & Da, along with the rest of the clan. http://highcrosses.org/kilkieran/index.htm

And if you do go to Kilkieran, drop in for a pint in Willie Moloney's as you pass. And be sure to go through Faugheen on the way in or out too.

The Ormonde Castle is a must see.
http://www.heritageireland.ie/en/south-east/ormondcastle/

And this one will give you a great overview to everything going on in Carrick ... http://www.carrickonsuir.info/

Make sure you spend some time wandering the Main Street and by the banks of the Suir. I hope the stories in this volume will add a little extra color and flavor to your adventures in Carrick-on-Suir. At the very least, you have a few stories of your own to share in whatever local pub you might choose to slake your thirst in.

Carrick ... For a Man or a Dog